Rach

9p.
24

"Look,
wrong,"

Cole said softly,   do with your
father. But taking   all the way across
Texas won't solve anything."

When Jessie made no response, Cole placed a
finger beneath her chin and lifted her face,
forcing her to meet his gaze. Inside, she felt her
heart lurch, felt the blood heat and rush to her
head, leaving her dizzy.

"Go home," he continued. "It's the only logical
choice."

"Choice?" she questioned, lifting her head in a
gesture of defiance. "What about your choice?
Why are you out here on the trail, drawing a gun
at every shadow?"

His tone hardened. "That's none of your
business."

"And what I do is none of yours."

Ruth Langan traces her ancestry to Scotland and Ireland. It is no surprise, then, that she feels a kinship with the characters in her historical novels. Married to her childhood sweetheart, she has raised five children and lives in Michigan, the state where she was born and raised.

Look out for TEXAS HEALER in July and TEXAS HERO in September.

TEXAS
HEART

Ruth Langan

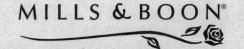

MILLS & BOON®

To my family,
those wonderful characters, who enrich my life.
To my aunt, Ella Quinn,
world's greatest cook, who, at my wedding,
was asked to duplicate the miracle of the loaves and fishes.
And especially to Tom, always Tom,
the main character in my life, who makes it all fun.

First published in Great Britain 1999
Harlequin Mills & Boon Limited,
Eton House, 18-24 Paradise Road, Richmond, Surrey TW9 1SR

© Ruth Ryan Langan 1989

ISBN 0 263 81659 1

Set in Times Roman 10 on 11 pt.
04-9905-90103-C

Printed and bound in Great Britain
by Caledonian International Book Manufacturing Ltd, Glasgow

Chapter One

Texas
August, 1870

"There's forty dollars here. Enough to see you through the next two or three months."

Jessie Conway carefully folded the bills and squeezed them through the narrow opening of the biscuit tin before placing it on a shelf. She turned toward the older of her two brothers, fourteen-year-old Danny, who was already inches taller than she was at seventeen, and continued.

"I checked all the corral fences. They're sturdy enough to hold the horses. But just to make sure, you'd better check them at least once a week." Hearing his sigh of impatience, she added, "And don't forget to milk the cow every night. You and Thad need the milk. It'll come in handy if you run short of supplies. Speaking of which…" She saw Danny roll his eyes and started talking faster. "If you have to go into town for supplies, don't let anyone know you're out here all alone. Just act like I'm busy with the ranch chores. And try to talk old Mr. Thompson into allowing you to take some food on credit. That way, you'll have this money in case I…" Her voice trailed off.

Danny swallowed. She was thinking the same thing he was.

What if she never made it back? Like Pa. Then there'd be just him and Thad.

He felt a surge of panic. "I want to go with you, Jess."

"You can't. Someone has to stay here with Thad."

"We'll take him along."

She glanced at their seven-year-old brother and, seeing the wide eyes so filled with fear, forced her voice to a low, soothing tone. "Pa could be anywhere from here to Abilene. That's almost six hundred miles. We can't take a little kid that far."

"I could do it," Thad chirped. "Pa said I'm the best rider he's ever taught. A real natural, Pa said."

Jessie dropped to her knees and drew her little brother into the circle of her arms. "I know, Tadpole. You're the best I've ever seen, too. But I can travel twice as fast alone. And it'll give me peace of mind to know you two are safe at home."

Home. Danny's eyes narrowed. This dirt-poor piece of land on the banks of the Rio Grande would never be home, not after the way it had slowly killed his ma. Danny studied the two of them—his older sister, his little brother. Both had hair the color of ripe wheat, eyes as blue as the Texas sky. Even though Jessie was the oldest, she was inches smaller than him and reed thin. Instead of wearing Ma's cast-off dresses like a lady, she wore a pair of Danny's britches tucked into her boots and a rough woolen shirt with the sleeves rolled above her elbows.

Of the three of them, she was the most like Pa. If Danny had to use one word to describe his sister, it would be *stubborn*. Ever since she'd made up her mind that Pa wasn't coming back, she'd been making plans to go find him. Stubborn. Like Pa. And tough. He remembered when their ma had died right after Thad was born. Their pa had suggested maybe the three kids should go East to live with an aunt. Danny had thought it would be great living in a real house instead of this sod shack, and going to school with other kids. But Jessie had lifted the squalling baby from the cradle and fashioned a bottle out of an old glove and cow's milk. And she'd said she wasn't leaving. This was her land now. Hers and Pa's. And though the work had nearly killed her, Jessie kept the place going just the way Ma had.

He glanced around the neat sod shack. There was a sturdy wooden table and four rough-hewn chairs. In the center of the table was a crocheted doily their grandmother had made before any of them was born. Over their beds of straw were colorfully woven afghans which their ma and Jessie had made years ago. Though they were worn and faded, they were clean. And though their meals weren't nearly as tasty as when Ma was alive, Jessie always found time to feed them no matter how tired she was after a day tending the cattle.

And now she was determined to have her way again. Pa had joined up with a cattle drive three months ago. The boss of the drive had convinced him that it was safer to join his herd with a big drive that would offer protection against Indian attacks, cattle rustling and the dozens of other things that could go wrong on a trek across Texas and Indian Territory all the way to the stockyards at Abilene, Kansas. Six hundred miles. The pay for a drive was enough to stake a man for a year if he was careful. But Pa should have been back weeks ago. And every day as she scanned the horizon, Jessie had grown more and more impatient. Nothing, she insisted, would keep Pa away from home this long unless he was in trouble. Or dead. Danny shivered. Either way, she had to find out, and that meant a journey across Texas. Someone, somewhere, would know about Pa.

"You're making a mistake, Jess. You're just going to end up the same as Pa."

She whirled on Danny, eyes blazing. "Pa's fine. He just got sidetracked." Lowering her voice, she reached out and touched her brother's arm, feeling the beginnings of muscles beneath the flesh. Sometimes she was amazed at how much he'd grown. In no time, she knew he'd be ready to fill their pa's shoes. Only now he was going to have to be a man sooner than nature had planned.

"I have to do this, Danny."

Pale green eyes, the color of their mother's, stared unblink-ingly into Jessie's. "I know."

She smiled and hugged him hard and fast. "Take good care of Thad. I'll be back. Promise."

He returned the hug awkwardly and turned away.

Jessie opened her arms to her little brother and drew him close for a last kiss. "Be sure to help Danny. Stay close to the house." She cradled his face between her hands, memo-rizing the slope of his brow, the upward curve of his lips. "Say your prayers, Tadpole."

"I will, Jessie."

She tucked the cloud of yellow hair beneath a broad-brimmed hat and picked up the pitifully small bundle she had packed. It was her intention to travel fast and light.

She crossed the dusty patch of earth and pulled herself into the saddle.

"Wait. Jess. You'll need this." Danny ran toward her, hold-ing out a heavy sheepskin-lined jacket. Since their pa had brought it back from Abilene after a successful cattle drive two years ago, it had been Danny's most prized possession.

"It gets cold at night," he said simply, pressing it into her hands.

Jessie swallowed down the lump that threatened to choke her. "Thanks, Danny. I'll bring it back soon."

"Yeah."

She watched as he stepped back and put his arm around their little brother. Jessie dug in her heels and felt her eyes sting as the horse's hooves sent up a cloud of dust.

As her mount crested a hill, she turned for one last glimpse of home. Damned dust, she thought, wiping the back of her hand across her cheeks. It always made her eyes water.

Cole Matthews reined in his horse and studied the barren hills. His grim odyssey had already carried him from San An-tonio to the Mexican border. Now it looked as if the trail was leading him back across Texas once more. He was saddle weary, but the anger simmering inside him spurred him on.

There was no way he would ever turn back. Or give up. He'd become a skilled hunter. And the bounty he sought was not animal. It was man.

He never allowed himself to think about what he'd left behind. The only soft bed he'd enjoyed recently was an occasional room above a saloon when he allowed himself a night's respite. Though he stopped at every town and settlement, he rarely stayed longer than it took to look over the strangers in the saloon or their mounts in the local stable.

Cole lifted his hat from his head and wiped the sweat from his brow. Daylight had already faded, and he'd been on the trail since before sunup. After a careful check of the area, he chose a well-protected spot to make camp.

Jessie stayed clear of the little settlement not far from her ranch, knowing her presence would cause speculation about where she was going and for how long. If the wrong kind of people knew she was gone, they might try to help themselves to the small herd left grazing on her land. Pa said the best kind of friends to have were no friends at all. That way there'd be no one to take advantage of your good nature.

Jessie wasn't at all sure she agreed with Pa on that, but she had no way of knowing. In their isolation, there'd been few chances to make friends. Her ma had spoken lovingly of their friends back in Missouri, before Pa had gotten the urge to head West. There'd been a church, Ma said, and Sunday afternoon picnics. But when Jessie thought about those things at all, she thought they were like the stories in Ma's books. In books, all the ladies wore beautiful dresses, and the men were all smooth-shaven and handsome. And they made each other feel strange but good somehow. Ma and Pa had been that way with each other. She remembered Ma blushing, and Pa laughing deep in his throat. And she'd heard them whispering together long after she should have been asleep. But now all Pa seemed to do was work. And sometimes get drunk on Saturday night and stay in town until dawn. And when he came home, he'd be whistling for a while, and then he'd go back to working around the ranch, cursing the heat and the dust and the cattle. For the most part, Pa had become a loner.

She shivered and drew on the heavy jacket Danny had given her. Danny. He'd do just fine alone with Thad. He was a good boy, strong and sensible even if he had inherited more of his ma's traits than Pa's. He was dreamy, always reading to her from Ma's books. And sometimes when he dropped exhausted into his bed at night, Jessie would find herself wondering what his life would be like if he could go East and study medicine like he wanted. Dr. Conway. The words made her smile.

What would little Thad be, she wondered, if he could go East and study, too? A lawyer maybe. Then they'd have a doctor and a lawyer. Now all they would need was an Indian chief. Her smile faded. There were plenty of them here in Texas. And one in particular had made it plain to Pa that he was interested in his golden-haired daughter. Pa had always said that when the time came, he'd find her a good husband. But Jessie wasn't interested even though she was way past the age of marrying. Hadn't her ma married Pa when she was only fourteen?

Jessie hunched deeper into the parka and slowed the horse to a walk. The shadows had lengthened until it was almost impossible to see more than a foot ahead of her. She'd have to stop soon and make camp.

What were Danny and Thad doing right now? She smiled in the darkness and pictured in her mind the little sod shack with its cheery fire. She'd left enough rabbit stew to last a week or more. Her stomach rumbled, and she thought about the meager supplies she'd allowed herself to carry. She hadn't eaten since she left home nearly ten hours earlier.

The sound of a twig snapping nearby brought her out of her reverie. Automatically her hand went to the gun in her belt.

"Who's there?" A man's voice called out in the night.

She swallowed and cursed herself for her carelessness. While she was daydreaming, she'd gotten too close to someone's camp. Drawing the brim of her hat low on her forehead, she gripped the bulky jacket around her to hide the soft curves that would reveal her gender. Though she'd never been with a man, she knew what could happen to an unprotected woman in this tough land. Her voice was naturally low. Fear now made it husky.

"A rider," she said softly.

She heard the click of a rifle. "Come into the light where I can see you."

Before she could dig her heels into the horse's side and make a run for safety, a hand shot out in the darkness, gripping the bridle.

"Going somewhere?"

She ran a tongue over dry lips. "I don't want to bother you. I'll just go on about my business."

"And what is your business?" The man was tall, with dark hair that hung to his shoulders.

"I'm heading for Abilene."

"Abilene." He was studying her closely. Too closely. "Where's your herd?"

"I'm joining a herd already on the trail." She lowered her head, avoiding his eyes.

"You may as well share our camp fire." Still holding the reins, he led her toward the light, where three other men were now standing.

The aroma of boiling coffee was strong, and Jessie noted the remains of dinner still giving off steam on tin plates.

"Didn't mean to interrupt your meal," she said. "Go on eating."

"I've had enough." The man holding the rifle stepped closer. "What I'd really like now is some good whiskey and a wicked woman."

The others laughed.

"What's your name?" the tall man asked.

"Jess. Jess Conway."

"Set a spell."

With one man holding her reins and the other aiming a rifle at her, Jessie had no choice. Easing from the saddle, she slid to the ground and wished she was taller.

"What are you going to do in Abilene, boy?" one of the others asked.

She relaxed a bit. She'd managed to fool them. "Joining a cattle drive. Got to earn enough to see me through the winter."

The man holding her reins led her horse away and tied it. When he returned, one of the other men had positioned himself behind her. She turned slightly, keeping him in sight while still watching the one with the rifle.

The man with the long hair grinned, revealing yellow teeth. "A cattle drive. Now that's a real hoot." His voice lowered. "Funny thing. I can smell a woman. Even with leather, horses, sweat all around me, I can always smell a woman."

Jessie's hand flew to the gun at her waist. In that same instant, the man behind her caught her arm in a painful grip. The gun clattered to the ground.

While the man continued to hold her, the other three circled around her. One of them lifted the hat from her head, and a cloud of shimmering hair drifted about her face and shoulders.

"God Almighty. Look at it." The tall man grabbed a handful of hair and watched as it sifted through his dirty fingers. "Did you say you wanted whiskey and women?" When the others laughed, he added, "Whiskey-colored hair and a woman. Just like that."

"What a nice surprise." The man holding her suddenly yanked the jacket from her and tossed it to the ground. Twisting her to face him, he grabbed both sides of her shirt collar and hissed, "I can't wait to see the rest of this female."

The others roared as he tore the shirt away from her, revealing smooth white flesh barely covered by a pale ivory chemise.

"Jess Conway, you just get better all the time," the tall one said, clutching her arm and tearing her away from the grasp of the other.

"I saw her first," the one with the rifle said.

"But I'm the one who kept her from bolting. The way you shoot, you'd have let her get clean away."

As the two men fought over her, a third man pulled a handgun from his belt and fired. The sound of the gunshot echoed on the still night air.

"This here gun says I get her first. After that, I don't care who gets her." The gunman fixed each of his companions with a hard stare. "Understood?"

Sullenly the others nodded. Tossing his handgun to his partner, the man said, "Blair here will see that you two wait your turn." Grabbing Jessie by the shoulders, he began dragging her toward a bedroll. "Come on, girlie. You and me are going to have some fun."

In the silence punctuated by the hissing of the fire, the only sound was Jessie's breathing as her heart slammed against her ribs.

Raw terror gave her renewed strength. Twisting, she brought her booted foot hard into the man's groin. Yanking free, she began to run. A hand caught at a tangle of hair, pulling her head back with a snap. Ignoring the pain, she plunged into a thicket and heard the crackle of leaves and twigs as the men followed.

Her breath was coming faster now as she forced herself to run in the darkness. Branches whipped against her, tearing at her flesh, but she ignored them and kept on running. She thought she saw a patch of sky through the maze of trees and stumbled forward, keeping her eyes on the distant light. Something shot out of the darkness. Suddenly she was tripping, then falling through space. When she landed, something heavy landed on top of her. She started to scream, but a hand covered her mouth, stifling the sound.

The heavy burden that was pinning her to the ground was a body. A man's body, from the size and weight of it. One of his hands pinned both of hers in a painful grip above her head. The other hand, rough and callused, was covering her mouth. Her breath was coming so hard now she thought she would choke. And still the hand continued to cover her mouth.

She heard a thrashing in the undergrowth nearby, and the hand on her mouth tightened. She swallowed the knot of fear that had formed a lump in her throat.

The footsteps came closer, and Jessie felt the figure on top of her stiffen. His breath was hot against her cheek.

The footsteps crunched directly beside him, and she forgot to breathe. She heard a voice cursing as the footsteps faded and were joined by the sound of others.

The hand suddenly left her mouth, and she took in great gulps of air, filling her lungs. The body that had been pinning her rolled aside. She went very still, fighting the dizziness.

"You all right?" The voice was deep, the tone abrupt.

"Yes. I'm…" She sat up, struggling against a wave of sickness.

"Better sit still a minute."

"I'll be fine." She came to her knees and pulled herself up, clinging to the branch of a tree.

Seeing her sway, he said gruffly, "My camp's not far from here. Think you can make it?"

"Yes." She stumbled forward and would have fallen if the stranger hadn't caught her.

Lifting her as easily as if she were a child, he cradled her against his chest and carried her to where a bedroll lay beside a fire. Situated between towering boulders, the campsite was completely hidden from view. As if, she thought with a sudden chill, this man was accustomed to hiding.

He laid her on the bedroll, then walked to the fire and poured a tin of steaming coffee that he offered to her without a word.

He saw the way she shrank from his touch. He was also able to see what she really looked like. In the firelight, her hair shimmered like spun gold. The face turned up to his was exquisite, with perfectly formed features. Her eyes were a little too bright. He recognized fear and shock in them. And her skin. He tried not to stare at the soft swell of breasts visible beneath the pale chemise. Very deliberately he turned his back on her.

She sipped the coffee and felt the warmth begin to course through her veins. Shivering, she sipped again before glancing up at him.

The stranger was tall, with wide shoulders and arms corded with muscles. His waist was slim, his stomach flat. Shaggy hair was as dark as midnight. His holster was slung low over his hips. Though he stood almost casually, feet apart, one hand resting at his waist, she sensed there was nothing relaxed about him.

He strode to his horse and rummaged through his saddlebag. "Here." He handed her a rough homespun shirt.

For the first time, Jessie realized the state of her undress. In her anxiety she'd been too distressed to notice. Her cheeks flamed as she accepted his offering. She fumbled with the buttons, then, looking up, felt his cool gaze study her.

"Thank you." It seemed inadequate, but she couldn't think of anything else to say.

"Save your thanks. We're not out of here yet." He doused the fire. "Are you strong enough to ride?"

"Ride? I guess so."

He led his horse closer. When she stood uneasily, he bent and began rolling the blankets.

"I'm betting your friends won't give up until they find you."

"They're no friends of mine. I stumbled into their camp by mistake."

He turned to give her a quick look, then stiffened at the sound of horses.

"Well, well, boys, look what I found." The man with the long hair stood silhouetted on a rock ledge just above their heads. A lariat snaked out, landing cleanly over the stranger's shoulders, pinning his arms to his sides.

Though still weak and dazed, Jessie bolted toward the stranger's horse, where she had spotted a rifle. Before she could reach it, she was grabbed from behind and yanked roughly into the arms of a man on horseback.

"Now we'll all go back where we started and have some fun."

While the men laughed and whooped, the stranger was tied

behind a second horse and forced to run as the horse was whipped into a gallop.

Jessie watched helplessly as the stranger fell and was dragged on the ground until they arrived back at camp. Once there, the four men left the stranger roped and tied behind the horse while they argued over who would get her first.

"She's mine," the long-haired man shouted. "I've waited long enough."

The others laughed their agreement and watched with glittering eyes as the long-haired man pulled Jessie roughly from the horse and gripped her shoulders.

"Now your hero can get a good look at what he might have had himself. My name is Knife," he said with a laugh that clawed at her nerves. "Know why? Because I like to carve my brand on a woman when I'm through with her." He held up the glittering blade of a knife and laughed again, and she saw in his eyes a mixture of cruelty and madness.

Jessie squeezed her eyes tightly shut, hoping to blot out as much of the pain as possible. She felt rough hands sliding along her arms and she cringed.

In the darkness a shot rang out. The hands on her body stilled. All four men turned toward the figure of the stranger, who had managed to cut the ropes binding him.

"Sorry to spoil your fun."

"How did you—" As Blair aimed his pistol, the stranger shot it cleanly from his hand.

Blair let out a yelp, and the long-haired man, Knife, made a dive for the rifle. Before he could reach it, the stranger kicked it aside and pressed a gun to his temple.

"Call off your friends, or I'll blow you apart."

Jessie felt a chill along her spine at the icy tone of the stranger. This was no rancher or farmer. And from the way he'd used his gun, he was no passing cowboy. Pa said there was a look about a man when he was a professional gunman. And this stranger had that look.

"I don't want to have to kill you. But unless you leave now, I'll have no choice."

"Kill us?" Blair, still holding his injured hand, gave a hollow laugh, and the others joined in. "There are four of us. And as I see it, there's just you and one skinny little woman. It hardly seems like a fair fight."

"Kill him," Knife shouted. "You're wasting the whole night jawboning. Get rid of him and grab the girl."

Jessie stared transfixedly at the stranger. He was coiled, ready to strike at the slightest provocation. The most compelling thing about him was the look in his eyes. He left no doubt he would kill them if they made the slightest move toward their guns.

"Looks like I'll have to—" As Blair aimed his pistol a second time, the stranger shot it cleanly from his hand.

"You." He pointed a finger at Jessie while keeping his eye on the others. "Take your horse."

Scrambling to her feet, she grasped the reins and hauled herself into the saddle.

"She's ours. You can't have her." Reaching into his boot, Knife fired.

Before the shot even rang out, he was clutching his shoulder. He whirled and leaped onto the back of a horse. Amid a swirl of choking dust, he disappeared into the darkness.

Jessie turned in time to see the stranger whirl as a second man fell on the rifle and fired. Dust kicked up near the stranger's feet, but he didn't flinch as he squeezed off a second shot and killed the man where he lay.

Blair reached behind his back and produced a second handgun. Before he could fire, he fell forward from a gunshot, barely missing the flames of the camp fire.

The fourth man sprang up and leaped onto her horse, hoping to use Jessie as a shield. Jessie watched in horror as the stranger calmly aimed his gun and fired, dropping the man directly behind her. An inch in either direction would have left her dead or badly wounded, but the stranger hadn't even hesitated.

When the carnage was over, Jessie stared dully around the

camp fire. Three lifeless bodies lay in mottled brown pools of blood and dust.

In the shadows a horse snorted and blew, then stood calmly while his master mounted. Bending in the saddle, the stranger plucked Jessie's sheepskin jacket from the dust and tossed it to her.

"Here," he said in that chilling tone. "You ride ahead of me."

Her horse shifted uneasily. The stranger looked directly at her for the first time, and Jessie felt a stab of fear. His eyes were slate, the light in them nearly opaque. There was no warmth in them, no compassion. Had he saved her out of a sense of honor? Or because he wanted her for himself? Or worse, because he simply enjoyed killing?

She'd been saved from a vicious attack. But her fate was now in the hands of a cool, calculating gunman.

Chapter Two

Cole filled a blackened pot with water from the creek, then added a measure of coffee before stooping to place the pot on the fire. Cocking his head to one side, he studied the figure of the girl asleep in the bedroll.

They had ridden for hours, until he was satisfied that they had put enough distance between them and any friends of the men he had shot. As soon as their horses were tethered, he had removed his holster, rolled himself into a faded army blanket and closed his eyes. He'd felt the girl watching him, assessing whether to stay or run; had finally heard the slight shuffling sounds as she'd arranged herself into her bedroll a short distance away. When her breathing became soft and steady, he'd satisfied himself that she was asleep and allowed himself to give in to an overwhelming exhaustion. He had slept soundly for three or four hours.

Now with the first pale fingers of light streaking the horizon, he crouched back on his heels and studied the figure in the bedroll.

Who the hell was she? And what was she doing alone in the middle of the Texas wasteland? Surely there was someone worried about her, searching for her. They would know that a lone woman was easy prey for every kind of vulture.

His gaze slowly skimmed her delicate features, taking in the arched eyebrows, the finely chiseled cheekbones, the slightly upturned nose sprinkled with freckles, giving her an impish appearance. A wisp of hair tickled her ear, and she lifted a hand in sleep to brush it aside. The blanket shifted, revealing a creamy column of throat and a shadowy cleft between high, firm breasts. He felt a rush of heat. Suddenly annoyed with himself, he turned away and tossed another log on the fire. A female had no place in his plans. He was a man in a hurry. A woman would only get in the way.

She sighed in her sleep, then stirred. Cole watched as her lids flickered.

Jessie inhaled. The first thing she was aware of was the bite of strong coffee in the morning air. Coffee and wood smoke. Pa. She smiled in her sleep. Pa was back, tending to his morning chores.

She sat up, brushing the hair from her eyes, and stiffened. The smile disappeared from her face. It wasn't Pa watching her; it was the stranger. She saw his eyes narrow before he spoke.

"I've got to be on the trail before the sun's up."

She nodded, too uncomfortable to trust her voice. He looked taller this morning and even more dangerous. His gun belt rode low on his hips. She had seen the way he'd handled the Colt Army .44. Like a man who'd been using it all his life.

Suddenly aware of her vulnerable position, she pushed aside the blanket and reached for her boots.

Cole tried not to stare as she flexed first one leg, then the other, shrugging into her boots. It gave him an odd sensation to see the rough fabric of his old shirt stretched tautly across her breasts. When she looked up he pulled his gaze away. Needing to be busy, he filled two tin cups with coffee. Handing one to her, he took a long drink from his own.

"My name's Cole Matthews. What's yours?"

She watched him over the rim of her cup. "Jessie. Jessie Conway."

"Where're you headed?"

"Abilene."

He looked at her as if she'd gone crazy. "That's hundreds of miles from here."

"That so?" She deliberately took a sip of coffee. "Strong. Good. That's the way I like it."

Damnable female. Cole decided to try again. "Where's your family?"

"In Abilene," she lied. There was no point in telling this stranger any more than she had to.

She had the impression that he was studying her much more closely than he let on.

"And you're heading there alone?" His words were clipped. "Your folks would probably whip you good if they knew what you were planning to do."

She swallowed the last of her coffee and bent to roll up her blankets. "You're probably right."

He watched her a minute, trying not to stare at her rounded bottom stuck up in the air as she fastened her bedroll. "Know much about this area?"

"Some." She carried her bedroll to her horse, tied it securely and reached for the saddle.

"Any towns nearby?"

She tightened the cinch. "There should be a town called Little Creek."

"Good. I'll ride with you as far as Little Creek."

She gave him what she hoped was a cool, appraising look. "I'll be turning off before we reach the town." She didn't add that it was her intention to avoid any towns nearby where someone might recognize Big Jack Conway's daughter. No point in telling the whole world that her father was missing and her little brothers were all alone on the ranch. They didn't have a whole lot worth stealing on their poor ranch. A couple of saddle horses and the few longhorns left to breed a new herd. But men had been known to kill for a lot less.

"Maybe you'll spot friends in Little Creek who'll take you in."

"Are you saying I need someone to take care of me?" Her

eyes darkened to the color of the sky just before a summer storm.

Fascinated, Cole half expected to see thunder and lightning.

"I don't need anyone coddling me. I can take care of myself."

"You did a good job of it last night."

She flinched. "I'm grateful that you rescued me last night. But I'll be just fine on my own."

The girl wasn't slow-witted; she had to be aware of the dangers. But whatever drove her was a need stronger than the need to be comfortable and safe. Though he hated to admit it, he'd probably do the same thing if he was missing his family. He admired her spunk. Still he'd hog-tie any female dumb enough to try crossing from Texas to Kansas herself.

Dousing the fire, he kept his thoughts to himself. This girl and her problems weren't his business. He had enough problems of his own.

"Sun's almost up. I've got to get moving. If you want to ride along, you can turn off before we get to Little Creek."

Jessie watched as Cole scattered the ashes and carefully brushed the area with a tree branch before mounting. As she pulled herself into the saddle, she shot a quick glance at the man beside her. He was examining the ground through narrowed eyes. Satisfied, he flicked the reins and took the lead. Jessie glanced back at their camp. All trace of human presence had been erased. A tiny tremble of fear sliced through her. There was no more doubt in her mind. Last night this man was too quick with a gun, too calm about killing three vicious men, to be an ordinary rancher or cowboy. This morning he was too careful, too cautious, to be a simple trail bum. Cole Matthews had to be a wanted man, a man on the run.

Jessie tightened her grip on the gun Pa had left her. Pa. What had he once told her? Tend to your own business. And let the other fellow tend to his. She would ride with Cole Matthews for a few hours, and that would be the end of it. She would never see him again. And what he did when they parted was no concern of hers. She swallowed back the little knot of fear and concentrated on the trail.

They rode in silence for several miles while the sun rose, touching the tips of mountains and buttes with a purple haze. As the sun rose higher, the mountains changed to pale mauve, then to palest pink. Even the grains of sand seemed touched with a shimmering light, causing them to glisten like fool's gold. With the rising sun Jessie felt her heart grow lighter. She would never tire of the sunrise here in the hot Texas countryside. And when she found Pa, they would return to this land that owned both their hearts.

They had eaten the dust of the trail for hours before Cole reined in his horse at the foot of towering buttes. Without a word Jessie slid from the saddle and pressed her hands to her back to ease the tension of saddle-weary muscles.

Cole handed her a canteen, and she took a long greedy drink before handing it back to him. He drank, then capped it before leading the horses to a cluster of rocks.

"We'll rest here a few minutes." Cole slumped down with his back against a cool rock. Wiping the sweat from his brow, he carefully removed his gun from the holster, cradling it gently in his hand, and closed his eyes. Jessie watched him a few minutes until she realized his breathing had become soft and steady. Could he be asleep so quickly? Sitting down beside him, she listened to the rhythm of his breathing, until, lulled, she could no longer fight her own weariness. She slipped quietly into sleep.

When she awoke, the sun was high overhead. Cool gray eyes were assessing her. For the briefest of moments, all thought scattered. She had no idea where she was or why. She knew only that the heat staining her cheeks did not come from the sun. And the erratic beat of her heart had not been caused by sudden wakefulness.

She came to her feet, brushing the dirt from her britches.

"Let's get moving," Cole said brusquely, turning toward his mount. "We've wasted enough time."

"If you're in a hurry, you can probably make better time alone."

Hearing the simmering anger in her voice, he didn't even bother to turn and glance at her. Tightening the cinch, he pulled himself into the saddle and waited while she saddled her horse. When she mounted, he took the lead without bothering to see if she was following.

Jessie rode in silence, fuming at his cold demeanor. It was obvious that he didn't want her around. Why was he bothering to stay with her? Why didn't he just ride on ahead and leave her to find her own way?

Up ahead, Cole waged the same argument within himself. Hadn't he done enough for her? Why take her under his wing now and try to steer her toward Little Creek? Because, he argued, she needed time to see how foolish her plan was. She couldn't possibly make it unharmed all the way across Texas and Indian Territory. If some lowlife didn't grab her, it would be the Indians or the heat or the vast isolation of this land that would finally destroy her. He just wanted to talk some sense into her. All he wanted was a chance to show her the error of her ways. If he could persuade her to stop in Little Creek, maybe she would turn tail and head back to wherever she came from. And he'd be free to move at his own pace.

As the horses' hooves kicked up the dust and the wind swirled it into their faces, he pulled the brim of his hat lower on his forehead and squinted into the sunlight. He knew that the girl, riding just behind him, would be eating even more dust. Hadn't she said she could take care of herself? Let her. He had no intention of playing nursemaid to a foolish, obstinate woman.

They rode all day without spotting another human. They stopped only twice. Each time, Cole disappeared behind rocks while Jessie fled in the opposite direction. Each time she returned to her horse, she avoided meeting Cole's eyes. Once, she thought he was almost grinning, but she couldn't be certain because she looked away as soon as she caught him watching her. They shared precious water and food, but little else. They spoke only when necessary.

When the sun began to cast long shadows on the desert floor, Cole reined in his mount and turned to wait for Jessie to catch up with him.

"How much farther do you think it is to Little Creek?"

She shrugged. "I've never been there. But Pa used to go once in a while. He made it there and back in three or four days."

"Three or four... Hellfire and damnation! Why didn't you just say you didn't know where the town was?"

She said each word slowly as if speaking to a child. "I figured it was in this direction. I didn't see how you could miss it."

"You didn't." He held her narrowed gaze for several seconds before turning away. It looked as though he would be forced to endure her company for another night.

While he pondered his situation, Jessie slid from the saddle and began to loosen the cinch. "I'm staying here for the night. You can ride on if you'd like. Little Creek is probably just over that ridge."

He saw a light winking in the distance. It could be a town or, he thought with a frown, a camp fire. It could be more of the kind he'd encountered last night. He wasn't in the mood for unwanted company tonight.

"No sense pushing the horses any harder than we have to."

Jessie piled some dried wood and touched a match to it. As it flickered to life and burst into flame, she turned toward her saddlebags. "I've got some stale biscuits here. You're welcome to share."

His mouth was watering for fresh meat, but he didn't want to risk a gunshot. "Thanks. I'll trade some of my dried venison for one of your biscuits."

They sat on either side of the fire and chewed their tasteless meal while coffee boiled and bubbled. When it was ready, they drank in silence. From a small sack in Cole's pocket, he produced tobacco and thin paper. With quick movements he rolled a cigarette, then held a flaming stick to the tip. He inhaled, drawing the smoke into his lungs. With a little sigh, he exhaled and watched the curl of smoke dissipate into the evening air. It was, Jessie realized, the first time she had seen him relax while he was awake. She leaned back, feeling tired and oddly pleased about the distance they had managed to cover since morning.

The sun was still visible on the horizon, casting long streaks of flame across the land. While Jessie set out her bedroll, Cole climbed to the top of a pile of rocks and studied the trail they had taken. For long minutes he stood unmoving, surveying the land in the distance. Suddenly he muttered a low savage oath. Looking up, Jessie saw him stiffen, then leap to the ground. Taking a rifle from the boot alongside his saddle, he made his way back up the rocks and dropped to his knees, his gaze fixed on something in the distance.

For long minutes her heart seemed to stop beating. She had been right about Cole Matthews. He was a wanted man. And whoever was trailing him was finally catching up with him.

What did she do now? There was still time to ride out of here before the gunfight started. There was, after all, a good chance that Cole Matthews, as good a shot as he was, would be done in by the man chasing him. In that case she could forfeit her own life as well if she was found accompanying him. Yet, despite her fears, she felt a sense of loyalty to this man who had risked so much to save her. She knew what Pa would do. And she knew without a doubt what she must do. Brushing aside her fears, she removed the old rifle from her saddle and hefted Pa's gun in the other hand. It was time for a decision, and she had just made hers.

Cole turned as she climbed up beside him. Seeing the gun in her hand, he hissed, "Get out of here. Go on back down and hide yourself behind those rocks."

"I owe you. And I know how to use this."

He dismissed her as though she were a schoolgirl. "This isn't your fight."

She gave him a level gaze and said, "You saved my life last night. That makes it my fight."

He turned to study her for long minutes. "You don't even know what I'm fighting for."

"I guess that doesn't matter."

His gaze bored through her. His eyes, she noted, held the same cold opaque look as the night before when he'd faced down four men.

He shrugged and turned toward the trail once more. "Just so you're warned. Keep your head down, and don't shoot until they're close enough to hit."

"They?"

"I count two of them." He pointed.

Jessie could see only the dust spewing upward from horses' hooves. As they drew closer, she could make out two shadowy forms. She checked her pistol before placing it within reach on a shelf of rock beside her. She rubbed her palms on her britches and grasped her rifle, keeping her finger on the trigger. She had killed plenty of game in her young life and was an excellent shot. But she had never deliberately taken aim at a man before.

The horses were moving slowly side by side. The figures astride them were compact, as though hunched deeply inside oversize coats. What sort of men tracked another man relentlessly, like an animal, with the intention of killing?

Jessie forgot to breathe as Cole calmly waited. A quick sidelong glance revealed a man completely in control. His hand rested loosely at his side, holding the rifle almost casually. Beneath the brim of his hat, she saw his eyes narrow. Keeping the figures in his sight, he tracked them as they drew closer. When the horses topped a ridge, Cole stood, prepared to return their fire if one of them shot first. In the glimmer of moonlight, something glittered in one of the rider's hands. Both Jessie and Cole spotted it at the same moment. Cole tipped his hat back from his face. He brought the rifle to his shoulder, taking careful aim. Just as his finger closed over the trigger, a ripple of boyish laughter wafted toward them. Instinctively Jessie brought her hand up, causing the rifle to discharge harmlessly into the air.

Swearing viciously, Cole caught her roughly by the shoulder and threw her against a wall of rock. Momentarily stunned, she shook her head to clear it, then ran at him as he took aim once more.

"No."

"Little fool. Are you crazy? Now that they know where we are, they'll come in with all guns blazing."

She made a desperate grab for his rifle. "Cole. Don't shoot. Please, don't shoot."

He shoved her aside even more roughly this time, then turned from the figure beside him to the two figures he had last seen astride the horses. The horses had trotted off a few paces. Both riders had dropped to the ground for protection.

Cole watched, waiting for one of the figures to go for a gun. Instead they continued lying motionless on the ground.

As Cole and Jessie watched, one of the figures reached out a hand. The gleam of metal was clearly visible in the grass, just out of reach.

With a cry of alarm, Jessie leaped from the rocks and began tearing across the space that separated her from the horses and riders. Cole stayed where he was, keeping all three figures now in his sight.

"Damned fool!" His voice echoed through the dusk, bouncing off canyon walls. "So you've decided to join them, have you, woman? What's wrong? Don't you like the odds?"

"You don't understand," came her breathless response. "I haven't turned against you. They aren't your enemies. They're my brothers."

Chapter Three

Brothers? Jessie's brothers, come to fetch her home where she belonged. Wherever home was. Skeptical, Cole kept the rifle cocked and ready to fire as he slowly made his way toward the three figures. Though the sun had already drifted behind the mountains, leaving the land in shadow, Cole kept them in his sight.

As he drew nearer, he watched the figures untangle themselves from the ground and rush into Jessie's arms. Only then did he lower the rifle.

At her shout, he had expected tall hulking brothers who would take Jessie to task for having run away from the ranch in search of her parents. Instead he saw two slender figures, one slightly taller than Jessie, the other much shorter.

He felt a wave of disappointment. Boys. Not men who would take her in hand and escort her home. Boys. One of them hardly into his teens from the look of him, the other little more than a baby. With a barely concealed look of disgust, Cole watched their reunion.

The taller one hung back, looking slightly embarrassed by his sudden display of affection. The smaller one was hanging on Jessie's neck as if attached by invisible cords.

"How'd you know it was us?" the taller one was asking.

"I heard Thad's laughter. I'd know that laugh anywhere." Her tone hardened. "What are you two doing here?"

"We decided to join you. It isn't safe for you to ride across Texas alone."

"You had no right. We agreed—"

"No, Jess. We didn't agree to anything. As usual, you just made your plans and ordered us to go along with them." Danny's voice betrayed both his hurt and his confusion. "After you left, Thad and I decided you needed us."

"Needed you. Humph." She gave a snort of derision. "Who's taking care of the ranch?"

"The Starkeys. They agreed to keep an eye on things until we got back."

The Starkey family had a ranch adjoining theirs, if twenty or thirty miles away could be called adjoining. Husband and wife and three strapping sons were hardworking, honest people.

"We can't afford to pay them for taking on the extra work load."

"Yes, we can. I promised them Bossy's calf in the spring."

"Pa'll kill you."

Danny met her look squarely. "I'll deal with Pa when the time comes."

Something in his tone told Jessie that her brother had thought this through. She could see the wisdom of Danny's plan. The tough Conway spirit of independence could be maintained by paying the Starkeys for their help. Still it rankled. She'd been counting on that calf to enlarge the herd.

Before she could argue further, Cole drew nearer, causing their conversation to fade. All three turned to watch his approach.

Cole's hand trembled slightly at the thought of what he'd nearly done. Another second and he might have killed a couple of innocent kids. His tone was harsher than he intended. "Hellfire and damnation! That was a stupid thing you two did. You nearly got yourselves killed. What the hell were you thinking of, coming up on us with no warning?"

Jessie's eyes narrowed with fury. It was perfectly all right for her to find fault with her brothers. After all, they were family. It wasn't all right for Cole to criticize. She became immediately defensive. "Don't you dare swear in front of my little brothers."

"I'll say any damned thing—"

"You will not swear in front of them. Or me." Her eyes blazed. "Furthermore, what did you expect them to do—shout out their names as they rode along the trail?"

His eyes narrowed, and he thought of several vicious swear words that would curl her hair. "I'd expect them to make camp before dark, like any sensible travelers."

"Who is this man, Jess?" Danny's gaze slid over the stranger, noting the gun and holster, the rifle cradled in his arm. The wide-legged threatening stance, the ripple of muscles did not go unnoticed by the boy. Nor did the cold, calculating look in the man's eye.

"His name is Cole Matthews. He saved my life last night. Which, I might add, doesn't give him the right to swear in my presence." She turned to him with a murderous look. "Cole, these are my brothers, Danny and Thad."

"Do you know where our pa is?" Thad chirped.

Cole was instantly alert. "I thought your sister said he was in Abilene."

Danny, carefully watching the stranger, made no move to offer a handshake. Instead he asked, "How'd you happen to save my sister's life?"

"He was camped nearby when some men pestered me."

Pestered. Danny wasn't fooled by the words. A boy like Thad might think nothing of it, but Danny was old enough to understand the implications.

He continued to stare at the stranger. "What did you do?"

Cole's voice was devoid of all emotion. "I killed them."

"How many?"

"Three. One got away."

Danny studied the man a minute longer, anger and relief churning inside him. What would four men do to a girl like Jessie? She wouldn't have stood a chance alone. He was glad the stranger had come to her rescue. He just wished the man didn't look so dangerous. Like a rattler coiled to strike.

He turned to face his sister. "I guess something just told me you needed us. That's why we're here."

She felt a wave of tenderness toward her sensible brother before she pushed aside such feelings. There was no place for tenderness now. She had to be tough.

"Well, you're going back in the morning. You know you and Thad can't make the trip all the way across Texas."

"We're not going back, Jess." Though his voice cracked, Danny's tone was determined. "You can't make us."

She glanced from Danny to Thad and watched as the little boy released her hand and stepped back in a show of defiance. He glanced uncertainly at his brother, then looked up to meet her steady gaze.

"Thaddeus Francis Conway. You'd disobey me, too?"

Cole watched as the little boy glanced quickly at his brother, then nodded his head. "We're family, Jessie. And Pa always said family sticks together."

Her eyes grew stormy. "How could you do this to him, Danny? You know Thad can't make this trip."

"He made it this far, didn't he?" Danny put a hand on his little brother's shoulder. "We've been riding since yesterday afternoon. We only stopped long enough to sleep a few hours before climbing into the saddle again. And Thad never complained once."

"But…"

"We're not going back, Jess. We have as much right as you to find out what happened to Pa."

At this, Cole found himself suddenly very interested. It was obvious that the girl hadn't told him everything.

Without waiting for her reply, Danny bent and picked up the rifle that had fallen from his hands when he'd leaped from his horse.

Seeing it, Cole gave a muttered oath. All three looked up at him questioningly.

"Where'd you get that rifle?"

"It's my Pa's," Danny said with pride.

"What were you aiming to shoot, a whole herd of buffalo?"

"What do you mean?"

Cole set his own Winchester on the ground and reached out a hand. Reluctantly Danny handed him the rifle. "This is a Sharps breechloader. It can bring down a buffalo from a couple of hundred yards. It you used it on a man, you'd blow him clean away."

"Good." Danny took back the gun and gave him a meaningful look. "That's what I'd do to anyone who threatened to hurt my brother or sister."

Cole's smile faded. The kid's message was loud and clear. "I think," he said, "we'd all better get some sleep. And in the morning, the three of you ought to head for home."

"Are we going home, Jessie?" Thad asked softly.

She stared at Cole for a moment, then turned her gaze toward her little brother. Wrapping an arm about his shoulders, she drew him close. "If I take you and Danny home, I'll lose two days. And even then, I can't be certain you'll stay there after I leave. You could just turn around and follow me again."

"Does that mean you're taking us with you?"

She studied the little boy for long silent moments. "I guess it means we've got a long way to go before we see home again. Come on. Let's get some sleep."

Cole watched as Jessie caught up the reins of the two horses and led them toward the camp fire. The little boy walked beside her, his exhaustion evident in the way he struggled to match her strides. Danny, hugging the rifle to his chest, brought up the rear.

As he retrieved his own rifle, Cole bit back a torrent of oaths. How the hell had he gotten himself into this? It was bad enough when he'd been stuck with the girl. But he had no intention of playing nursemaid to a pint-size version of Jessie and a young bull who was itching to test his manhood with a buffalo gun.

He watched in silence as Jessie fixed her brothers' bedrolls beside hers.

"Did you two have anything to eat?"

Danny nodded. "I heated up some of the rabbit stew you left us." He held up a leather pouch tied to his saddle. "And I brought along as much milk as I could carry. But it curdled in the heat. Now it's more like buttermilk."

Jessie chuckled at the look of revulsion on Thad's face. "Don't worry, Tadpole. I won't make you drink it. I never could abide curdled milk myself. Looks like you'll have to settle for coffee in the morning."

"I'd like that," the little boy said before adding softly, "Pa always drinks coffee."

Jessie saw the tears that sprang to his eyes before he could blink them away. She knelt and ruffled his hair before drawing him close against her. "I know you miss him, Tadpole. So do I." Forcing a cheerful note to her voice, she added, "Won't Pa be surprised to see how much you've grown?"

"Yeah." He sniffed against her shoulder. "Maybe by the time we find him, I'll be as big as you."

"Maybe." She kissed the top of his head before standing. "Now I think you two had better climb into those bedrolls and get some sleep. We've got a long ride ahead of us in the morning."

"How about you, Jess?" Danny asked, keeping an eye on Cole, who was pouring coffee into a tin cup.

"I'll just see to your horses before I sleep."

She watched as the two boys slipped off their boots. Thad curled up in his blanket and closed his eyes. Within minutes he was sound asleep. Danny set the buffalo rifle in the blankets beside him and clasped his hands beneath his head. His eyes, she noted, followed every movement Cole made. There was no doubt that Danny had no intention of trusting the gunman.

When the horses were fed and carefully tethered, Jessie watched as Cole drained the last cup of coffee from the pot and handed her a steaming cup.

"Thanks."

She wrapped her hands around it, inhaling the warmth.

Cole glanced toward Danny and saw the boy struggling to keep his eyes open. Nodding toward him, Cole murmured, "You're not really going to take them along, are you?"

"Looks like I don't have a choice."

"People always have choices." His voice was low with repressed anger. "Take them home where they belong. Where you belong."

"It won't be much of a home without Pa, will it?"

"Feel like telling me about what's going on?"

"I can't."

He stared at her and saw for the first time all the fear and hopelessness she was feeling. Without thinking, he rubbed his knuckles across her cheek.

The flare of heat was so sudden, so shocking, he was nearly rocked back on his heels. His eyes narrowed as he studied her. The smooth flesh beneath his hand was the softest he'd ever felt. Softer even than a newborn foal.

Without realizing it, his hand opened until his callused fingertips were caressing her cheek.

Jessie stood frozen to the spot. It was as if someone had tied her hands to her sides, rendering her unable to move. Strange stirrings rippled through her, constricting her throat, making it impossible to speak.

The breeze lifted a strand of her hair and Cole caught it. Silk. Silkier even than those dresses Maud Hennings's whores wore when they were working the saloon. He watched, fascinated, as the strands sifted through his fingers. He had a sudden, almost overwhelming desire to plunge both his hands into her hair and savage her mouth with kisses.

Jessie glanced up in time to see the way Cole's eyes narrowed. Whatever was he thinking? Did he have any idea what his touch was doing to her? Did it affect him the same way it was affecting her? Or was a man immune to such feelings?

Tiny pinpricks of pleasure shot along her spine, leaving her trembling inside. She lowered her gaze, afraid to look at him, afraid her feelings might be mirrored in her eyes. Nobody had every touched her with such tenderness. It made her want to melt against him and hang on for dear life.

His tone softened. "Look, I know something's wrong, and it has to do with your father. But taking two kids all the way across Texas won't solve anything. Go home, Jessie."

When she made no response, he placed a finger beneath her chin and lifted her face, forcing her to meet his gaze. Inside she felt her heart lurch, felt the blood heat and rush to her head, leaving her dizzy.

"Go home," he said softly, coaxingly. "It's the only logical choice."

She could stand here like this all night, feeling his fingers on her flesh, his gaze boring through to her very soul. But if she did, she would forget how to breathe. Her heart would forget how to beat.

"Choice." With a supreme effort she twisted her head to free herself from his touch. She took a step back, breaking contact. She felt her mind beginning to clear. Lifting her head in a gesture of defiance, she fixed him with a steady gaze. "What about your choice? Why are you out here on the trail, drawing a gun at every shadow?"

His tone hardened. "That's none of your business."

"And what I do is none of yours."

He clamped his mouth shut on the words that sprang to his lips. Damned obstinate female.

"You choose to follow the trail, knowing that someone is out there in the darkness, sniffing at your heels. Well, Cole Matthews, I choose to go across Texas, knowing it's the only way I can find out what happened to my pa."

"You don't know where he is?"

When she looked away and shook her head, he continued. "You could wire the sheriff in some of the towns and forts. Give a description of your father and ask to be notified of anyone who fits that description."

"I guess you haven't had much dealings with sheriffs," she said with a note of derision.

"And you have?"

She shrugged. "Not me. My pa. He always said the two things he was determined to keep away from were fast women and men who wore badges."

"Why?"

"He said both are quick on the draw, and both feel their profession gives them the right to do anything they want to a man."

Despite his frustration, Cole nearly laughed aloud. Did she have any idea how beguiling she looked when she was angrily spouting her father's ramblings without having any idea what they meant?

Stung by his laughter, she tossed the bitter dregs of the coffee on the fire and watched as the flames hissed and snapped. Turning on her heel, she walked ramrod straight to the bedroll and pulled off her boots. Climbing in beside her two brothers, she rolled over and closed her eyes, ignoring the soft rumble of laughter still issuing from Cole.

As soon as she had fallen asleep, Cole climbed up to the craggy outcropping of rock, his rifle in his arms, watching the trail below. While he kept watch, he thought about the three Conways sleeping peacefully in their bedrolls. This strange, primitive countryside bred strong, independent people like them. Imagine one skinny little woman trying to comb half the West for a missing father. What was worse, she intended to drag two fool kids along. He thought about his own childhood on a windswept stretch of Texas soil as he rolled a cigarette and leaned his back against the cool rock. Taking a deep drag, he filled his lungs and slowly exhaled. Whether he sympathized with her or not, he wanted no part of Jessie Conway and her brothers. He had no time for their problems. He'd tried to talk to them like a friend. He'd pointed out the dangers, had urged them to go home where they'd be safe. There was nothing more he could do for them. He had no intention of being their damned nursemaid.

He thought of Jessie's soft skin and found he was itching to touch her again. Dangerous thoughts, he warned himself. He'd been too long without a woman. Life on the trail could turn a man into something resembling the coyotes who cried their mournful songs to the moon. Out here men and animals often behaved in the same way in order to survive.

He closed his eyes, allowing himself to recall for just a moment longer the way her skin felt against his fingertips. Soft. So damned soft he'd wanted to crush her in his arms and take her right there beside the fire.

Beneath a canopy of stars, he smoked until the cigarette burned his fingers. Dropping it, he crushed the butt beneath his heel and walked to his bedroll. He would grab an hour or two of sleep before hitting the trail. By the time Jessie Conway and her brothers awoke in the morning, he told himself firmly, he'd be long gone.

Chapter Four

Jessie lay in that soft gauzy twilight between waking and sleeping. Drifting on a cloud of contentment, she snuggled deeper into her blanket.

Nearby a twig snapped and she thought about opening her eyes, but the need for sleep was too powerful an urge. Rolling to her side, she drew the blanket over her head to blot out the shuffling sounds that intruded on her comfort.

Shuffling sounds. Like muted footsteps. Instantly alert, she slid the blanket from her head and opened her eyes. A tall wiry figure moved among the horses. Raising her head slightly, Jessie peered through the gray light of dawn. The figure was too gaunt, too thin to belong to Cole. It was a stranger. A stranger who was tying their horses to a rope.

God in heaven! Someone was stealing their horses.

She lay perfectly still, agonizing over what to do. Her gun. Jessie felt around the blanket for the gun she had carelessly set beneath her head before falling asleep. Where was her gun? Her fingertips brushed cold metal. She closed her hand around it and wondered if she dared to use it. She couldn't risk having a trail bum kill her little brothers. But without their horses, they would be helpless against this harsh land and elements.

When the stranger finished tying the last of their horses, he turned. Lying perfectly still, Jessie tracked his movements through partially closed lids.

He walked around the embers of the fire and stopped at the foot of their bedrolls. Jessie's heart was pounding so loudly in her chest, she was certain the stranger could hear it.

Garbed all in black, with a black hat pulled low over his face, he peered intently at Danny, whose blanket covered all but one slender hand. Just below that hand, Jessie knew, lay the buffalo rifle. Thankfully it was not visible from the stranger's vantage point.

Next the stranger scanned the tip of Thad's blond head poking out from his bedroll. In sleep he looked like an angelic cherub.

Squeezing her eyes tightly shut, she tensed, knowing that the stranger's gaze was now scanning her figure. With the blanket pulled up over her face, she prayed he would think she was just another skinny kid. Her hand, closed tightly around her pistol, trembled slightly. Cold beads of perspiration formed on her forehead. She waited, fearing that the stranger would yank the blanket away and discover the gun in her hand. He would aim and she would be forced to do the same.

A slight movement alerted her that the stranger had moved away. With terror gripping her heart, she opened her eyes. The man was now standing over Cole's bedroll. Please, God, Jessie prayed, don't let Cole wake up. If he did, the man would certainly shoot him where he lay.

Cole sighed in his sleep. A familiar click sounded beside his temple. Sleep vanished. His dreams disappeared. Cold reality had him instantly alert.

With eyes tightly shut, he assessed his situation. His gun rested just under his left shoulder. He was lying on his left side, with his right hand resting on his chest. Even though his eyes were still closed, he knew that someone stood over him with a drawn gun. He had heard that sound often enough to know that there was no other sound like it. And he knew with icy certainty that the slightest movement of his hand toward his gun would bring death. What he didn't know was whether or not the person standing over him would kill him if he continued to pretend to be asleep.

Was it a trail bum after horses and supplies? Or was it the one who'd been eluding him for so long? He could smell the stranger. He smelled of horses, leather, sweat and the overpowering stench of stale whiskey.

Cole's hand itched for his gun.

How would he know? With his life hanging in the balance, he had to know who was standing over him, aiming a pistol at his head. Did he take the chance that it was someone who would walk away? Or did he act on the assumption that it was someone who would kill a sleeping, unarmed man just for the fun of it?

Jessie. Jessie and her brothers. Until this moment he'd forgotten about them. If the gunman standing over him killed him, he would kill them, as well. Or maybe kill the boys and take Jessie with him for sport. No matter what the cost to Cole, he couldn't risk all of their lives. He had told Jessie that everyone had choices in life. His choices had just been narrowed considerably. In fact, Cole knew that he no longer had any choice.

His eyes blinked open. In that first split second, he had the impression of a thin man bundled inside a heavy coat. The man had long dark hair that reached nearly to his shoulders beneath a broad-brimmed hat. He was bending close, straining against the semidarkness to determine whether or not Cole was awake. With quick, practiced movements, Cole reached beneath his shoulder for the Colt Army .44.

At his sudden movement, the gunman blinked, straightened and leveled his gun at Cole's face.

"No! Cole! Beside you."

At Jessie's cry of alarm, the stranger twisted around toward her. In that instant, she saw his eyes. They were glittering feral eyes. The eyes of a predator. The wide, haunted, hate-filled eyes of a monster. The same monster who had once threatened to carve his initials into her flesh.

The gunman pointed his gun at Jessie and she froze. Cole felt the gun in his hand, felt the surge of adrenaline as he lifted the gun from beneath his shoulder. At the slight movement the gunman whirled back toward Cole. With his finger on the trigger, Cole knew he was a second too late. He heard the terrible explosion, felt his body rock backward with the force of a powerful blow.

For long moments Cole felt nothing. And then pain seared through him, ripping through his flesh, tearing through his mind. He tried to hold on to something, anything. But he was falling, falling through darkness. He heard voices shouting, crying. He heard another terrible explosion. And then he lapsed into blessed unconsciousness.

''Dear God, no!''

Jessie was on her feet, aiming her pistol at the man as he ran toward his horse. She fired and saw him stagger.

Beside her, Danny sat up, rubbed his eyes, then reached for the buffalo gun.

''It's Knife, the man who attacked me. He's killed Cole. He's stealing our horses.''

Danny heard his sister's plaintive voice and watched as she aimed and fired again. The man screamed and cursed as blood spread in a widening circle along the back of his coat. With a last desperate effort, he pulled himself into the saddle and caught up the rope holding the string of horses.

''We have to stop him.''

Danny had never fired his father's rifle. In fact, he had never even held it in his hands until the day before yesterday. But he had seen his father handle it often enough to know what to do. Setting the trigger, he took careful aim and fired. The rifle roared like thunder. The powerful report sent him flying backward. He landed in the dirt with a force strong enough to leave him dazed.

With a shriek, the man dropped the rope and spun his mount away. Within minutes there was nothing left of him but a cloud of dust. The horses, free of their ropes, milled about in confusion before slowly drifting back toward the camp fire.

While Danny and Thad watched in silence, Jessie ran to where Cole lay and dropped to her knees beside him. She placed trembling fingers on the side of his throat. For a moment she felt nothing, and a wave of terrible desperation washed over her. Then, haltingly at first, she felt a feeble, thready pulse.

"He's still alive." She looked over at her brother. "We have to save him, Danny. We have to."

Cole heard a voice very close to his ear. But the words made no sense. They drifted in and out of his mind like the soft musical notes of a bird. Maybe it was a bird, he thought. Or maybe it was the voice of an angel. Maybe he had died.

It had always been Danny who had been called upon to practice his healing arts when any member of the family had been hurt. But the worst thing he'd ever had to deal with was Pa's busted leg when the mule had kicked him through the wall of their sod shack.

Danny knelt beside Jessie and looked down at the blood spilling out of Cole. He knew that the gunman had missed Cole's heart, because Cole was still breathing. But from the blood and ragged tissue, it looked as if half of Cole's shoulder and chest had been blown away.

This was no simple cut or scratch or broken limb. This was a man's very lifeblood slowly slipping away. Danny would hold a man's life in his hands. And the boy teetering on the brink of manhood, for all his fascination with doctoring, had never faced anything like this before.

Jessie, noting the pallor of her brother's cheeks, put a hand on his shoulder. "We've got to save him."

He met her steady gaze. "I know." Forcing himself not to think about the blood, Danny said firmly, "We'll need to get the fire going."

Jessie nodded and sent Thad scurrying about for firewood. It would be good to give their youngest brother something to do. The poor little thing hadn't said a single word since awakening to the sound of a terrifying gunfight.

Danny thought about all the books he had read: *Doctor Cooney's Guide To Health*, *A Primer of Home Medicine*, *Journal*

Of A Western Doctor. In each one, alcohol and boiling water played a major role in healing the patient.

"Check Cole's saddlebags and bedroll for a bottle of whiskey," he said.

Jessie looked up from the fire and nodded. A few minutes later she produced two bottles.

"Good." Danny gently peeled away the last of Cole's shirt. "As soon as the bucket of water boils, I want you to bring it here. I'll need my pocketknife and some soap and long strips of clean cloth."

Jessie assembled the items he'd requested, then hauled the bucket of boiling water and set it on a blanket beside the still figure of Cole.

"We're going to have to roll him over. The bullet's inside him. He'll never stop bleeding if I don't get it out. He'll die of blood poisoning." Danny mopped at the blood with a rag.

"What if you can't find it?"

Danny looked up at her, then brought his attention back to the man who lay as still as death. "I'll find it, Jess. I have to if he's going to live. Come on. Help me roll him over."

Cole made no sound as they struggled to roll him on his stomach. Even Thad helped, pulling and tugging until Cole was completely turned. Jessie found herself wishing he would moan or even swear. Then she'd know that he was still alive.

"Hand me my pocketknife," Danny said.

With a bent stick, Jessie fished it out of the boiling water and handed it to Danny. Thad ducked behind Jessie, peering out every few minutes at the still figure of the man, only to duck once more behind his sister's back.

Jessie knelt beside her brother, feeling her throat go dry as Danny plunged the blade of the knife into Cole's flesh. Blood spurted and flowed freely as Danny probed beneath the skin.

"Uncork that bottle. Pour some of that whiskey here. Quick," Danny added as her fingers fumbled.

Jessie poured a liberal amount of the whiskey and watched in horrified fascination as it mingled with the blood to form a river that flowed between his shoulder blades before pooling in the small of his back.

"Catch that blood," Danny urged.

Instantly Jessie lifted a rag and began sponging the blood. As quickly as the wound was clean, it filled again with fresh blood.

"Hurry, Danny," she whispered. "If he doesn't stop bleeding soon, it will be too late."

"I'm trying, Jess. I'm trying."

Jessie glanced at her younger brother. His face was stiff from the strain. His long and tapered fingers were smeared with Cole's blood. With the blade of his knife, he probed gently, gently, until suddenly he felt the tip of the knife scrape against metal.

"Here it is."

At his words, Thad peeked out from behind Jessie's back. Catching sight of the raw flesh, he quickly moved back and buried his face against his sister's shoulder. While Jessie continued to sponge the blood, Danny cut deeper below the bullet and lifted it to the surface. Dropping it unceremoniously in the dirt, he wiped his knife on his pant leg, then poured whiskey into the open wound.

Dipping a small cloth into the boiling water, Danny lathered on some of Jessie's homemade soap, cleansing the wound and the area around it. Then he poured more whiskey over it. When the wound was clean and disinfected, he bound it tightly with strips of cloth.

"Now we'll have to roll him over and tend to the rest of this."

Straining and struggling, the three of them managed to roll the heavy, muscled body over. Blood streamed from the gaping hole left by the gunshot.

Once again Danny washed the wound and poured generous amounts of whisky over the jagged flesh. Working quickly, he bound the wound with the rest of the cloth strips.

With Thad's help, they managed to slide Cole from his soaked, bloody bedroll and into their clean dry blankets.

"We'll have to keep him warm," Danny said.

"At least the worst is over," Jessie muttered, glancing at the still figure wrapped in blankets.

"All we did was remove the bullet and clean up his wounds. The worst is still to come."

Jessie looked at him with alarm. "What could be worse than removing a bullet from all that bloody flesh?"

"Fever, chills and shock. According to Dr. Cooney, that's when most patients are lost."

Jessie studied the unmoving figure covered with their blankets. What if all their efforts had been in vain? She turned away quickly, annoyed at such thoughts. Cole would live. He had to live. He had saved her life. Now she owed him the same favor.

Touching a hand to Danny's cheek, she whispered, "You go wash up. I'll make us something to eat. We have a long day ahead of us. Thad, you tend to the horses."

As they walked away, Jessie called, "Danny."

He turned toward her.

"You did a fine job. You're going to make a good doctor."

He gave her a weary nod before stumbling away. In the bushes he bent over and retched. For long minutes he knelt, heaving and retching until the sickness passed.

"Jess." Danny touched a hand to his sister's shoulder. In her sleep, she sighed then was instantly alert.

"Is it Cole? Is there any change?"

"No. But I can't keep my eyes open any longer. It's your turn to tend him."

She sat up and shivered in the predawn chill.

"Don't forget to keep the fire going. He has to be kept warm."

She nodded. "I'll take care of it."

As she stood up, Danny took her place beside Thad in the warm bedroll. He was asleep as soon as he stretched out.

Earlier that day, Jessie had washed Cole's blankets in the bucket of boiling water, and draped them over rocks to dry.

The three of them would share Cole's bedroll since Cole was wrapped in theirs. At bedtime she and Danny had agreed to take turns keeping watch over Cole and keeping the fire going to make certain that he was warm. Thad had wanted to take his turn, as well, but Jessie had insisted that he needed his sleep.

She walked to the fire and threw another log on the glowing coals. Flames licked along the bark and blazed skyward.

Filling a tin cup with coffee, she sat down beside the still figure of Cole and touched a hand to his forehead. His skin was on fire. The fever raged through his body, leaving him soaked and trembling. Despite the heat, his teeth chattered uncontrollably. Every so often he mumbled incoherently. Jessie leaned close, straining to catch a familiar word.

"...kill you. Don't...hide..."

Cole turned his head from side to side like a man possessed. Sweat beaded his forehead, and Jessie mopped at it with a cool damp rag. Gradually his breathing became softer. The words, the torment, abated for the moment.

Who was he? she wondered. And who was it he watched for in the shadows? His whispered words disturbed her. He spoke of killing, hiding. Had she helped save the life of a wanted gunman? No matter. For now, he was her responsibility. Who he was, what he was, made no difference.

She picked up her cup, drained it and poured a second. The hours from now to dawn would be long, but she had to stay awake. Walking the perimeter of the campsite, she stooped to pick up fallen branches for the fire. In the distance she heard a coyote baying to the moon. The mournful sound sent shivers along her spine even as it brought a measure of comfort. This vast wild land was home to her. As long as she could watch the sun set over a distant mountain peak or hear the much loved sounds of the wilderness, she was content. She shivered again, forcing herself to dismiss the fear that tugged at her. She would not dwell on the dangers ahead. She would get through this night and face another day. It was the creed by which Jessie lived her life.

Stacking the branches near the fire, she warmed herself, then crouched beside Cole's still figure.

He moaned.

Bending close, she whispered, "Cole. Are you all right? How do you feel?"

His eyes flickered open, and he squinted against the light of the fire.

"Jessie?" His throat was so dry the words would hardly come out. "Is that you?"

She leaned closer. "Of course it is."

"You're not...dead?"

She laughed low and deep in her throat, and Cole thought it was the most beautiful sound he'd ever heard. "No. And neither are you."

"I thought..." He coughed, and pain crashed through his chest and shoulder, leaving him gasping. He had seen the gunman aim at Jessie That was what had caused him to lose his timing. Jessie. He'd been so desperate to save her from the gunman's bullet, he'd hesitated just long enough to allow the stranger to gain the upper hand. So the gunshot hadn't found Jessie. At the moment, nothing else seemed important though he didn't know why. What the hell was the matter with him? She was just a girl, a stranger he'd met along the trail. A burden he'd hoped to be rid of as soon as possible.

"Don't talk anymore," she said. "Here. Drink this." Cradling his head against her chest, she held a dipper of water to his lips.

As she laid him gently back against the blanket, he became aware for the first time of the dressings that bound his shoulder.

"The bullet...got to get..." The words were raspy. Jessie worried that he was using up too much energy talking.

"You took a bullet in the shoulder. Don't worry. Danny got it out. The wound is clean."

"The kid?" He stared at her as if he couldn't believe what he'd heard.

She placed a hand on his lips to silence him. The touch of

her fingers on his lips caused a tiny spark of heat in the pit of his stomach. So he wasn't dead after all. He could still react to a woman's touch. He could still feel.

"I'll tell you all about it later. After you've slept. Right now, you need to rest."

Rest. Her voice washed over him, lulling him. He was so tired. So damned tired. It was too much effort to keep his eyes open. He wanted to ask her if she'd keep her fingers on his lips. It would be so nice to fall asleep with her touching him. It had been a long time since he'd savored a woman's tender touch. But he didn't have the strength to get the words out. All he could do was lie there clinging to the thought that the gunman hadn't killed her. She wasn't dead after all.

So much killing. So much pain. The pain began radiating from his shoulder to his chest to his ribs. Soon his whole body seemed to be a mass of pain. But the pain only served to reinforce one fact. Only a dead man would feel no pain. Jessie wasn't dead. And, by God, neither was he.

Chapter Five

Pain. Cole touched a hand to his shoulder, hoping to ease the pain that engulfed him. That slight movement only brought more pain. He couldn't tell where the aching began or where it ended. His chest was on fire. His shoulder felt as if hot knives were being thrust into it. His head throbbed. His back ached. His whole body was a mass of searing pain. The slightest movement made it worse. Yet it seemed impossible to lie still and absorb any more pain.

Light. As Cole opened his eyes, sunlight stabbed, causing him to blink them shut. Overhead the sun was a harsh brilliance reflecting off rocks and sand. Hot needles of light pierced his eyes even after his lids were closed.

Cold. So cold. Despite the heat of the day, several layers of blankets had been wrapped around him. A fire crackled nearby. He shivered. How he could be chilled when he was surrounded by warmth? Why was his body failing him?

"Good. You're finally awake. How are you feeling?" Jessie knelt beside him and touched a hand to his forehead.

"Do you really want to know?"

"Of course."

"I feel like hell. If this is what it feels like to live, I'd rather be dead."

She grinned. "I can see you're feeling much better."

"Better? How the hell can you tell?"

Her smile grew. "Because you're swearing. The last time you woke up, you were still too weak to swear."

"Sorry. I'm not used to being around a lady. Or a pack of kids."

"I can tell. Want something to drink?"

He nodded, and she filled a dipper with water, lifted his head and held the dipper to his lips. He drank and felt the liquid soothe his parched throat.

"More?"

He nodded. When he had drunk his fill, she gently laid his head back down on the blankets. Dipping a clean rag into the cool water, she began sponging off his face and neck.

In an instant the pain was forgotten. He closed his eyes, and she pressed the cloth to his hot lids.

"That feels good."

His voice was deep and raspy. He lay absolutely still, feeling the soft caressing movement of her hands. She smelled clean like rainwater, and he knew that she had visited the creek for a morning bath. As she bent close, her clothes gave off the fragrance of evergreen, and he guessed that she had washed them and spread them out on tree branches to dry. A soft sigh escaped his lips.

While his eyes were closed, Jessie studied him. Life beneath the western sky had turned his skin to bronze. His brows were thick and dark, his forehead wide and slightly furrowed from squinting against the sun. Fine little lines fanned out from the corners of his eyes. His nose was perfectly formed, his lips wide and sensual. Her gaze lingered on his lips a moment, and she found herself wondering what it would feel like to have them pressed against hers. The thought stunned her. Where in the world had such a thought come from? Yet, even while she berated herself for allowing such thoughts to creep into her mind, she felt a strange curling sensation in the pit of her stomach. As she brought the cloth across his cheeks, his lids flickered open. She found herself staring into those hypnotic gray eyes.

"You have a nice easy touch, Jessie," he muttered.

She felt the beginnings of a blush sweep across her throat and along her cheeks.

Striving to keep the conversation light, she said, "I'll bet the trail bum who attacked you last night isn't saying that."

"Why?" He hoped she would go on touching him forever.

"I shot him."

"You? You shot him?" He caught her hand, stilling her movements. Cole's eyes narrowed fractionally. "Is he…?"

"Dead? No." The touch of his hand on hers left her feeling disoriented. Such a gentle touch for such a strong man.

She dipped the cloth into the bucket, wrung it out and touched it to his forehead. "But he left a clear trail of blood."

Cole closed his eyes, willing himself to relax. "I thought I heard an explosion after I was hit."

She thought a moment. "That was probably Danny. He fired Pa's buffalo rifle, causing the thief to drop his rope. If he hadn't, we'd probably still be chasing after our horses."

Cole felt a wave of relief. "He didn't get the horses?"

She shook her head, and he watched the way her hair danced with the movement. "All he got for his troubles was a gunshot in the back or shoulder. In all the confusion, I couldn't tell where my bullet hit him."

"He ought to be easy enough to spot then. I'll keep an eye out for a wounded man along the trail."

"From the looks of your wounds, you won't be hitting the trail for quite a while."

"I'll be fine by tomorrow," Cole said matter-of-factly.

"By the way, your attacker wasn't just a trail bum," Jessie said as calmly as she could manage. "He was Knife, the man who escaped on the night we first met."

"Knife." Cole tested the name, immediately hating it. "I remember him. Long dark hair and yellow teeth."

She nodded and found she couldn't even speak of him. Jessie drew the blankets around Cole's shoulders and watched as his eyelids drooped. Standing, she wiped the sand from the knees of her britches and picked up the bucket of water. Even before she made it to the creek, Cole was fast asleep.

* * *

When Cole awoke again, the sky was ablaze with millions of stars. Darkness enfolded the land like thick black velvet. The only sounds were the hiss and snap of the fire, the whir and chirp of the night insects and the far-off song of a coyote.

Shifting slightly in his bedroll, he caught his breath at the wave of pain that took him by surprise. Instantly Jessie was at his side.

"Feeling worse?"

"Worse than what? Being kicked in the head by a mustang?"

Jessie swallowed back the laughter that threatened.

"Here," she said, holding up the bottle of whiskey she'd taken earlier from his saddlebags. "Danny said you might need this when you woke up. Especially since we don't have any laudanum."

"He did, huh?" Cole eyed the bottle and nodded. When Jessie tipped it to his mouth, he felt the warmth snake through his veins before settling low in his stomach. He lay very still, willing the pain to subside. "How about another?"

He watched in dismay as Jessie corked the bottle and set it just out of his reach. "Not until you have some food in you." As she ladled steaming broth into a tin cup, Cole watched the way the firelight turned the ends of her hair to flame.

Returning to his side, she supported his head with her arm while holding the cup to his lips. He sipped, swallowed, then sipped again.

"That's good. What is it?"

"The broth from rabbit stew."

"How'd you catch the rabbit?"

"The same way anybody would. I shot it."

He arched an eyebrow and regarded her more closely as she laid his head gently against the blanket. "Your pa teach you to handle a gun?"

She nodded. "After Ma died, I was alone a lot at the ranch, looking after my little brothers."

So, he realized, another piece of the puzzle had just slipped into place. With no mother, she would be even more desperate to find a father hundreds of miles away in Abilene.

"Pa was often away, seeing to the herd," Jessie continued. "He knew I had to learn how to protect myself." She slid her arm beneath his head once more. "Drink before it gets cold."

As she cradled his head, Cole suppressed a grin. Damned if he wasn't starting to like being pampered. Was there anything in the world to compare with a woman's touch?

She leaned over him, concentrating on feeding him without spilling a drop. Up close she smelled good, like the earth after a summer storm. He knew that if he turned his head just a fraction, he'd find her breast. The thought left him weak.

When he drank his fill, she set the cup on the ground and folded her sheepskin jacket to pillow his head.

"Are your brothers sleeping?"

She nodded. "Danny's been tending you most of the day." She saw him run a hand over the clean dressing on his chest and shoulder. "He told me to let him know when you were awake, but I figure he needs his sleep more than you need him right now."

"I'm fine. Let the kid sleep." He lay quietly a moment, his eyes closed, his ears alert to the night sounds. Watching him, Jessie thought he was dozing. But suddenly his lids lifted, and she saw the pain he couldn't mask.

"I'll have some more of that whiskey now."

She uncorked the bottle and eased his head up before lifting the whiskey to his lips. He took a long pull before signaling that he'd had enough.

"Do you know where my tobacco is?"

She rummaged through his saddlebags and produced the little pouch and thin papers. With one hand he skillfully filled the paper, sealed it with his tongue and placed it between his lips. Jessie touched a stick to the fire and held it to the tip of his cigarette. He inhaled, filling his lungs, then lay back and studied the stars.

"We'll hit the trail in the morning," he said casually.

"Danny said you'll need another couple of days before you're strong enough to ride."

His voice was low with anger. "No fool kid is going to tell me what to do."

The flickering flames cast Cole's face into light and shadow. Jessie studied him a moment, seeing the barely controlled fury in his eyes. Where was it he had to be in such a hurry?

"Danny knows what he's talking about."

"Maybe. But I don't have time to lie around and be coddled." He took a long drag on his cigarette and exhaled a stream of smoke.

"And I don't have time to stand here and argue with a fool drifter, either." The wave of anger caught her by surprise. For endless hours she'd been worried sick about this man. Now his arrogance lit the short fuse of her carefully banked temper. Jessie sprang to her feet and glared down at him. "Every day I stay here with you is another day I could be closer to my pa."

Needing something to do, she walked to the shadows, then returned to the fire, staggering under the weight of a tree limb. While Cole watched helplessly, she managed to drop the log on the fire. Within minutes the bark smoldered and flamed. Despite the warmth of the fire, he felt chilled as he berated himself for taking out his anger on her. How could he have forgotten? He'd intended to abandon her and her brothers on the night he'd been shot. He'd planned to creep away before the first light of dawn, leaving them to fend for themselves. And now they were suspending their own plans in order to care for him.

How could he repay them? Cole smoked the cigarette until he could no longer hold it in his fingers. Flicking it aside, he frowned. He refused to be coerced by guilt into taking a female and two dumb kids along on the trail. He would escort them to the nearest town and leave them. And he'd slip a few dollars into Jessie's saddlebag when she wasn't looking. That was payment enough. Especially if it forced them to do the sensible thing and go home.

He glanced toward the fire and watched while she struggled with a second log. Damned obstinate woman. She knew just how to take all the pleasure out of being coddled. It made him furious to see her working like that while he was lying here as helpless as a newborn.

He rolled to his side to blot out her figure and swore at the pain such movement caused.

She was trouble, he told himself as he began to doze. Jessie and those little brothers. Nothing but trouble. And the smartest thing he could do would be to ride out of here as soon as he was able. And never look back.

Cole awoke to sunlight streaming across his face. His eyes, when he opened them, felt gritty. A fire raged through his body, leaving his skin clammy, his blankets soaked. Some distance away, he heard the whinny of a horse. Turning his head, he saw Thad leading a string of horses away. Cole tried to speak, but his voice was a weak croak. He watched helplessly as the horses faded from his line of vision.

Into his blurred sight came two figures moving toward him. He tried to remember where his gun was, but his mind was too muddled. As they drew nearer, he recognized Jessie and Danny hauling buckets of water on poles that they carried across their shoulders Indian style. When they reached the fire, Jessie sank to her knees and deposited the heavy buckets.

Seeing Cole watching her, she hurried to his side and touched a hand to his forehead.

"His fever's worse," she called to her brother.

Immediately Danny was beside her. "We'll have to take turns sponging him."

Cole drifted in and out of delirium. Someone was attacking him. Someone armed with a soft whispery voice and gentle hands that would choke the life from him unless he fought back. He struck out blindly.

At Jessie's frightened look, Danny said, "That's the fever. It makes a body half-crazy. Come on. We have to cool him down."

Stripping away the blankets, Danny and Jessie dipped cloths into a bucket of water and began sponging Cole's fevered body.

"He's on fire," Danny muttered. "We can't let the fever get any higher, or…"

Jessie's heart skipped a beat. Wringing out a cloth, she pressed it to Cole's throat and felt the feeble heartbeat. "He seemed to be mending just fine."

"Fever's a funny thing," Danny said, sponging water across Cole's chest. "I cleaned his wounds as much as I could. But sometimes even the cleanest wounds can become infected. Then the body will reject that infection any way it can."

Jessie thought about all those nights that her brother had sat beside the fire, his nose buried in medical books. How she had berated him for giving up his sleep in order to read. How grateful she was now that he had defied her.

Brother and sister worked together for nearly an hour while Cole struggled, slapping away their hands and cursing them. Whenever he struggled too fiercely, the pain would stop him and he would lie back, gathering strength for a fresh attack.

Finally glancing at the sky, Danny muttered, "I'd better get down to the creek and help Thad bring back the horses before dark. If Cole gets too violent, back off. Or tie him up."

Jessie nodded.

Danny got to his feet. Giving a last worried glance at his patient, he turned away.

The fever broke during the night. Cole lay very still as fragments of memory washed over him. Someone had attacked him. Someone had forced him to lie still when he had wanted to get away. Someone who matched him harsh word for harsh word while pinning his arms down. Someone who offered cool water when he had thought his burning body was a funeral pyre.

With a jolt, Cole awoke to find Jessie lying beside him. She lay facing him, her head cushioned on her arm. Shifting slightly, he studied her in the firelight. Pale golden hair drifted like a veil across half her face. Her lips were parted, her breath warm and sweet as it feathered across his cheek. Fascinated, he studied the soft rise and fall of her breasts as she slept. How gentle she seemed in repose. Not at all like the little she-cat that had kicked and fought her attackers that first night they'd met. Not at all like a woman capable of firing a gun and driving off an armed thief.

His gaze came to rest on the damp rag in her hand. He felt a wave of remorse. Jessie had been his attacker. An imaginary attacker. She had been trying to soothe him, and he had fought her every step of the way. Ashamed, he noted the tiny purple bruises about her wrists. And he recalled squeezing them until she had cried out in pain.

His body was covered with a damp sheen, his blanket soaked with sweat. A cool breeze ruffled Jessie's hair, and he lifted a hand to touch it. A shiver of pleasure passed through him. Soft. So soft. Lifting the corner of his blanket, he drew her close and covered her. She didn't stir. Content, he closed his eyes and slept.

Cole awoke to the wonderful aroma of coffee boiling over a fire. In a skillet, rabbit meat sizzled and snapped. He touched the blanket beside him. It still bore the warm imprint of Jessie's body. He lay still, watching as she moved about the fire. From beneath a mound of hot stones, she removed a pan. When she lifted the lid, the fragrance of freshly baked biscuits wafted on the breeze.

He sat up and the world tilted at a crazy angle. Bringing a hand to his head, he waited until everything came back into focus.

Jessie turned, and he saw the way her lips curved into a surprised smile.

"I'm glad you're back in the land of the living."

He gave her a sheepish grin. "Yeah. Me, too."

"Hungry?"

Cole realized he was ravenous. "I guess I could eat something." Like a small deer. Raw.

She hurried over to him. "It'll take a while to get your strength back. Here." Shoving a saddle behind him, she eased him back against it until he was sitting upright. Then she returned to the fire and poured him a steaming cup of coffee. While he sipped it, she filled a plate with meat, gravy and biscuits and watched as he devoured it. When she filled his plate a second time, he emptied that, as well.

"Whatever you did for me," he said, mopping up the gravy with another biscuit, "it must have been magic."

"I didn't do anything. Danny was the healer."

He set down the plate and picked up his cup of coffee. Watching her over the rim of his cup, he said, "I don't think your brother did it all alone. I seem to remember fighting you last night."

"It wasn't you fighting. Danny said it was the fever."

"All the same, I'm sorry."

Embarrassed by the awkward silence that followed, Jessie stood. "If you're feeling strong enough, you'd better wash your wounds. Danny said they have to be kept clean."

"Whatever the doctor orders. Who washed me yesterday?"

At her flushed cheeks, he knew the answer. Tossing back his blankets, he saw that he was naked. His pants and shirt lay neatly folded beside his boots and gun belt.

Covering himself, Cole accepted her offer of a bucket of water, a clean rag and a glob of yellow soap.

Jessie turned away quickly, embarrassed to have him know that she had been the one who'd stripped him. Somehow, Cole awake and feeling strong again was not at all like the Cole who had lain still as death in his bedroll.

As Jessie turned away, he fumbled with the rag tied about his shoulder. "I think I'm going to need some help with these dressings."

Jessie knelt and began untying the rags. As soon as her fingers came in contact with Cole's skin, she felt a rush of heat. Before, it had been easy to concentrate on his wounds. He had been unconscious. But now, as she bent over him, she could feel his gaze burning into her. Her cheeks flamed, and she fought to ignore the fluttering of her heart. It was the same feeling she'd had earlier when she awoke beside Cole in his bedroll. In her confusion she had rolled away from him and hurried to the creek, where she could escape this stranger and be alone with her thoughts.

"Call me when you've finished washing," she said, turning away quickly, "and I'll dress these wounds."

Sensing her discomfort, Cole swallowed back his laughter. The look in her eyes spoke volumes. She was aware of him as a man now, and not a wound to be tended. What was worse, in the days since the shooting, he'd become aware of her as a woman. He could not deny the stirrings he'd felt when she touched him.

He smeared the soap over his chest and let out a torrent of oaths. Hearing him, Jessie gave him a murderous look. "It's a good thing Thad is at the creek. Otherwise I'd wash out your mouth with that soap."

"Soap. It burns like lye. Where the hell did you get this stuff?"

"I made it."

"I should have known. What did you make it with?"

"Kitchen fats and wood ash."

"And lye. Don't forget the lye. It just took off a layer of skin. What did you hope to do? Burn me alive with this?"

"It can't be that bad. My brothers and I use it all the time."

He gritted his teeth as he splashed water on his chest and rubbed vigorously until the soap was removed. "No wonder you're all so tough. You'd need elephant hides to bathe with this."

She shot him an angry look.

Without another word, he washed and rinsed quickly, then toweled himself dry. He struggled into his clean pants and pulled on his boots.

It cost him a tremendous effort to stand. For several seconds he stood very still, until he was certain his legs would support him.

''I'll have to ask for your help one more time,'' he said, holding up a clean strip of cloth.

She stood beside him and poured a liberal amount of whiskey over the wounds before binding them. She heard his hiss of pain.

Odd, she thought as she tied the cloth at the back of his shoulder, she hadn't noticed the way the muscles of his arm flexed and bunched as he moved. Odd, too, that she hadn't noticed the width of his shoulders, the slope of his chest, the narrowness of his waist.

While her hands moved over him, his weariness vanished. She was so close. Too close. A little pulse began throbbing in his temple. His throat went dry.

Last night when he drew her against him and covered her with his blankets, he'd felt the passion rise in him and threaten to swamp him with desire. But sleep had come unbidden to rob him of his strength. Now, by simply pulling her into his arms, he could do what he'd wanted to do last night. He could taste her lips. He could feel the softness of her melt against him.

Slowly, ever so slowly, he drew her into his embrace. Jessie's eyes widened, and he saw the surprise that gradually turned to knowledge. The knowledge that he was going to kiss her. Her lashes lowered, veiling the fear that coursed through her veins.

''Jessie.'' With his thumb and finger he lifted her chin, forcing her to meet his steady gaze.

''Don't, Cole.'' She started to push away, and he tightened his grip on her shoulders.

''One kiss.'' He drew her closer until they were nearly touching. He lowered his head and she felt the warmth of his breath on her cheek.

Her hands were balled into little fists that she kept firmly between them as a protective barrier.

When his lips touched hers, she froze. Icy needles skittered along her spine, leaving her shocked and trembling. When she tried to pull away, he held her firmly while his lips moved over hers.

"Don't hurt me." The words were out before she could stop them.

Remorse flooded him. How could he forget what she'd been through with those men in the woods?

With great tenderness, he lifted his big hands to frame her face. He stared into eyes that were wide with fear.

"Jessie, I won't hurt you. I promise."

Once more he lowered his head and touched his lips to hers. It was the merest whisper of mouth to mouth. Slowly, gently, he rubbed his lips over hers until her mouth softened, opening to him almost against her will.

Jessie forgot to breathe. Her heart skipped a beat, and then another, until it began a wild rhythm in her breast. With a will of their own, her hands opened and splayed across his ribs. At the first contact with his naked flesh, she jerked her hands away. But as he continued to kiss her, she was forced to lean lightly against him. There was nothing to do but allow her palms to rest on his chest.

She tasted clean and fresh like cold water on a sultry day. As his lips moved over hers, he felt the wild racing of her heart like the flutter of a caged bird. She smelled of evergreen and wildflowers, and he yearned to lie with her here in the sand and love her until both were sated. The thought brought a new rush of heat, and he had to exert all his willpower to keep from crushing her in his arms.

From the way she hesitated, he knew that she'd never before been kissed with any tenderness. It worried him. It exhilarated him. It frustrated him.

He had to take it slowly, he warned himself. If he tried to rush her, she'd run like a frightened deer.

There was no pressure, no force, no touching, except his hands on her face and her hands splayed across his chest.

"Jessie." He spoke her name against her lips, and she felt the warmth of his breath mingle with hers. And again, "Jessie,'' and she thought no one had ever said her name with such reverence.

So this was what it felt like to kiss, to be kissed by, a man. Such tenderness. Such gentleness. Such feelings flooding her mind. She wanted to run away so that she could sort out her feelings. She wanted to stay here forever so that this kiss would never end. She wanted… Oh, she wanted so much. And yet she didn't know just what she wanted anymore. She knew only that all her life she had wanted to hear a man speak her name this way, and kiss her as if she were the most beautiful, desirable woman in the world.

She heard the sound of the horses' hooves a moment before they registered in her brain. She jerked and pushed away.

''My brothers. They're coming.''

She hurried to the fire, where she tried to look as though she'd been busy serving up their plates.

Cole slumped down on his bedroll and sat with his back against the saddle, watching her through narrowed eyes. What the hell was the matter with him, acting like some fool dandy courting the town beauty? He had no right. Not with a girl who had her whole life ahead of her. He felt a wave of bitterness. He was a man with no future. A man on the run who couldn't stop.

For the first time, he wished he could end the chase long enough to get to know her. Now he knew what she tasted like. Knew the sweetness of her lips, the softness of her skin. What was worse, he could imagine the way her body would mold itself to his. He was aware of the way she responded to his touch. Though she was afraid and far too innocent, there was fire there, carefully banked. And there was, just below the surface, smoldering passion and wild, willful desire.

Trouble, he reminded himself again. He rolled a cigarette and drew the smoke deep into his lungs. Jessie Conway was going to cause him nothing but trouble unless he got rid of her soon.

Tomorrow. He made himself a promise and exhaled a stream of smoke. By tomorrow he'd be strong enough to ride. He'd thank her for her trouble and get out of her life. For good.

Chapter Six

"What are you doing?" Seeing Cole rummaging through his saddlebags, Jessie rolled from her blankets and struggled to pull on her boots. Though barely awake, she forced herself to move quickly.

"Getting ready to hit the trail."

Beside her, Danny and Thad sat up, rubbing sleep from their eyes.

"Is your fever gone?" She had to resist an urge to touch a hand to his forehead. Instead she crossed to the camp fire and poked at the glowing coals before adding a log.

"I feel fine." The truth was, he felt like hell. But he wasn't certain whether it was because of his injuries or because of the expectant look on her face that had just disappeared at his first words. All he knew was, he had to get out of here.

"Want some coffee before you ride?" Jessie set the pot over the fire.

"I'd like that." Cole tossed his saddle over his shoulder and caught his breath at the thrust of pain. Gritting his teeth, he walked to his horse, then turned toward the two boys who were shrugging into their boots. It went against the grain to ask for help, but the pain was coming in waves. "Can one of you give me a hand? I guess I'm not as strong as I thought."

Ignoring him, Danny hung back, deliberately staring at the toe of his boot. Little Thad ran toward Cole, eager to help.

Within moments he'd neatly tossed Cole's saddle blanket over the stallion's back. Cole set the saddle over the blanket and stood aside as the little boy led the horse to a boulder. Climbing on top for height, Thad secured the cinch, then deftly applied bit and bridle before jumping down and leading the horse back to Cole. When he handed him the reins, Cole couldn't hide his surprise at the little boy's skill.

"Where'd you learn to handle a horse like that, boy?"

"My pa taught me all about horses as soon as I could walk," Thad said proudly. "Pa said I was born to be a horseman."

The stallion nudged the boy's hand until Thad ran his chubby fingers over the velvet muzzle.

"Your pa's a smart man." Cole ruffled the boy's hair.

Thad beamed at the unexpected praise.

From the other side of the camp fire, Danny rolled their blankets and watched through narrowed eyes. The buffalo gun lay menacingly at his feet.

"Coffee's done," Jessie called.

She handed Cole a cup and poured three more. She heaped four plates with the last of the rabbit meat, leftover biscuits and warm gravy.

Cole ate slowly, enjoying his final meal with the Conways. If it killed him, he intended to be civil on this last morning together. He cleared his throat. "You're a good cook, Jessie."

While Jessie blushed at the compliment, Thad and Danny seemed surprised at Cole's words.

"Pa says she's not nearly as good a cook as Ma was."

"Does he now?" Cole glanced at Thad. "To my way of thinking, it doesn't seem fair for Jessie to have to compete with a memory."

"You calling my pa a liar?" Danny's face was nearly as purple as the shadows creeping upward over the mountains in the distance.

Cole swallowed back the words that sprang to his lips. It was obvious that this awkward youth was spoiling for a fight. Cole searched for a way to deflect Danny's anger.

"I'm just saying a man's memory of something long past is often a lot sweeter than the actual thing. Maybe your ma was the best cook in all of Texas. Or maybe your pa's memories of your ma just make her seem that way now."

"I'm old enough to remember my ma's cooking," Danny said with pride. "And no one could come close to her biscuits."

"I'll lay money that in a couple of years you'll meet a young lady whose cooking will make you forget everything you've ever tasted up to that moment."

"Is that what Jessie's cooking does to you?" Thad asked innocently.

Cole nearly choked on his biscuit. Flustered, Jessie sprang to her feet and poured the last of the coffee, then busied herself at the fire until the heat had left her cheeks.

"Are you riding with us to find our pa?" Thad was unaware of the embarrassment he'd caused.

"I'll ride with you until I turn off at Little Creek." Cole said. "Then you'll be riding alone."

"Can't we go to Little Creek, Jessie?"

Danny and Thad turned to her. Annoyed, she said, "I'd hoped to avoid it, but now that there are three of us traveling, I'll need some supplies. I guess we can make a stop in town."

When Jessie looked up, she found Cole studying her closely. She knew what he was thinking. Once in town, she'd change her mind and take her brothers back home. But Cole didn't know the depth of her determination.

Being careful to show no emotion, she lifted her chin in a defiant gesture. "But we'll only stop in Little Creek long enough to get what we need."

They ate quickly. When they were finished, the three saddled their horses while Cole extinguished the fire. He meticulously swept the camp with tree branches until it was clean. Pulling himself into the saddle, Cole surveyed their campsite. Satisfied, he flicked the reins and took the lead. Thad rode directly behind him, with Jessie following. Danny stayed a

short distance behind them, the buffalo rifle resting across his
saddle.

It took them nearly six hours to reach Little Creek. The
town consisted of a couple of run-down buildings that turned
out to be a stable, a saloon, a general store and several houses
that had been hastily thrown together. On a distant hill were
six or seven more houses and a wooden building with a cross
on the roof.

"Looks like the churchgoing people of Little Creek don't
want to live too close to the riffraff."

Thad glanced at Cole. "What's riffraff?"

"People who swear and drink and don't bother to go to
church on Sunday," Jessie said before he could answer.

Thad glanced innocently at Cole. "Do you go to church?"

"I figure the church building might fall down if I set foot
in it."

"And I've heard you swear. Does that make you riffraff?"

Instead of getting angry as Jessie expected, Cole laughed
low and deep in his throat. The sound danced across her
nerves.

"I guess it does, Half-pint."

Thad smiled, as much at the gift of a new nickname as at
Cole's easy agreement. All his life he'd been called "Tadpole" by his family. When they called him "Thaddeus" or
"Thad" in a certain tone of voice, he knew he'd done something to rouse their anger. When they called him "Tadpole"
he knew they were pleased with him. Coming from a tough,
mysterious man like Cole, "Half-pint" sounded like a benediction.

They dismounted in front of the stable. A tall thickset man
with a thatch of white hair peered out from behind one of the
stalls and eyed them warily.

"We'd like to leave the horses for an hour or two," Cole
said, handing the man several coins. "How much to feed and
water them?"

"Half a dollar extra."

"Done." Cole handed the man his money and stepped inside the darkened stable, studying each stall and horse carefully.

When he was satisfied with his inspection, Cole ambled from the stable and headed toward the saloon while Jessie and her brothers walked to the general store. Over the door was a sign: Murphy's Mercantile.

"Morning, young lady." A hard-eyed man in a soiled gray apron looked up from his ledger. Seeing Danny and Thad he added, "Boys. What can I do for you today?"

"We'll be needing a few things." Jessie eyed the sacks of flour and wished they had a pack mule. "Sugar, flour, coffee, dried meat. Just enough to carry in our saddlebags."

Mr. Murphy seemed surprised. "You don't have a wagon outside, miss?"

"No, sir." She shot a glance at her brothers and said, "We're meeting the rest of our family in two or three days. We just need enough to tide us over."

"You three riding alone?"

Something in the tone alerted her to danger. Was it his eyes, where the smile never reached? Or the way he had looked her over as she'd entered?

"No, sir." Now that she had started, Jessie found the lie growing. "My pa's younger brother is with us." She swallowed. "He just stepped into the saloon. He'll be here in a little while."

The shopkeeper nodded and began selecting the items Jessie'd ordered. While he measured sugar and flour into smaller cloth sacks, Jessie mentally calculated her meager funds. If only she hadn't been so frugal. But she had taken only as much as she dared, leaving the rest of Pa's savings in the cookie tin in case she and Pa never returned. That way, she'd reasoned, Thad and Danny would have enough, with the sale of the cattle, to return East and settle with relatives.

While Jessie and the shopkeeper dealt with her supplies, Danny and Thad wandered about the store. Danny picked up a book about the use of herbs in healing and wished for the hundredth time that he was the son of a millionaire so that he could buy every book ever written about healing. It wasn't fair, he thought, scanning the pages, that only the rich and the educated could share the knowledge. He wanted so badly to know everything. He walked to the open doorway and in a spill of sunlight began devouring the words. There was so much he wanted to know.

Thad studied the jars of wild strawberry preserves and felt his mouth water. Last year a stagecoach had delivered four jars of strawberry preserves from his aunt in Boston. Pa had said that such things grew wild in the East, and that people could pick them right off the plants and eat them. When they were cooked with sugar and water, they made the best tasting sweets a body had ever experienced. For weeks after, they had strawberry preserves with biscuits, with fresh sweet cream, with just about everything Jessie could think of.

Moving on, Thad pressed his nose against the glass counter and studied the rock candy. Pa had brought them rock candy once from town. He could still recall the tart-sweet taste. And now he was actually in town himself. He had to have some of that candy. He just had to.

When Cole entered the store, Jessie didn't look up. She went on ordering her supplies, annoyed with the thoughts that kept interfering with her concentration. Had Cole stood at the bar with other men, drinking his whiskey, staring at the half-dressed women who always seemed to work such places? She had seen one of the women in the doorway, waiting to greet Cole as he entered. She was plump, with heavy, sagging breasts barely covered by a filmy wrap. Her hair was the color of red clay and had been held away from her face with two combs. Beyond the door, Jessie had seen a second woman, younger, with long dark hair and a gown that displayed more than it covered.

Had there been time for Cole to go upstairs and pleasure himself with one of them?

Jessie knew what went on between a man and woman. She'd grown up on a ranch with cattle and horses mating each season. But from what she'd seen, it didn't look like much fun for the female. She'd long ago decided that marriage wasn't for her. Even now, recalling the feelings she'd experienced when Cole kissed her, she told herself that she'd been too confused to know what she felt. But she knew one thing, one thing she couldn't deny. She'd never felt anything quite like that before. And she'd give a whole lot to feel like that again.

From the corner of her eye, she saw Cole cross the room and stand behind Danny.

"A book on medicine?"

At the sound of Cole's voice, Danny stiffened. Without looking up, he nodded. "Sort of. It's all about herbs that can heal."

"The Indians use herbs. A lot of white men think they're crazy. But I've seen the results. They really work. Maybe you can learn some of their tricks from that book."

Danny snapped the book shut. Without looking at Cole he said, "We'll be back on the trail in a little while. And the book and the knowledge will still be here in Murphy's Mercantile."

He returned the book to the shelf and dug his hands into his back pockets. Through narrowed eyes, Cole watched the way the boy's shoulders hunched. He seemed too young to be so intense.

At the tone of Jessie's voice, Cole turned to watch her deal with the owner.

"That's all," she said to the shopkeeper.

"Can I have some rock candy?" Thad was already mentally picking out the pieces he wanted.

Mr. Murphy glanced at her, eager to please. She shook her head and began counting out her money on the countertop.

"That'll be four dollars and fifty cents, miss."

Jessie bit her lip. The sixteen dollars still left in her saddlebags wouldn't take them far. "Take out the dried meat," she said softly. They'd eat rabbit until they choked on it.

With a look of disdain, the shopkeeper returned the meat to a shelf.

"Three dollars even," Mr. Murphy said.

"And one rock candy. Please, Jessie." Thad's voice held a pleading note to it.

"We can't, Tadpole." She handed the bills to the shopkeeper and said politely, "Thank you."

"The candy's only a penny." Seeing the pleading look in the boy's eyes, Mr. Murphy decided to press his advantage. "Isn't it worth that much to see the lad happy?"

"No. Thank you." Her tone held a note of finality.

"Give the boy what he wants," Cole said, striding forward.

Mr. Murphy's eyes crinkled into a smile. "This the uncle traveling with you?"

Uncle? Cole shot a questioning glance at Jessie, which the shopkeeper instantly noted.

Jessie swallowed convulsively. "Yes." Turning to Cole, she refused to meet his eyes, staring instead at a spot somewhere beyond his shoulder. "Pa gave the money to me before we left, Uncle Cole."

The shopkeeper coughed discreetly.

Jessie shifted her gaze until she was staring directly into Cole's eyes, daring him to argue. "Pa said I wasn't to let you pay for a thing."

He bit back the grin that tugged at the corner of his lips. She was so damnably independent he wanted to throttle her. "It's only a penny, Jessie." His tone was low, coaxing.

Her chin lifted fractionally. He saw the little points of flame that came into her eyes. It had become a matter of pride. "No." She turned, completely shutting him out. "Thank you, Mr. Murphy. That will be all."

With her head held high, she walked from the store with her precious supplies. Behind her, Danny caught Thad's hand and forcibly led him away from the counter. From inside the store, Cole watched as they trudged along the dusty trail toward the stable. He felt an instant kinship with them. They had chosen a long hard trail. And a lonely one.

Cole made his purchases quickly and just as quickly strode toward the back side of the stable. By the time Jessie and her brothers arrived, Cole had their horses saddled and was leading them out.

If Jessie was surprised at his sudden appearance, she said nothing. Tying her supplies behind her saddle, she watched as Cole approached her brothers.

Cole had planned his leave-taking. It would be swift. And as painless as he could make it.

"So long, Half-pint," he said, lifting Thad onto his pony's back. "Do as your sister tells you."

"Yes, sir." In the saddle, Thad was eye level with Cole.

"If she's tough with you, it's because she loves you. Don't you forget that."

"No, sir."

Cole turned to Danny, who was watching Cole as warily as he had since that first night they met.

Cole stuck out his hand. "Thanks, Danny, for all you did."

The youth shrugged, not wanting to accept the handshake, but not knowing how to refuse. "I just did a little doctoring."

"Your sister said you saved my life."

Reluctantly Danny accepted the handshake and for the first time met Cole's direct gaze. He was startled by what he saw there. He'd expected dark, simmering anger or at least mocking humor. Instead he sensed respect. The respect of one man for another.

Confused, he blurted, "I'd have done as much for anyone."

"That's all a man could ask."

As he dropped his hand, Danny stood a moment longer, measuring himself against this leanly muscled gunman. How many years before he could match him? Too many, he thought miserably, wishing he could be anything but young and gangly and awkward.

Though he still resented everything Cole stood for, Danny had to admit that this stranger had treated them fairly. He hadn't tried to take their meager supplies or their horses. He'd accepted their help when it was needed. And he was man enough to thank them. Yet Danny felt a sense of relief that they were parting company. Cole's presence made him uneasy.

Jessie's reaction to the gunman worried him though he couldn't say why.

As Danny pulled himself into the saddle, Cole turned to Jessie.

She was dressed as always in a pair of her brother's cast-off britches and a plaid shirt with the sleeves rolled to her elbows. Her hair had been tucked up under an old wide-brimmed felt hat. The top of her head barely reached his chin. Yet there was nothing small or frail about her. Her chin was lifted in that familiar air of defiance. She stood with one hand on her hip, the other hand clutching the reins.

"Goodbye, Jessie," Cole said evenly. The warmth of his smile was hidden behind a polite mask. "It's been... interesting knowing you."

She felt the beginnings of a blush sweep across the base of her throat and spread upward to her cheeks. She stuck out her hand. "Goodbye, Cole. Thanks for saving my life."

He took her hand in his and felt the sexual pull as compelling, as insistent, as anything he'd ever felt in his life. The warmth was instantly gone from his voice, from his face. He said gruffly, "You did the same for me. Now we're even." He released her hand quickly, jamming his hands into his back pockets to keep from touching her again.

She reached up to her bedroll and turned back to him. "I'm returning the shirt you loaned me."

He accepted the freshly laundered shirt. It smelled of creek water and evergreen, and he knew that he would always be reminded of her whenever he wore it.

As she turned to pull herself into the saddle, Cole touched her arm and said, "Jessie."

She reacted to his touch as if she'd been burned, wheeling toward him expectantly.

He cursed himself for his clumsiness. Prolonging the agony was only making it worse. "You really ought to take your brothers home. It's where you belong."

He hadn't meant to be so abrupt. All he'd wanted to do was

point out the obvious. But now that the words were out, there was no way to recall them.

He saw the way her eyes darkened. Twisting away, she pulled herself into the saddle. She refused to meet his glance, looking instead toward the two boys on horseback. ''Let's go. We have a lot of miles to cover before making camp tonight.''

Very deliberately Cole refused to watch as they made their way along the dusty trail past the stable toward the mercantile and the saloon. Feeling a fresh wave of annoyance, he stuffed the shirt into his bedroll and strode back into the stable. For several minutes he spoke with the big beefy man in charge, until he was satisfied that the one he was seeking had not been in Little Creek. With a brusque word of thanks, he walked outside and pulled himself into the saddle. He caught a glimpse of Jessie pausing beside the saloon. The tall owner of the saloon had hold of her reins and was pointing. Now why would she stop there? If she'd needed directions, why hadn't she asked the stable owner before leaving?

Puzzled, Cole mopped at the sweat beneath his hat and pulled the hat low on his forehead in a gesture of finality. Jessie Conway was not his responsibility. What did it matter if she was talking to the oily man who owned the saloon? Cole had seen his kind hundreds of times. Soft hands. Smooth voice. A way with women. They dealt in liquor and cards and men's lust. They dealt women a line of pretty words and easy money. And a life of pain.

He turned his mount in the opposite direction, refusing to look again at the little female who could make him angry with a single word or look. Jessie Conway was a burr under his saddle. A burr he had just dislodged.

He dug in his heels and felt his horse break into a run as if the animal sensed his need to get away from this place.

Above the thunder of hoofbeats he heard a sound. A cry? A shout? Or the shriek of a bird? Pulling in the reins, he slowed his mount and turned in the saddle. At that same moment, he heard the thunderous report of a rifle. The unmistakable sound of a buffalo gun.

He jerked the reins, causing his mount to wheel in mid-stride. A cold razor of fear sliced his heart before the adrenaline began pumping through his veins. There was only one reason why Danny would fire that rifle. He'd vowed that he would blow apart any man who threatened harm to his sister. That had to mean Jessie was in trouble. Again.

Jessie prided herself on her inner strength. For one so young she had faced plenty of crises: her mother's death, her father's long absences on ranch chores and cattle drives, her isolation far from the company of others. She had felt from her earliest years that her gender need not set her apart. Though her pa expected her to care for her little brothers and keep house the way his wife had, he also expected her, as the oldest, to share all the ranch chores. She branded cows, searched for strays and mended fence. She worked alongside her father and brothers or her neighbors to the south without ever thinking of them as men. And though she usually fell into bed too exhausted to even dream, she never complained.

Why then, she wondered as she followed along the dusty trail leading out of Little Creek, did she feel so strange, so disoriented, in the company of Cole Matthews? He was just a man. And not a very nice once. But one word, one touch from that man, and she felt all weak and whimpery inside. She wasn't sure what those feelings meant. Was it just part of growing up? If that was the case, she wanted no part of it. It was too confusing.

Cole. He had gone his own way. And she had gone hers. Cole liked to talk about choices. They seemed to have few. She had to find her pa. And Cole had his own demons to chase.

She was thinking about Cole and about Pa, when the man from the saloon stepped into her path, startling her.

"That man who was with you," he said, reaching up to catch her mount's bridle. "Kin?"

Her eyes narrowed. Was Cole wanted for some crime here in Little Creek? If so, she and her brothers wouldn't want to be connected with him. She glanced at Murphy's Mercantile, just across the dusty road from the saloon. She had made a foolish mistake. Mr. Murphy would have repeated her lie.

"Why are you asking?"

His sly smile gave him a deadly appearance. "No reason. I just noticed that he wasn't riding with you."

When she said nothing, his glance slid to Danny and Thad. "Yours?"

"My brothers."

"Brothers." He dismissed them as harmless and turned his attention back to Jessie. His look raked her. "The way I hear it, you could use some money."

Mr. Murphy again. There were no secrets safe in a town as small as this.

The man was looking at her in a way that made her uncomfortable. She leaned down to take the reins from him, but his hand closed over hers.

His tone was low, intimate. "I could always use a new girl in my place."

She glanced at the closed doors of the saloon. From within came the sound of men's voices. Above them could be heard a woman's laughter.

"I don't need money that badly."

His eyes narrowed. Before she could pull away, he caught her by the front of the shirt, nearly yanking her off her horse. Her hand went to the gun in the waistband of her pants, but his hand was quicker. Before she could move, he had disarmed her and sent her sprawling in the dust.

Terrified, Thad let out a cry and turned to his brother for solace. Seeing the man reach for Jessie, Danny lifted the rifle skyward and squeezed off a shot that echoed and reechoed through the town. Before he could aim and fire again, the rifle was shot cleanly from his hand. With a shriek of pain Danny clutched the singed hand to his chest and watched helplessly as the saloon owner stood leering at his sister.

Heads poked from open doorways. Men stood at windows, watching the scene without emotion. Across the street, Mr.

Murphy quickly closed his doors and hurried to the back room where he lived behind the store.

"Now," the saloon owner said, holding Jessie's pistol against her temple, "as I see it, this boy threatened my life. I have the right to defend myself against attack."

"And what about my rights?"

He gave her a wicked smile that caused her heart to stop. "These are your rights. You can step inside and agree to work for me, or you can watch those two brothers of yours die. Afterward, you'll work for me anyhow just to pay their burial fee."

Jessie lay, still sprawled in the dust, feeling her breath coming in short quick gasps. What kind of town was this? Was there no one who would stop this man? Would they all hide behind their closed doors and allow this terrible thing to happen?

A wave of self-loathing swept her. How could she have been so careless as to daydream when she should have had her wits about her? This was the second time her carelessness had managed to get her into big trouble.

Thad was crying harder now. The sound nearly broke her heart.

"Speak up, missy. Are you going to cooperate?"

Before she could respond, a cold unrecognizable voice said, "Now you have two choices, big man. Drop the gun and step away from the woman, or die where you are."

"What…?" The man looked up and saw Cole Matthews astride his horse, aiming a gun directly at him. He knew from the look in those eyes that this was a man who would never back away from a fight. He blinked, then made a hasty, foolish decision. He pressed the cold steel against Jessie's head and snarled, "Don't try it. I'll kill her."

"I guess you've made your choice." Slowly, deliberately, Cole aimed his pistol and fired.

Everything seemed to be happening in slow motion. Jessie heard the sound of the gun being fired, heard the shrill scream of her little brother, felt the warmth of the man's blood as it spilled across her shirt.

As the man toppled into the dust, Jessie was grasped by firm hands. She found herself staring into the steely eyes of Cole. Seeing the blood on her shirt, he ripped it open, searching for a wound. Seeing none, he realized it was the saloon owner's blood and let out a long hiss of breath.

She heard someone crying but didn't realize it was Thad, heard the distant murmur of voices but had no idea where they were coming from. She felt strong arms lift her, heard a voice say, "Hellfire and damnation! Get your rifle, Danny. Thad, take the reins of your sister's horse. Both of you move out ahead of me. Now. Before the whole damned town comes gunning for us."

Cradled in Cole's arms, her face was pressed against a rough, scratchy shirt. She inhaled the musky scent of Cole. And as a horse moved in a loose, easy gait beneath her, she heard his deep voice say, "Woman, it seems like all I've been doing since I met you is hauling your hide out of trouble."

She wanted to say something cutting, something that would let this man know that she would have handled it herself if she'd been given more time. But she humiliated herself by clinging to him, by burying her face against his throat. And worst of all, by crying.

Chapter Seven

Cole's arms tightened about Jessie as she struggled with the sobs that shook her. He shivered slightly as her warm tears traced the hollow of his throat. It tore him up to hear this fierce little female crying. What was worse, she was fighting every tear, every sob. She had been through too much these past days. It was all catching up with her. It frustrated Cole that there was no time to comfort her, to say the words she needed to hear.

While he led the way to safety, he continued to look over his shoulder. In a gunfight, he knew he could count on only himself. And though he hadn't wanted this to happen, he was now responsible for the safety of these three innocents.

The Fates were playing tricks on him, he thought angrily. The last thing he needed in his already complicated life was one more obligation. But for now, he had no choice.

They rode for hours beneath a scorching sun. When Jessie was strong enough to ride alone, Cole helped her into the saddle and took the lead. None of them spoke. After the first hours, he stopped looking over his shoulder. Maybe this time good luck had favored them. Maybe the saloon owner had no friends willing to avenge his death.

Jessie and her brothers never questioned where they were headed. Cole had assumed the role of leader. They were more than willing to follow him. For now.

By sundown they had crossed the Pecos River and made camp on the far side. The horses drank gratefully, then began grazing nearby.

Jessie untied her bedroll and laid out their fresh supplies. But when she attempted to put together a meal, a heaviness seemed to envelop her, slowing her movements. She managed to mix up a batch of dough and set the pan of biscuits over hot rocks to bake slowly. She lifted a pot of boiling coffee from the fire and set it aside. But as she bent to the task of cutting strips of dried meat, she felt perspiration bead on her forehead and upper lip.

It was merely the heat of the fire, she told herself, pressing her arm to her face. She was warm. Too warm. She looked up, shaking her head from side to side to ward off a feeling of dizziness. Near the river she saw a shimmering halo of light. For a moment the light disappeared and she recognized Danny and Thad watering their horses. Then the light appeared brighter than before, and she felt the world spin in circles.

Alarmed, she sat perfectly still and waited for the moment to pass. When her head finally cleared, she leaned back against a rock and closed her eyes. She was tired. So tired. She would rest, she promised herself, for only a minute or two. And then she would call the others to supper.

Half an hour later, Cole saw her sitting quietly, her face lifted to the sky. When he walked closer, he realized that she was fast asleep.

For long minutes he stood over her, enjoying the vision. If possible, she was even more beautiful in repose. By the light of the fire, her lashes cast long shadows over high cheekbones. Her lips were parted slightly, and as he knelt beside her, he felt the warmth of her breath against his hand. Touching a strand of hair, he marveled once more at its softness. Up close he could count the freckles that paraded across her nose, and he had an almost unreasonable desire to kiss every damned one of them.

He lifted her easily in his arms and carried her to her bed-roll. When he settled her gently among the blankets, she sighed softly. Her lips lifted in a smile, and he wondered what she was dreaming about. Tucking the covers about her shoulders, he knelt a moment longer, savoring this last chance to watch her without her knowledge. Then hearing the voices of her brothers as they returned from the river, he stood and began dishing up their meal.

It was Thad who innocently told Cole the truth about their search for their father.

"Do you think we'll find Pa soon, Danny?" Thad asked.

Cole looked up. "I thought you knew where he was."

Thad shrugged. "Jessie said he could be anywhere between Texas and Kansas," he said between bites of supper.

"I thought he was in Abilene." Cole poured a cup of coffee and watched as Danny and Thad exchanged a glance.

Jessie stirred and noticed that her brothers seemed uncomfortable and that Cole had gone very still. She struggled to stay awake long enough to hear what they were saying.

"Pa left on a cattle drive about three months ago," Danny explained.

"Three months is a long time." Cole rolled a cigarette and held a flaming stick to the tip. Though he assumed a casual pose, he was alert to every word.

"That's what Jessie said. That's why she decided to find him."

"Did your father know the others on the drive?"

Danny shook his head. "He joined up with a bunch of strangers. The top drover said theirs would be the biggest drive in all Texas before they were through. He said it was safer going through Indian Territory with a lot of men."

Cole was frowning, deep in thought. "Maybe your father's just taking his time coming home."

Danny's voice trembled with intensity. "We know our pa. Nothing would keep Big Jack Conway from coming home."

Cole could think of a couple of things, and one in particular. Death.

These kids weren't addled. They would have thought of that. What Jessie was probably searching for was proof of her father's death. Though he hated to admit it, Cole admired her spunk. He'd do the same thing. Still, alone, these kids didn't have a snowball's chance in hell of making it to Abilene. But with the right assistance...

For an hour or more he waged a losing battle with himself. He'd make much better time riding alone. And he didn't need to take on anyone else's troubles. Still they were heading in the same direction. And besides, now that he knew the facts, he'd just found a compelling reason why he ought to be the one to accompany them on their journey.

Jessie woke to the still, incandescent light of predawn. She was instantly alert. The lethargy with which she had been burdened last night was gone. She remembered clearly everything that had happened to her the previous day. She had been careless. And that moment of carelessness had nearly cost the lives of her brothers. She would remember well the lesson learned.

She glanced about the camp fire and saw that the others were still asleep. Touching a hand to her stiff bloodstained shirt, she pushed aside the blanket and sat up. Before anyone awoke she needed to wash away the blood of the vile saloon owner. His blood and his touch.

Her boots were standing neatly beside her blanket. Had she prepared supper last night? Had she taken time to eat?

She remembered sitting quietly, waiting for the dizziness to pass. She could recall a feeling of floating, of drifting, of strong arms cradling her. At the time, she'd dreamed that Pa was carrying her to a loft in the barn. But now she realized it could not have been Pa. She touched a hand to her suddenly warm cheeks. It must have been Cole.

Then she remembered something else. Cole had been questioning her brothers about Pa. She felt a moment of panic. She hadn't wanted him to know much about their business. But she remembered the way he had gone all quiet when Danny mentioned the cattle drive.

She brushed aside her worries. Cole would soon be leaving them. In fact he was eager to get away.

Rummaging through her saddlebag, her fingers encountered the soap. But when she removed it, she discovered that it was not the yellow soap she had used since her childhood. It was round, having been poured into a mold. It was pink. And it gave off a fragrance reminiscent of crushed rose petals.

She stared at it for long moments before realizing what it meant. She turned toward the man sleeping beside the glowing embers of the fire. Cole had hated her soap. And he had been in the mercantile after she left.

Was it possible that a gunman would take the time to buy her something so wonderful? She felt a lump rise in her throat and quickly swallowed it. She had never had a gift from a man before. Oh, her pa had once brought her a lace handkerchief from San Antonio. It still lay under her pillow, untouched. It was too beautiful to ever use. It was enough to look at it, to know that it was hers. But nothing could equal this. She lifted the soap to her nose and breathed deeply.

Ma had once had a bottle of rose water. Jessie had thought it was the prettiest fragrance in the whole world. Whenever she smelled it on her mother, she was reminded of the woman she would one day become. But she had long ago used all of it to bathe the tiny babe her mother had left behind. It would, Jessie had reasoned, keep Ma's memory alive for Thad. Besides, she would never be the beautiful creature her ma had been. She would always be just plain Jessie.

Digging into her saddlebags, she pulled out the gob of yellow soap. It just didn't seem right to use something as wonderful as rose-scented soap on her grimy clothes.

Moving silently, Jessie walked to the river and removed her shirt and britches. Rubbing the stained shirt with sand and then with lye soap, she was able to remove most of the blood. Spreading the wet shirt on a low-hanging bush, she walked into the river until the water was as high as her shoulders. Holding her breath, she ducked beneath the water and came up sputtering. Carefully working the rose-scented soap through her hair, she lathered, then ducked once more beneath the water until all the soap floated free.

She breathed deeply, loving the fragrance that seemed to envelop her. She couldn't remember ever feeling this pampered. Moving the soap along her body, she marveled at the way it felt on her skin. When at last she strode from the creek, she felt truly cleansed.

Shivering slightly, she dried herself and pulled on her chemise and britches. She touched a hand to the freshly washed shirt. It was still damp. Without a breeze, it would take another hour to dry.

"Looking for this?"

Jessie looked up to see Cole leaning against a tree, one foot crossed carelessly over the other. In his hand was a clean shirt, the one she had returned to him.

With a look of disdain, she snatched the shirt from his hand and turned away before pulling it on. "How long have you been watching?" she called over her shoulder.

He bit back a grin at the angry tone. "Not nearly long enough."

She turned around, still tucking the ends of the shirt into her britches. He tried not to stare at the way the shirt strained across her breasts.

"You smell good, Jessie."

She felt herself blush clear down to her toes and was grateful that the dawn light had just begun to cover the land. "I— thank you for the soap, Cole."

"Isn't that better than lye soap?"

She couldn't help returning his smile. "Much better. Why did you buy it for me?"

"I thought you'd like it." He rolled a cigarette and held a match to the tip. He exhaled a stream of smoke and added, "Besides, I wanted to pay you back somehow for the way you took care of me when I was shot."

"Pay me..." He saw her smile fade. Fool, she berated herself. It wasn't a gift. It was payment. So that he could walk away from her without owing a debt.

All the warmth left her. In a flat voice she said, "I hope

you didn't spend too much on it. Because what I did for you, I would have done for a dog.''

He tossed the cigarette aside and bit back a torrent of oaths. ''Hellfire and damnation!'' Why did he have to say too much? Why hadn't he kept his mouth shut? And why did she always have to be so eager to fight?

''Look,'' he said, grabbing her roughly by the shoulder. ''I didn't come out here to argue.''

''No.'' She twisted away from him and took a step backward. ''You probably came out here to catch me naked in the river so you could have another laugh at my expense.''

His hands gripped her painfully by both shoulders, and he nearly shook her as he fought a wave of frustration. ''Believe me, woman, if I saw you naked, I wouldn't be laughing.''

Startled, she looked up and saw his gaze focus on her mouth. He drew her perceptibly closer until she could feel the warmth of his breath as he released it on a long slow sigh of impatience.

''And neither would you.''

No, nor was she laughing now. Her throat was as dry as the desert. Her heart seemed to still for a moment before it began a wild pounding in her chest. She stared at him, mesmerized by the hunger in his eyes.

''You shouldn't...''

''Shouldn't what?''

''Touch me like this.''

He ran his hands along the tops of her arms, across her shoulders. ''Like this?''

His voice had gentled until it was a mere whisper. She thought it the most wonderful sound in the world. His touch, too, seemed gentler though she could feel his barely controlled tension just beneath the surface.

She wanted him to kiss her as he'd kissed her before. And yet she was afraid. Her emotions were still too close to the surface. Feelings she'd never even known existed were tumbling about as he held her. They frightened her. And she had always dealt with her fears through anger. Anger and action.

She lifted her head a fraction, assuming the tone of voice she always used with her brothers when she wanted swift obedience. "Take your hands off me."

"When I'm good and ready."

Her voice was pure ice. "Now, Cole."

He leaned closer, and she saw the little pulse beat at his temple. "I'm not Danny or Thad. Don't try ordering me about." His glance swept her face, taking in the narrowed gaze, the tight, hard line of her mouth. "When I see something I want, I go after it."

"No one can have everything they want." Her gaze was drawn to his mouth, and she saw the beginnings of a smile on his lips.

"Want to bet?"

"I don't gamble."

His smile grew. "I know. Or swear. Or back away from a fight." He surprised her by drawing her firmly against him. "Let me give you some advice. Don't push me too far, Jessie. I've been patient with you. And I'm not, by nature, a patient man."

"Advice? It sounds more like a warning to me."

"Then be warned."

She thought about struggling but discarded the notion. He was physically stronger. She had no chance of besting him. Words were her only weapon now.

"I won't be bullied by you. We're even now. You saved my life; I saved yours. My brothers and I will go on our way, and you can have your precious solitude back."

"Wrong."

She looked up at him as if he'd gone mad. "What do you mean?"

"I mean I came to a decision last night. I'm not letting you out of my sight. Every time I do, you get yourself in trouble. I've decided that if you and those two brothers of yours are ever going to survive the trek across Texas, I'll have to accompany you there myself."

For a minute she was swamped with conflicting emotions.

Distrust. What had caused him to suddenly change his mind? From the beginning he had wanted nothing more than to be free of her. And now he was insinuating himself into their plans.

Then the distrust vanished and she experienced a feeling of intense joy. Cole would be guide, protector, savior. She swallowed back the happiness she felt and allowed her sense of independence to take over.

"We don't need you."

"Woman, you and your brothers need a wet nurse."

Insulted, her hand swung in a wide arc. Before it reached his face, he caught it and twisted it behind her.

"You have no business playing with the grown-ups," he hissed.

"You'll see—"

Before she could say more, his mouth covered hers in a savage kiss.

All the words she had been about to hurl were forgotten.

It was the only thing he'd thought of since he'd first seen her by the river. In that single kiss he found all that he desired. She tasted sweet and wild and forbidden. Her slender body, young and firm, fit against his like the missing piece of a puzzle. He changed the angle of the kiss, taking it deeper, and heard her little moan of protest.

She smelled of cool fresh water. And roses. The fragrance of roses drifted from her hair, from her skin, until he was drowning in the scent of her.

Jessie's hand clutched wildly at his waist as she found herself trapped in the savageness of his kiss. Before, he had been tender, coaxing, gentle. There was no tenderness now, only passion and wild, pulsing needs.

For the first time, she sensed the danger that lurked just beneath the calm surface of this man. His lips were seeking, demanding. His hands moved along her body, giving her no time to relax her guard.

"Maybe I was wrong. You sure as hell don't kiss like a sheltered little farm girl, Jessie."

The words were whispered against her mouth before his lips closed once more over hers.

For the first time she became aware of the many ordinary things that had suddenly become extraordinary. The sun rose above the mountaintops, shooting ribbons of flame across the spot of land where they stood. Insects hummed, birds sang, as if in harmony to the song in her heart.

His lips were warm and moist. There was the lingering bite of tobacco on his tongue. The hands at her back were strong, so strong that they could break her in two. But they moved with sensual softness along her spine. His clothes smelled of horses and leather—scents she had known since infancy. Scents she loved.

He plunged his hands into her damp hair and pulled her head back before pressing his lips to her throat. Against the sensitive skin he murmured, ''You kiss like a woman, Jessie. A woman who could make a man enjoy being a man.''

She had to end this. End it before she got caught up in something she couldn't control.

Taking a deep breath, she pushed against him and took a step backward, breaking contact. Her breathing was labored, as was his. She waited a moment until she was certain she could speak.

Her voice was low, still husky from desire. ''I'll...start breakfast now. We could use some wood for the fire.'' She turned away, then looked back. ''Oh. thanks for the use of your shirt.''

He felt a flash of annoyance at the cool way she walked away. Damnable woman would only lead him into more trouble than he needed. Still, he couldn't help admiring her spirit. Or the way her backside looked in her brother's britches.

Cole was grateful for the chance to be busy. He gathered an armload of firewood and coaxed the coals into a blazing fire. Then he touched the toe of his boot to the two figures still rolled in their blankets.

''Let's get moving. I expect to be on the trail within the hour.''

While Thad rubbed his eyes, Danny sat up and squinted at Cole.

"You riding with us today?"

"Yeah." Cole tried not to watch as Jessie bent over the fire. "I figure since I'm heading the same way as you, I may as well tag along."

Danny wondered why he didn't feel disappointed at Cole's announcement. After all, Danny made no secret of the fact that he didn't trust Cole. Still, after yesterday's incident, he felt a sense of relief. If it hadn't been for Cole, there was no telling what would have happened to them. He couldn't help wondering what had happened to change Cole's mind.

"Come on, Thad," Danny said, shaking the boy's shoulders. "Help me roll these blankets."

Danny discovered his gift first. Last night he'd been too drained to think about anything but sleep. Now, as he tied his bedroll behind the saddle, he was alert enough to notice the bulge in one of his saddlebags. Inside he found the book. With a look of surprise, he turned and found Cole watching him. Instantly he knew.

"Why'd you do this?"

"I wanted to thank you for doctoring me. Besides," Cole added, rubbing his stiff shoulder, "I figured I might need you again some day. And I'd like you to learn all you can about healing."

Almost reverently Danny opened the cover of the book and began devouring the words.

They ate quickly and broke camp. Cole watched admiringly while the three imitated him, dousing the fire and scattering the warm ashes over the earth until there was no trace of the people who had been there.

A wind blew up from the south, sending the dry earth swirling about in little dust devils. Thad reached into his saddlebag for a handkerchief to tie about his lower face. His fingers encountered something small and round. Puzzled, he lifted the object up for his inspection. For a moment he could only stare.

Then he let out a whoop that caused the others to turn and stare.

"It's rock candy." His eyes widened. "Jessie, it's rock candy."

Jessie shot a sideways glance at Cole. Not even a hint of a smile tugged at the corner of his lips.

"Now how do you think that got in your saddlebags, Half-pint?"

"You put it there," Thad chirped. "I know you did."

"Me? Why would I do a thing like that?"

Thad took a lick and unable to resist the temptation, thrust the entire piece of candy into his mouth and struggled to get the words out around the delicious obstruction. "I don't know, Cole. Why'd you do it?"

"I remembered how much I loved rock candy when I was a pup."

Jessie felt an unreasonable flare of anger. It had hurt her not to be able to give her little brother the only thing he'd wanted. But even a penny could prove necessary on this long journey. And now Cole had become a hero in Thad's eyes.

"It couldn't be because you wanted to ease your conscience about holding us up along the trail and then leaving us, could it?" The words were out before she even had time to think.

Cole gave her a withering look. "I did want to thank you. All three of you. But don't flatter yourself that I felt any guilt at all about leaving you on your own." He urged his horse ahead, passing her with barely a glance. If he noticed the fragrance of roses, he chose to ignore it. "As you're fond of reminding me, you can take care of yourself." He flicked the reins, taking the lead. "Come on. We have a long hard day ahead of us."

Behind him, Thad wiped the drool with the back of his hand and fell into line behind Cole's mount. He didn't care how far they rode this day. The tart-sweet taste of rock candy would keep his mind off any discomfort.

Danny rode behind his little brother, the buffalo rifle slung across his knees. As he rode, he kept only one eye on the trail.

Most of his attention was held by the precious words in the open book. Cole Matthews might be a dangerous man on the run. But he had given Danny a special gift this day. The gift of knowledge. And for that, the boy would be eternally in his debt.

Jessie took up the rear position, keeping a sharp watch on the rocks and boulders to either side of the trail. While she rode she fought a rush of feelings. Anger, jealousy, guilt. Just when she thought she'd figured out this strange man, he surprised her again. Why had he been so thoughtful? Was she right? Was it mere guilt because he'd slowed their journey? Or was it something more? She let out a long sigh. The day had just begun, and already she was weary of trying to sort out all the mysteries that surrounded Cole Matthews. For now she would merely accept the fact that he was here with them. For at least another day, she felt safe.

Careful, she warned herself. She was safe as long as she didn't get too close to him. Up close Cole posed another kind of danger altogether.

Chapter Eight

"Look. A horseman."

Jessie pointed to a cloud of dust on a ridge. Instantly Cole led them to the shelter of tall boulders, where they reined in their mounts and watched until the rider drew near. The man, sitting tall in the saddle, was powerfully built, with guns on either hip and a rifle slung into a boot by his saddle.

Jessie glanced at Cole. Though he was watching the man carefully, he made no move to be seen. Was the stranger's life in danger? Did Cole intend to ambush him from the cover of the rocks? Though his eyes were narrowed in concentration, there was no hint of anger, only curiosity. Was there a price on Cole's head? she wondered. Were there "wanted" posters in towns and settlements? She glanced at her brothers and made a barely perceptible shake of her head, then touched a finger to her lips. Danny and Thad nodded their understanding. None of them would break the silence.

The horse and rider drew abreast of the rocks, and Jessie watched as Cole's hand closed around the gun at his hip. Her throat went dry. What if one of their horses gave away their place of concealment? She and her brothers would be caught in the cross fire. Or killed, if the other gunman was quicker than Cole.

When the horse and rider were out of sight, she let out the breath she had been unconsciously holding. Cole led them from their shelter and set a hard, fast pace in the opposite direction.

They had ridden for days without seeing another human being. In Texas that wasn't so unusual. But even in the most desolate areas of the land, there were occasional signs of civilization. A wagon wheel, cracked and broken, lay discarded beside a rotting wagon, whose horse or mule had probably been unhitched and used for transportation or food. A child's doll, its head missing, lay in the dust along the trail. Jessie glanced at her little brother, so young, so fearless in his innocence. She felt a cold shiver along her spine. What had happened to the child who owned this toy?

A shirt still flapped in the breeze over the bleached bones of a human skeleton. Someone, a traveler in need perhaps, had removed the pants and boots. All were mute testimony to the danger of man's determination to master the wilderness.

Pioneers left their war-torn farms and plantations to seek a better future. Two and three generations of families turned their backs on their past to seek a land of peace, a land of promise. But what they often found was a land that was desolate, natives who were hostile and weather that was forbidding.

Jessie began to notice that whenever Cole saw a ranch in the distance, whether it be sod hut or cabin, he steered them away from it. She no longer suspected that it was her imagination. Cole was doing everything possible to avoid all human contact.

Was he tracking someone? Or was someone tracking him? Fears often invaded her thoughts, but she forced herself not to dwell on them.

"Oh, Jessie. Look!" Thad reined in his mount and stared from his vantage point on a grassy mound toward the plains below.

Though the settlers were beginning to thin the herds of buffalo, the magnificent animals still roamed the prairies in herds that stretched for miles. Each time they spotted a herd, they would pause to watch the amazing spectacle. For as far as the

eye could see, the land was alive with the shaggy beasts, plodding, slowly plodding, in search of grassland. When something
caused them to stampede, they were an awesome, terrifying
blur of speed and motion.

Most nights they were asleep before darkness covered the
land. The long hours in the saddle, beneath a blazing sun, left
them drained. But they were blessed with water in the form
of mountain streams and half-dried creeks, as well as fresh
meat and cool star-kissed evenings.

While Danny and Thad merely watched, Jessie and Cole
took turns killing enough game to keep them well fed. They
dined like royalty on deer, boar, ducks, doves and quail.

One night while Jessie and Danny prepared supper and
Thad tended to the horses, Cole slipped away. By the time
venison sizzled in a skillet and coffee boiled over hot coals,
he returned with a leather pouch brimming with fresh cow's
milk.

"Where'd you get that?" Jessie hadn't seen any sign of life
for days.

"A couple of miles back. I spotted a small herd. Didn't
figure the rancher would miss a little milk." Cole handed the
pouch to Jessie, who promptly poured the milk into cups.

Cole watched as Thad drained the cup and started on a
second. "A growing boy shouldn't drink coffee every day."

"I like coffee," Thad chirped, wiping a milky mustache
from his upper lip. "It's what my pa drinks."

"Fine. But whenever it's available, you should drink milk."

Cole wasn't aware of Jessie's startled look. What a puzzle
he was. For a moment he almost sounded like a man who
cared about such mundane things.

Cole sat on the ground and leaned his back against a saddle.
He wanted to offer a cup of milk to Danny, as well, but hesitated. The boy was trying so hard to be a man. All Cole had
to do was say the wrong thing and they'd be right back where
they'd started.

He accepted a plate of supper from Jessie, then surprised her again by asking for some of the milk.

"Milk? You don't want coffee?" She'd watched him down gallons of coffee since they'd first met.

"Not when I can have fresh milk." He drained the cup and turned his attention to Thad. "Who milked the cows at home?"

"Jessie, mostly. But I helped," the little boy said proudly.

"I'll bet you did." Cole bit into the tender venison and wondered what Jessie did to make it taste so good. He'd have to remember to ask her sometime. "Did you and Danny help your father with the ranch chores?"

"Some. Pa was trying to teach Danny everything he needed to know to run a ranch of his own some day. But Danny'd rather sit under a tree and read his doctoring books." Thad gave an affectionate glance at his brother and was rewarded with a rare smile from Danny. It was obvious that the two brothers, so different, shared a bond of love and trust. "So mostly it fell to Jessie. 'Specially when Pa went to town for supplies. Sometimes he wouldn't come back for a week or more."

Cole glanced at the girl who sat between her two brothers. She stared pointedly at her plate. It was obvious she didn't like being the object of discussion.

Cole bit into a warm biscuit. "Good thing the Comanches didn't know you were alone at your ranch. Nothing they like better than helpless women and kids."

"Jessie's had dealings with the Comanches," Danny said. His voice held a note of pride.

Cole's smile faded. He turned to study the silent girl. "What does he mean, 'dealings'? Nobody deals with the Comanches. They take what they want."

"Not around Jessie." Danny reached for the pouch and poured himself a cup of milk. If it was good enough for Cole, he reasoned, it was good enough for him.

Cole pretended not to notice.

Wiping his mouth on his sleeve, Danny added, "The Indians keep a respectable distance from our ranch."

"Why? What hold do you have over the Indians?"

Thad and Danny exchanged a look. Danny shook his head as if to caution Thad about saying more. But the little boy loved talking.

Thad grinned. "The chief of the Comanches wants Jessie for his wife."

"Two Moons?" Cole was suddenly alert.

"Yeah. Two Moons. How'd you know that?" Thad asked innocently.

"I know a little about the Comanches." Cole knew also that Two Moons was shrewd, cunning and ambitious. He was a chief who answered to no one. The other tribes in the area feared and respected him.

"He offered Pa a dozen Indian ponies for Jessie."

"A dozen ponies?" Cole set his plate aside. With studied casualness, he rolled a cigarette and lifted a flaming stick from the fire. Inhaling deeply, he tossed the stick on the fire and leaned back. Through narrowed eyes he said softly, "The Comanches value their horseflesh. They'd kill a farmer and burn his crops and livestock just to steal his horses. They would consider it the highest honor to offer twelve in exchange for one wife."

Jessie felt her cheeks burn, but continued to stare at her plate. Whenever she thought about the Indian chief, she felt a flutter of fear. He had made it quite clear that one day, either her father would accept his offer, or he would take what he wanted without permission. Was this the reason she so desperately wanted to find her Pa? Did she harbor the secret terror that once Two Moons found out that her pa had not returned, he would come to claim what he had already decided was his?

"What did your father say to Two Moons about the offer?" The girl, he noted, had gone very still, lost in private thoughts.

Eager to share his store of knowledge, Thad chattered like a magpie. "Pa told him he needed Jessie to help with the ranch. So Two Moons offered Pa a squaw to replace her. But Pa said he wasn't interested."

Danny stood. From his agitation, Cole realized that the boy knew much more than he let on. More than his innocent younger brother, who expressed no fear as his words tumbled out.

"You didn't finish your supper," Jessie called to her brother's retreating back.

"I'm not hungry." Danny disappeared over the ridge, heading toward the creek.

"Can I go with him?" Thad mopped up the last of his gravy with a biscuit and handed his tin plate to his sister.

"I guess so." She took the plate from his hands and stood.

As the little boy disappeared from the circle of light, Jessie plunged the plates into a bucket of water over the fire, deliberately keeping her back to Cole. When her brothers were around, she felt easy enough in Cole's company. But when they were alone, she felt clumsy and awkward.

His voice was low, blending with the sounds of the night. "Would you ever consent to be the bride of Two Moons?"

"Not if I get a choice." She bit off the words.

Now why should that statement please him? He released a sigh and watched her stiff angry movements as she washed the dishes and dried them.

"Have you told your father how you feel?"

She turned. Cole's face was in shadow, outside the circle of firelight. In the darkness she saw the red glow of his cigarette, then smelled the hot acrid smoke as it dissipated into the night air.

"Pa said not to worry. He'd find me a husband when it was time."

He noticed that she avoided answering with a simple yes or no. "Whose time? Yours? Or your pa's?"

He saw the way her eyes rounded before narrowing in anger. Apparently he'd hit a nerve.

"My pa wouldn't sell me for a dozen Indian ponies."

"And a squaw," Cole added softly.

''Not even for two or three squaws. He gets along just fine with what he has. I can do the work of any squaw.''

His voice, coming out of the darkness, sent a shiver of fear along her spine. ''There are things a squaw can do that a daughter can't.''

With great effort she lifted the kettle from the fire and dumped the contents into the nearby grass. In the darkness Cole could hear the hiss as hot water met cool earth.

He broke the uncomfortable silence. ''We could have used that water.''

She shot an angry look in his direction, then picked up the empty bucket and swung away. ''I'll go to the creek and get more.''

''Jessie.''

Before she took three steps, Cole was at her side. With a hand at her shoulder, he stopped her.

''I understand your need to be busy.'' His voice was deep, soothing.

''No, you don't. You don't understand anything.'' She tried to pull away, but was no match for his strength.

''Did your father say that when he returned he was going to find you a husband?''

She felt her heart contract. She lowered her head, refusing to meet his eyes. ''Pa warned me that if I waited much longer, I'd be too old to be worth anything to a man.''

As Cole opened his mouth to speak, she looked up and said quickly, ''But he promised me that as long as he was around to protect me, he wouldn't let Two Moons have me unless I agreed.''

And now it was out. The truth. The terrible, awful truth. If her father never came back, she would be at the mercy of the Comanches. And for the sake of her brothers, she knew what she would have to do.

''Do the Comanches know?''

''That Pa's gone?'' She nodded her head. ''They came by after Pa left on the drive. I told them that unless they left us alone, I'd tell Pa, and Two Moons would never get his chance to have me.''

''What did they say?''

He felt her shiver. She stared down at the ground. ''Two Moons said that until my pa returned, my brothers and I were under his protection.''

''And you trust him?''

She looked up into his eyes and nodded. ''I have no choice. Besides, he's never broken his word to us. I figured that Danny and Thad would be safe while I was gone. The Comanches would never disobey their chief.''

''Maybe.'' Cole's eyes narrowed. ''But the Comanches could decide to take all of you into their tribe in order to keep you safe.''

''Would they do that?''

He shrugged.

''You've had dealings with the Comanches?''

He laughed low and deep in his throat. ''Enough.''

When he offered no explanation, she took a step back. ''I'll get the water now.''

He took the bucket from her hands. ''I'll carry it. From what Thad said, you've had your fill of chores. Sounds to me like your ranch would fall apart without you.''

''We all do our share.'' She walked along beside him, matching her steps to his.

''Some people always seem to carry a bigger load than others.''

''I don't mind hard work. Ma used to say, 'It isn't hard, it's just life. To survive, we all do the necessary.' ''

Cole smiled at her words. ''You seem to do more than the necessary.''

''Pa has a lot on his mind, with Ma dead, and the herd straying, and the ranch needing so much of his time. I don't mind being needed.''

''Neither does a pack mule. Unless he's pushed beyond his limit. Then he just sits down in the middle of the trail and refuses to go another step.''

"I'm not a pack mule."

"Sounds like someone forgot to tell your father."

Bristling, she stopped and balled her hands into fists at her sides. "Stop blaming Pa. And don't believe everything Thad says. He's just too little to understand. The chores I do around the ranch are the same things everybody else does."

"I don't know too many women who'd willingly take on all the things you do."

"And I'm sure you know lots of women." In the moonlight, her eyes blazed.

"I've known enough." His voice had grown dangerously soft.

"I suppose all the women you know wear frilly dresses, and their hands are soft, and they smell good."

"Some of them." Standing this close to Jessie, he couldn't remember a single one.

She felt a shaft of pain in her heart. What did she know about being a woman? Look at her. She wore her brother's clothes, and her hands were rough and calloused, and she smelled of sweat and horses. Some of the pain was evident in her voice. "Maybe Pa's right. Maybe I ought to consider Two Moons' offer." She gave a hollow laugh. "It's probably the only one I'll ever get."

He let out a hiss of anger. "Don't sell yourself short, Jessie." She felt the sting of his hot breath against her cheek.

Before she could react to his angry outburst, he tossed the bucket aside and framed her face with his big hands. Her eyes widened at the intimate contact.

"You're some kind of woman, Jessie." He lowered his face until their mouths were touching. She felt his breath warm, and his lips moist, as he breathed. "Some kind of beautiful, desirable woman."

For a moment she went rigid, letting the words he'd just whispered wash over her. The mere touch of him left her paralyzed. But as his lips closed over hers, her body refused her commands. Her arms slid around his waist. She clung to him, thrilling to his lean muscled strength.

This time he wasn't gentle. His kisses weren't tender. His kisses took her on a wild ride of emotions, by turn soaring through the skies, then plummeting wildly to earth. Her heart had become a tumbleweed, churning inside her breast as if it would break loose and fly away.

"Cole." She meant to push away, but when he lifted his head, she found herself drawing him closer.

He loved the sound of his name on her lips. Her voice was soft, breathy. It was the kind of voice that a man dreamed of on long lonely nights beneath the stars.

He kissed the corner of her lips and laughed when she tried to draw his mouth back to hers. Instead he pressed kisses to her cheek, her temple, the tip of her nose. When she closed her eyes, he pressed his lips to her lids and felt the soft flutter of her lashes against his skin.

"You taste so good, Jessie." His lips plundered her mouth, taking the kiss deeper, then deeper still, until both of them were lost in it.

His hands moving along her spine were so strong. And yet they caressed with a tenderness that surprised her. She leaned into him, loving the way his body seemed to mold itself to her softness.

As his lips moved over hers, his tongue invaded the intimacy of her mouth. After a moment's hesitation, she followed his lead. He tasted dark and mysterious, with a flavor like nothing she had ever known before. His mouth was tempting. Too tempting. With great effort she pushed away, taking in great gulps of air.

"I need more of you, Jessie."

He dragged her against him and ran openmouthed kisses along the sensitive hollow of her neck. He felt her tremble and knew that he needed to go slowly. But needs, hard driving needs, made him bolder. His mouth moved lower to the soft swell of her breast. He heard her suck in her breath. Her hands pushed against his shoulders, straining to break contact.

"What's wrong?" His words were whispered against her throat.

"You—shouldn't touch me like that." She was surprised at how difficult it was to speak.

"It's how a man wants to touch a woman, Jessie." His hands gripped her shoulders, drawing her so close she could feel the imprint of his hard body on hers. "It's how I want to touch you. Like this." He pressed his lips to her throat, then lower until his lips encountered the hardness of her taut nipple through the rough fabric of her shirt.

She gasped as spasms jolted through her body. Somewhere deep inside she felt a tightening, as though her entire body was being pulled by strings. Strings controlled by Cole's lips and fingertips.

She knew she should end this now, before it went any further. But never, never had she felt such needs. Needs that clouded her mind, took over her reason.

Cole was stunned at the depth of his passion. He'd intended merely to comfort her. But the minute she was in his arms, the minute he'd tasted her lips, he'd lost control. He wanted her. God in heaven, how he wanted her. But a voice in some dark corner of his mind called out a warning. It was too soon. He was taking this innocent too far, too fast.

He lifted his head and pressed one last kiss to her mouth. He felt her breath tumble from her lips and mingle with his. With his hands on her shoulders, he forced himself to lift his head and take a step back.

Feeling strangely disoriented, Jessie struggled to stand very still. Gradually the ground beneath her feet settled, becoming firm once more. Slowly, ever so slowly, her ragged breathing became steady.

When she was certain she could speak, she said, "I'll let you get the water. I think I'll be safer back at camp."

He caught her chin in his hand and forced her to meet his steady gaze. "You won't be safe from me anywhere, Jessie."

At his words she felt a little thrill. Fear? Or anticipation? Without another word she turned and made her way back to the camp fire.

He watched as she bent to pour a cup of coffee. Then he picked up the fallen bucket and headed toward the creek. He was sweating, he noted, and it wasn't because of the heat of the night.

Chapter Nine

Cole was still smiling as he headed into the darkness toward the creek. The bucket swung in loose easy movements by his side. He was thinking about Jessie, about the way she tasted fresh and slightly wicked. And about the way she felt in his arms, soft, so damned soft.

It would be easier if he quit fighting these feelings for her and just accepted them. If they just gave in to the temptation to love, all the tension between them would dissolve.

He thought about lying with her in the tall cool prairie grass. A frown touched his lips. Once wouldn't be enough. Or twice. He knew, just from the way she tasted, that he'd never have enough of a woman like Jessie. She'd take him clear over the top of a mountain and send him soaring through space. And then he'd spend the rest of his life wishing he could soar like that again.

No, once would never be enough with Jessie. Nor a hundred times. Jessie Conway was the kind of woman who made a man start thinking about home and family and forever.

Forever. That was about as reliable as Texas weather.

Lost in thought, he never saw the figure leap from the shadows until it was upon him.

Cole heard the growl of anger low and deep in the throat, a split second before he was hit. With a wild thrashing of fists and feet, he went sprawling in the dust with a half-crazed creature on top of him.

Reflexively his hand went to the gun at his waist. Jamming it into the midsection of his attacker, he hissed, "Move a muscle and you're dead."

His attacker paused. A nearly unrecognizable voice choked with fury said, "Go ahead. You may as well kill me. Because if you don't, I aim to kill you."

"Danny?"

Cole dropped his hand and strained through the darkness to make out the figure of the boy who had attacked him. "Son, that's the second time you nearly got yourself killed by my hand."

"Don't call me that. I'm not your son. And I'm not afraid of you."

"What's this all about...Danny?"

"It's about you and my sister. You had no right taking liberties with her like that."

Liberties? Cole didn't know whether to laugh or let loose with a stream of oaths. Just how much had the boy seen? And heard?

Cole peered at the creature, half boy half man, who stood with fists clenched, his breath coming in short angry spurts. Tossing the gun to the ground, Cole shrugged.

"All right, Danny. I can see that you're feeling pretty upset about what you think I did to your sister. Go ahead. Take the first punch."

As soon as the words were out of Cole's mouth, a fist landed squarely on his jaw. He felt himself reeling backward until he came to rest against a boulder. Shaking his head, he felt it slowly clear. Where had that strength come from? The gangly youth with long thin arms and hands as soft as a woman's must have been storing up a lot of hatred to pack such a wallop.

Rubbing his jaw, Cole stepped forward. "I allowed the first one. But that's all you get. From now on, it's a fair fight."

Danny landed a second blow to Cole's face and the muscled

gunman felt the sting as his eye began to swell. But when Danny swung again, Cole ducked and landed a punch to the boy's shoulder. He heard the grunt of pain before Danny began swinging wildly. The next three punches barely grazed Cole's body, while two of his landed cleanly on Danny's jaw and temple.

The youth was panting now, his breath coming faster as he tried to dodge Cole's fists. As he moved back for another punch, his feet slipped in the grass and he went down on one knee. Cole waited while the boy lumbered to his feet.

"What are you waiting for," the boy called, his voice cracking with emotion. "Go ahead and hit me, Mr. Gunman. It ought to make you feel real big."

"This is your fight, Danny. Now finish it."

Danny charged him, and both of them fell to the ground. As they rolled around, fists flying, the air was punctuated with grunts and curses.

Cole got to his feet and waited until Danny did the same. Blood spilled from the boy's nose, and there was a cut above Cole's eye that had trickled blood down his face and onto his shirt. He was stiff and sore, especially around the shoulder that had still not completely healed from the horse thief's bullet. But he intended to see this thing through to the end.

"I didn't trust you the first time I laid eyes on you," Danny spat.

"I thought this was about your sister."

"That, too," the boy cried. "I don't like the way you look at my sister."

"And how is that?"

"The same way Two Moons looks at her."

Cole felt a sudden twinge. Jealousy? Impossible. Why would he be jealous of the way a Comanche chief looked at Jessie?

"I want you to show some respect to my sister," the boy said, raising his fist.

Cole braced himself for another blow. When it came, it glanced off his temple.

He landed a punch on Danny's already bloody nose. Fresh blood spurted. With a cry of pain, Danny dropped his fists.

"Keep 'em up, boy. You're leaving yourself wide open to attack." Cole waited until Danny raised his fists, then landed another blow to the boy's midsection, doubling him over with pain.

"Always remember, in a clean fight, keep your fists in front of that part of the body you want to protect. If it's a dirty fight—" he paused a moment, wondering if the boy could even hear him through the blur of pain "—go for your opponent's most vulnerable spot. Hit him hard, hit him quick, and make it count."

He stood over the crumpled form of the boy, feeling disgust at what he'd been forced to do.

"Had enough?"

In reply, Danny caught him by the ankles and brought him down. Instantly the boy pounced on him and started punching him about the head and face.

Caught by surprise, Cole swore viciously and brought his hands up to ward off the blows. Within minutes he could feel the boy's strength ebbing. Finally spent, Danny rolled aside and lay gasping for air.

Cole sat up and watched the boy struggle to control the tears that were very close to the surface. Then he lumbered to his feet.

Standing, he offered his hand to Danny. For long silent moments the boy stared at him with contempt.

"For a first fight, you did good."

In tense silence Danny glared at him.

"I'd like you to accept my apology," Cole said solemnly.

He saw the boy's eyes widen. As the words sank in, Danny asked, "You mean it?"

"Of course I do." He extended his hand again and this time Danny took it, coming slowly to his feet.

The two stood facing each other, each seeming to take measure of the other.

Danny stared into the gunman's eyes, determined to make his point. "I think my sister, Jessie, is special."

"So do I."

"You do?" For a split second, Danny's voice was tinged with surprise. Then his tone hardened. "I want you to promise that you won't touch her like that again."

"What?" Cole withdrew his hand, staring at the boy as if he couldn't believe what he'd just heard.

"I said—"

"I heard you." Cole studied the boy for a few seconds longer, weighing the issue. Maybe by tomorrow he'd find the trail of the one he was seeking. If so, the promise would be a simple one to keep. He'd never see Jessie Conway and her brothers again. On the other hand, he could find himself in the company of Jessie for several days or weeks. In that case, this promise could prove to be sheer torture.

"Promise?" Danny asked. He stuck out his hand.

"Promise." Cole took the boy's hand, then added with a sly grin, "Unless, of course, Jessie makes the first move. If she wants me badly enough, then I figure I'm obliged to do the lady's bidding."

At his words, Danny's face darkened with fury. He raised a fist and Cole saw his eyes narrow. Then he brightened. "It's a deal. Hellfire, I'll put my money on Jessie to want something better than a tumble in the dirt with a stranger who's quick with a gun."

A half grin touched Cole's lips. Damned if the kid wasn't sharper than he'd thought. He'd just been roundly insulted by a kid who was still wet behind the ears. And the kid had just exacted a stupid promise out of him. A promise he didn't want to make. But now that he had, there was no backing out. He'd just have to live with it.

"You drive a hard bargain." Cole picked up the fallen bucket and dropped an arm around the boy's shoulders. "Come on. I was on my way to the creek for water. Let's wash off this blood before your sister sees us and throws a fit about two bulls fighting."

"You mean that's the end of it? You don't hold a grudge?"

Clutching the boy's shoulder, Cole drew him close against his side. "When two men shake hands, that's the end of the matter."

Danny beamed with pride. Men. Cole had said two men. It was the first time anyone had ever called him a man. He was feeling so good right now, he could probably take on two more gunmen and whip them with one hand behind his back.

The sky was awash with soft feathery clouds. Pale pink rays of light touched the horizon. As Jessie made her way back from the creek, she was surprised to see the others awake and moving about. Bedrolls had already been tied behind the horses. Coffee bubbled and steamed over the fire.

Cole looked up at her approach and quickly looked away. But in that brief glimpse, he saw the way her damp hair streamed down her back in soft waves. And he was achingly aware of the soft womanly curves beneath the faded shirt and britches.

Kneeling, she poured herself a cup of coffee, then stared at his face.

"What happened to your eye?"

"Bumped into something last night." He ladled food onto his plate and turned away.

"Danny, Thad, come and get something to eat before we start out."

As her brother accepted a steaming plate, she caught sight of the purple bruise on his cheek. "You look awful. How did that happen?"

"Hit something in the dark," he mumbled, stuffing his mouth with stale biscuit.

"You hit something. Cole bumped into something." She looked from one to the other. "What have the two of you been up to?"

"Getting acquainted." Cole finished his meal in two bites and strode toward the horses. Without a word, Danny gave her a sheepish grin and followed.

Jessie stared at them for long silent minutes. Something had happened last night. They had obviously been fighting. Yet neither of them seemed the least bit angry at the other. In fact Danny seemed in better temper than he'd been since he first joined her on this journey.

Men. She stood and began the task of clearing the camp. She'd never be able to figure them out.

"We'll bypass San Antonio," Cole announced. "We can pick up the Chisholm Trail across the Colorado River near Waco, then head on up to Fort Worth. Brace yourselves. It's going to be a rough trip."

Rough. The word was too simple. They had been over a week without a single sign of civilization. They rode beneath a blistering sun and shivered under blankets on cold dark nights.

This day as they rode up over a rise, they reined in their horses and stared at the sight of a buffalo herd that stretched as far as the eye could see.

For long minutes they watched the spectacle.

"Jessie," Cole called, "You and Thad wait here. Danny and I are going hunting."

"Me?"

Jessie saw the startled look on her brother's face. Always before, Jessie and Cole had taken turns hunting game for their meals.

"You and that Sharps breechloading rifle are going to take care of supper," Cole said. "Come on."

With a grin splitting his face from ear to ear, Danny urged his horse to follow Cole's lead.

They approached the herd, then when they were near enough to be seen, left their horses and continued on foot. While Jessie and Thad watched from the safety of a grassy knoll, Cole and Danny dropped down on their hands and knees and crawled to within twenty yards of the herd.

Cole touched Danny's shoulder and whispered, "When you aim, go for the lungs. If you hit him in the heart, he'll run three or four hundred yards before he goes down and take the whole herd with him.''

Danny's Adam's apple bobbed up and down. ''Wouldn't you rather borrow my rifle? That way you can be sure of hitting at least one. I might drive the whole herd away.''

Cole shook his head. ''It's your shot, Danny. Pick out the buffalo you want and give it your best.''

Sweat trickled along Danny's forehead and spilled down the corner of his eye, blurring his vision. He took a moment to wipe his wet palms on his pants before looking through the sight of his rifle. A huge shaggy beast lifted his head at that moment and seemed to stare directly at the lad. He felt his heart skip a beat, but before he could contemplate what he was about to do, he saw the animal take a tentative step closer.

''Better get him quick, before he decides to walk clear over us,'' Cole whispered.

Meeting the animal's curious stare, Danny took a moment longer to aim. Sweat beaded his forehead and upper lip. His hands were trembling, and he knew that the man beside him could feel his fear. It was a palpable thing. He could smell the fear, taste it.

How could Cole trust him with such an important task? What if he embarrassed himself by missing? Putting aside such thoughts, he gave one final look through the sight and pulled the trigger. A sound like thunder echoed and reechoed through the skies, and the herd shifted uneasily.

Danny fell backward from the force of the report, and when he sat up, he was astounded to see the huge brown beast lying perfectly still. The rest of the herd grazed around him, completely unaware of any danger.

''Good shooting,'' Cole called, slipping his hunting knife from his belt.

Danny beamed with pride. It was the first time he felt almost equal to the stern gunman who so intimidated him.

''Yeah.'' On trembling legs Danny edged closer until he stood over his trophy. ''It wasn't bad, was it?''

''I couldn't have done better myself.''

Danny could have died from sheer happiness. His pa always treated him like a foolish dreamer, because he preferred his books to ranch chores. Pa had disdain for anyone who couldn't carry his own weight. His own weight. Danny felt a swelling of pride at his accomplishment. If Pa had been here, he'd have seen for himself that his son could do plenty of things, given half a chance.

"We'll have enough food for a week," Cole said. "Not to mention the warm buffalo hide. That will belong to you."

Danny felt his head swim with the knowledge. He'd killed a buffalo. He had just carried his share of the load. Maybe he and Cole weren't so different, he thought. He could hunt. And like Cole, Danny rarely initiated a conversation. He and Cole were both more content with their own thoughts than with words.

The thoughts that were tumbling through Danny's mind startled him. It wasn't that he wanted to imitate a gunman, he realized. But there was something about Cole that Danny admired. He just couldn't put it into words yet.

Jessie and Thad scrambled down the embankment and stared in awe at the size of the dead beast. Jessie threw her arms around her brother's neck and embarrassed him by kissing him on the cheek.

"That was wonderful."

Danny shrugged. "I just did what Cole told me."

"Were you scared?" Thad asked.

"Naw." Danny glanced at Cole's arched eyebrow and added, "Well, some. But I knew I couldn't waste time being scared or I'd lose my shot at him."

"That's an important lesson everyone needs to learn in life," Cole said quietly. "It doesn't matter whether or not you're scared. Everyone is afraid at some time in his life. But you can't let fear keep you from doing what's needed."

Cole reached into his belt and withdrew a second knife. "Since this is your kill, you ought to help me carve it up, Danny."

The boy felt a tightening in his throat as he accepted the knife. Cole needed his help. Cole trusted him.

As he knelt, Jessie noticed the dark sticky stain trailing the back of Danny's shirt.

"What's this? You've been hurt."

"It's nothing," he said, shoving away her hand.

"You're bleeding. Let me look at that." Ignoring his protest, Jessie lifted his shirt from his waistband. She gasped at the purple welt surrounding a deep cut.

"I—fell backward when I fired the rifle. Guess I cut my back on a rock." Danny wished the earth would open up and swallow him. Now Cole would realize that he was just a dumb kid trying to play at being grown-up. He couldn't even properly use his father's gun. "Leave it alone, Jess." He twisted away from her touch. "It's nothing."

"I think you should let me treat that wound."

Danny pushed her hand away. "I don't need my sister treating me like a helpless little kid."

Jessie watched in startled silence as the boy bent to his task of gutting the buffalo and stripping away its hide.

"I don't understand what's made you so moody."

When Danny didn't respond, Cole said softly, "Sometimes a man just wants to be left alone."

A man? Danny? Danny was her brother. Her younger brother. "Fine. I'll leave him alone. I'll leave everyone alone."

Annoyed by Cole's unexpected coldness and puzzled by Danny's recent unexplained behavior, she pulled the precious soap from her saddlebag and went off in the direction of the creek.

As she disappeared below a ridge, Cole swore softly. He'd just begun to make peace with Danny, and now he had Jessie riled. But that wasn't what bothered him. What really rankled was that for the rest of the night he'd have to fight off visions of Jessie naked in the creek. Not that it wasn't a pleasant thought. But staying alive required a certain amount of concentration. He couldn't afford the distractions. And ever since his promise to Danny, he'd had to fight doubly hard to keep away from a certain tempting diversion.

Chapter Ten

The day was hot, the sun a searing ball of flame in a pale unblemished sky. As the horses moved across the plains, the dust rose up in clouds to choke their riders.

This day Jessie took the lead, with Thad and Danny riding single file some distance behind. Cole brought up the rear, keeping a sharp eye on the high buttes that rose on either side of the trail.

Glancing at the rocky ridges, Cole felt a prickling along the back of his neck. He was a man who had always trusted his instincts. Though he could see nothing out of the ordinary, he was certain they were being watched.

He checked the bullets in his pistol, then ran a hand along the Winchester resting in the boot beside his knee. As the sun beat down mercilessly, he pulled the brim of his hat low on his forehead. They would need to reach higher ground before sundown. He wanted a clear view of the trail before they stopped to make camp for the night.

If he was alone, he realized, he would have been able to ride without revealing himself. Four horses raised a cloud of dust visible for miles.

By midday they were forced to take refuge from the relentless sun. When Cole gave the order to stop, Jessie slid gratefully from the saddle. She watched as Thad dismounted and sank to his knees. Instantly she was beside him, lifting him in her arms.

"You all right, Tadpole?"

The boy smiled up into her eyes, and Jessie could see the heroic struggle he made to keep going. "I just got dizzy for a minute."

"You rest here." Jessie deposited him in the shade beneath an outcropping of rock.

"What about the horses?" The boy's voice was little more than a croak.

By mutual consent the others had allowed Thad to assume the care of their mounts. He was conscientious, always seeing to it that the animals' needs were seen to before he allowed himself to eat supper each night. And in the morning, while the others broke camp, Thad saw to it that the animals were fed and watered and ready for another day on the trail.

"Don't worry about it. I'll see to them," Danny said, taking Thad's reins.

He led the horses to a shady spot and unsaddled them, then tethered them within reach of tufts of prairie grass.

Jessie ordered Thad out of his sweat-drenched clothes and spread them out on a rock to dry. When she returned, Thad was already sound asleep. She turned to study Cole, who was standing in the shade, staring intently at the trail behind them. When she came up behind him, his attention remained focused on the surrounding countryside.

"Maybe we should stop here for the rest of the day," she whispered.

"Not yet. As soon as we reach the high ground up ahead."

Jessie's gaze swept the trail that seemed to stretch endlessly before them. "I don't think Thad can go much farther."

"We'll keep going until I give the word to stop."

"Just like that?" She stared at his back and felt resentment begin to grow. She was hot, tired and feeling pushed to the limits. It was her fault her brothers were being forced to endure such hardships. The guilt of that knowledge made it all the more painful for her.

When he didn't respond, she spat, "Fine. You can go if you want. My brothers and I will stay here until we're rested."

"Jessie, listen to me." He turned his attention from the trail and lowered his voice so the others wouldn't hear. "There's someone following us. Our safest bet is to get to high ground as soon as possible."

He saw the sudden flash of concern before she said in a controlled voice, "We don't need to stop at all then. We'll go on."

His tone was low, commanding. "Grab a quick rest. We need it to keep our minds sharp. We'll be leaving as soon as the sun's behind that butte."

He removed his gun belt, sat down and closed his eyes. His gun, she noted, was held firmly in his hand, his rifle in the dirt beside him. Though his breathing gradually became soft and easy, she had the distinct impression that he was attuned to the slightest change in the rhythm of nature's sounds around them.

Despite her fears, she dropped down beside her brothers. Within minutes, she was sound asleep.

The sun had long ago bled into the western hills. Long stretches of shadow drifted across the land. A hawk circled overhead, hungry for a late-night meal. At the end of a long hot day, Danny and Thad were rolled into blankets, their breathing steady.

Jessie banked the fire and crawled into her bedroll, listening to the comforting sounds of the night. Even in childhood she'd never been afraid of the dark. It was her friend. With darkness came an end to the chores. Lying in her bunk in the little sod shack, she had been free to think, to dream, to plan. She'd had grand plans for her life. Like her father, she would be a rancher. But her ranch would be big. She would own half of Texas and stock it with a herd of longhorns that would stretch as far as the eye could see. Like the herds of buffalo they'd seen on the prairie, she thought. Vast swarms of steers would cover the land. And her house would be the finest house in

Texas. It would be a grand mansion like the plantation houses she'd seen in her mother's picture book. No more sod shacks with an earthen floor and sod roof. There would be a winding staircase, and windows on the upper floors that looked out over the land. Her land. Sometimes she would wear a beautiful gown like the ones her mother had described to her when she was a little girl.

Her mother had talked about church socials and farm parties and dances, where all the ladies wore lovely gowns and whirled around in the arms of handsome suitors. When she felt like it, Jessie thought, she would look like a fine fancy lady. But mostly she'd wear buckskins and ride the range, keeping track of her empire. That was what she dreamed of. An empire in Texas.

She closed her eyes and tried to conjure up an image of her mother. For a brief moment, she saw in her mind's eye a fragile woman with pale yellow hair and laughing blue eyes. The image faded. Jessie squeezed her eyes tight and willed herself to remember, but the image would not return. She tried so hard to keep her ma's memory alive. By using the lilac water, by keeping the handmade quilts on their beds. But each year it grew more and more difficult. What frightened Jessie even more was the loss of Pa. He'd only been gone a few months, and already there were times when she couldn't see him clearly. What if he was gone forever? Would his image fade like Ma's? She thought of Danny and Thad. For their sakes she had to keep the memories alive. And the dreams.

Sitting up suddenly, she turned to study Cole keeping watch some distance away. Ever since they had made camp, he'd been keeping his attention fixed on the trail below. Climbing from her blankets, she made her way to the fire. She poured the last of the coffee and walked toward him.

He accepted the cup, drank, then glanced at her empty hands. "You're not having any?"

"That's the last of it."

He nearly reminded her that it was her frugality that caused them to cut back on rations. But there was a sadness in her eyes tonight. This was not a time for teasing her.

"We'll share." He handed her the cup and watched as she took a long drink before handing it back.

"Not tired?"

She shook her head.

"Sit a while."

She sat with her back to a boulder and watched as he rolled a cigarette. His fingers were long and bronzed and callused like her own. The thought of those same hands touching her skin caused a little pulse to flutter deep inside her.

"See any sign of a visitor?"

His eyes narrowed. He emitted a stream of smoke. "Nothing so far. But someone's out there."

"How do you know?"

He shrugged. "I just know."

She felt a slight tremor of fear. "You think it's smart camping out in the open like this? Having a fire?"

"If someone's trying to find me, I'd just as soon be found here. Up there—" he pointed to the towering buttes, "—he could shoot from behind cover and never show his face."

"What's the difference? If he kills you, you're just as dead."

"I want to see the man who kills me. I want him to face me like a man, not hide behind cover like a coward."

Something in his tone chilled her. There was a seething bitterness festering inside him. She had no doubt that Cole Matthews was a man who would face death with the same arrogance he displayed in life.

"You think someone killed my pa?"

He filled his lungs with smoke. Why the hell did she have to bring up that subject? "Your father sounds like a man who'd be home if he could."

She stared at him, wondering if the anger in his eyes was directed at her or at himself. "So you think he's dead."

"I didn't say that."

"It's not like you to dodge a question."

"I'm not dodging." Damn her! He was. He didn't want to add to her burden. "I just don't have any answers. And neither do you." He swung his head away, scanning the darkness. "Why don't you try to get some sleep."

"Yeah." She stood, but before she could turn away he was on his feet, catching her by the shoulder.

"Jessie." He'd forgotten how small she was, how delicate her bones.

She turned, and he saw the way her eyes widened in surprise.

He'd only meant to soften the blow. But now that he was standing this close, inhaling the soft scent of her, he had a desperate urge to take her in his arms, to kiss her until she was weak and clinging.

His tone was low and rough. "When a man's been on the trail for a long time, he forgets how to be civilized. I'm used to my own company."

"Then I'll leave you to it."

"No. Wait." His thumb dug into the soft flesh of her upper arm, and he saw her flinch. Frustrated, he swore and dropped his hand to his side. His tone deepened. "I'd like you to stay."

Her heart quickened. She felt the beginnings of a blush and was grateful for the darkness. She craved his companionship. Maybe because she was afraid of whoever was out there watching, waiting. Maybe because her own thoughts this night were sad, dreamy. Or maybe because she was never able to forget the way it felt to be held in his arms. So many nights she'd lain awake thinking about him. The things that flashed through her mind made her cheeks hot. Yet in the daylight, Cole treated her with less regard than his horse.

It wasn't daylight now. Darkness covered them, making them both bolder.

"I'll stay." Her voice was a muted whisper on the night breeze. "But you ought to sleep a while, and I'll keep watch."

"I'm not tired." He was so alert now, all of his senses were humming.

The wind danced through her hair. He caught a strand and

allowed it to sift through his fingers. His gaze centered on her mouth.

The promise he'd made to Danny crept unbidden to his mind. How could he have been so foolish? At the time, the promise had been made almost casually with no regard to cost. But with her lips mere inches from his own and her eyes full of promise, he'd give anything to be relieved of the handshake and the vow.

There was one small consolation. If this was what she wanted, he needn't be the one to stop her.

The danger lurking just beyond the circle of light was forgotten. The only thing that mattered at this moment was the woman who stirred his blood as no one else ever had.

"I'm not tired, either." She swallowed and found herself watching his lips. They parted in a half smile and she felt her breath catch in her throat. Such perfectly formed lips. She'd never seen such a beautiful mouth on a man before. Of course she'd never taken such pains to study one before.

"You should see what moonlight does to your hair." He touched a finger to it and his smile grew. "So pretty. Like holding a candle up to a glass of whiskey."

Jessie's throat went dry. No one had ever said such words to her. No one had ever before made her feel pretty.

"In sunlight it shines like spun gold. But in moonlight." He shook his head, lost for words, and grabbed a handful of her hair.

He pulled her head back and studied her for long silent moments, fighting the desire to crush her in his arms. The need for her was becoming an unbearable ache.

"Cole." Her mouth had suddenly gone so dry she couldn't swallow. She saw his eyes narrow as she ran a tongue over her lips. She felt his fingers tighten as they tangled in her hair, and she felt a little thrill at the realization of the power she possessed.

Why was he holding back? Why was he prolonging this agony when the only thing she wanted was the taste of his lips on hers?

She looked up at him with a puzzled frown and saw his gaze center on her mouth. Was it anger she saw? Dismissal? Desire? The thought left her stunned and reeling. Desire. The same desire that curled along her veins.

Slowly, carefully, she drew herself closer to him and stood on tiptoe to reach his mouth. Still he made no move to hold her. Puzzled, she pressed closer and touched her lips to his. As their lips grazed, she felt his quick intake of breath. Her sense of power grew. He wanted to kiss her. She was certain of it. But something held him back.

Curiosity and her own growing sense of power made her bold. For whatever reason, he was allowing her to make the first moves. Now she wanted to test him, to push him to the limits of his control.

Shyly, tentatively, she moved her lips over his, nibbling, tasting, until she heard his drawn-out intake of breath. With a boldness that surprised even her, she touched her tongue to his mouth and traced its fullness.

God in heaven, how much could a man be expected to take? He had tried, honestly tried, to live up to his promise. But the woman was driving him over the edge. A wisp of her hair brushed his cheek and he pushed it aside, then plunged his hand into a tangle, pulling her head back. He stared down at her for the space of a heartbeat, seeing the invitation in her eyes. On a moan he plunged both hands into her hair, crushing her to him. His lips claimed hers in a savage kiss, plundering her mouth until they were both gasping for breath.

"Do you know what you do to me?" The words were ground out against her lips. Before she could respond, he kissed her again with a hard, lingering kiss that left no doubt of his feelings.

A horse nickered, but neither of them noticed.

Cole lifted his lips a fraction and murmured, "You are the most…"

A shadow flitted between two of the horses. The words Cole had been whispering died in his throat. How could he have been so careless? The creature in his arms had him so distracted, he'd forgotten the simplest rules of survival.

With one hand he shoved Jessie behind him into the shadows; with the other he drew the pistol from his holster. In quick strides he threaded his way among the tethered horses and pressed the cold steel against the head of a shadowy figure.

"Don't try it." His voice held the edge of steel.

The figure turned. In the moonlight, wide dark eyes stared unblinkingly into his.

With her own gun drawn, Jessie came rushing toward him. Seeing the figure, she came to an abrupt halt.

"Cole, don't shoot." Her voice was low pitched with terror. "It's a girl."

At the sound of Jessie's voice, the girl whirled and lifted a hand. In her hand was the hilt and broken jagged blade of a knife. She left no doubt that she intended to bury it in the woman facing her.

Cole's hand snaked out, catching her wrist in a painful grip. He twisted her hand until the weapon fell to the earth. Though he swore viciously, the girl spoke not a word as she kicked and fought until she was subdued in Cole's arms.

He studied the fallen weapon. "Not just a girl," he said through gritted teeth. "An Indian. Comanche, from the looks of her and her knife."

Hearing the commotion, Danny and Thad rolled from their blankets and hurried toward them. The girl gave a snarl like that of a ferocious animal and twisted free of Cole's grasp. She stood facing these new strangers who studied her with a mixture of fear and curiosity. It was obvious that she was prepared to fight all of them with teeth and fingernails rather than meekly give up.

"We don't want to hurt you," Cole said in English. When she made no response, he repeated the words in a language Jessie and her brothers didn't know.

"You speak Comanche?" Danny asked.

"Not much. Enough to get by."

He turned toward the girl. "You understand? We don't want to hurt you. But we're sure as hell not going to sit by and allow you to steal one of our horses."

Sensing that he was the leader of this group, the girl slowly faced him. As she did, the glow of the fire illuminated her clearly. Her dirty buckskin dress was smeared and stained with blood. Fresh blood oozed from her shoulder and soaked her sleeves and lower arm.

"She's hurt," Danny said.

As he took a step toward her, she whirled and would have attacked him if Cole hadn't stopped her. It took all of his strength to subdue the kicking, biting girl.

When at last they lay panting and choking, Cole straddled her and held her arms above her head. While the others watched in consternation, he tore away the sleeve of her buckskin dress.

He swore loudly, viciously.

The wound was deep and badly infected. From the looks of it, it had been several days since the wound had been inflicted, and she had lost a considerable amount of blood.

"She must be half-crazy with the pain," he muttered.

The others stood by helplessly, staring in dazed fascination at the ugly wound.

"We have to help her." It was Danny who broke the silence.

"She won't let you," Cole said quietly. "She'd rather die than submit."

"Then we'll just have to force her to accept our help." Danny had spent hours poring over every word of the medical book Cole had bought him. Though her wounds appeared to be badly infected, he felt a strange sense of calm acceptance. He'd dealt with Cole's wounds; he could deal with hers. "I'll need your whiskey, Cole. Jessie, I'll need boiling water and strips of clean cloth."

"What should I do?" Thad asked.

"You'll keep your distance," Cole said loudly, casting a meaningful look at the girl. "Otherwise, this little wildcat will cut us all up for stew and have us for supper. I tell you, Danny, the girl will never allow you to touch her.''

Danny gave no reply. He was already spreading out a bed-roll beside the fire.

Jessie gave a last look at the girl before hurrying off to fetch the necessary items. Now that she was lying quietly, the poor thing looked more like a wounded kitten than a wildcat. But she had seen the way the girl had fought.

Wouldn't she do the same? she thought with sudden insight. If she were caught by hostile people, wouldn't she do anything to escape them? But she and her brothers weren't hostile. They wished the girl no harm. They merely wanted to heal her wound before allowing her to be on her way. Now they would have to find a way to convince her of their intentions. With time and luck, they might be able to earn her trust.

As she set the bucket of water over the fire, she fretted over this latest incident. They had brought a strange new enemy into their camp. And added another element of danger to their already perilous journey.

Chapter Eleven

By the light of the camp fire, Cole laid the Comanche girl on the bedroll, then very deliberately drew his pistol, hoping to subdue her.

"You'll lie still, or I'll shoot." He aimed the gun at her head.

If she understood, she gave no indication. The girl watched as Danny assembled the items he needed. When he knelt beside her, she sprang up, determined to escape or die trying. In the confusion that followed, she managed to knock Danny backward and began scrambling over him to freedom. Just as she was about to sprint, he caught her by the ankle, bringing her down on top of him. With the breath knocked from her, she lay atop him, gasping. Wide dark eyes stared into narrowed green ones. Her breasts were flattened against his chest; her slender hips pressed firmly against his thighs. For one terrible moment they stared at each other with a look of stunned surprise. Before either of them could react, Cole's arm encircled her throat. With his other hand he pinned her arms behind her back and lifted her off Danny.

"There's only one way to do this," Cole said through clenched teeth. "If you're determined to help this girl, we'll have to tie her."

Before the others could protest, Cole produced a length of rope and bound her hands and feet. When she was completely unable to move, he stood up, withdrew his pistol from his holster and calmly sat down on a nearby rock.

"All right, doc. Do what you have to."

Danny was visibly trembling by the time he knelt beside the girl a second time and bent to examine her wound. For long moments he studied her dark eyes, wide and unblinking. He picked up a knife and saw her eyes narrow fractionally. With the knife, he slit the top of her garment and folded it back to lay bare the entire wound.

The flesh of her shoulder was torn and jagged, indicating a bullet. As he gently probed, he saw the signs of raging infection.

"She was shot," he said to the others. "Some time ago, from the looks of it. Bullet's still in there. I'll have to dig it out. Jess." He motioned to his sister. "I'll need your help."

Instantly Jessie was at his side, fishing out the hunting knife from the boiling water.

Seeing a leather strip about her neck, on which dangled a copper disk, Danny cut it away. Instantly the girl cried out something unintelligible. Danny pressed it into her open palm. She snatched at it and curled it tightly into her fist.

"That's an amulet," Cole explained. "It's supposed to bring the wearer good luck."

Danny wished he hadn't been so rough with the girl. "She'll need all the good luck she can find."

As Danny probed, Jessie saw the girl wince. Jessie laid a hand on the girl's arm and squeezed gently. Though the girl showed no further emotion, she kept her gaze firmly fixed on Danny's face.

Sweat beaded his forehead. He knew how much pain his probing caused, but it couldn't be avoided. Deeper he probed, then deeper still, until he felt the scrape of metal against the tip of the knife.

"Here it is." He brought the tip of the blade below the bullet and inched it upward until Jessie could grasp it with her fingers.

Working quickly, he poured whiskey on the open wound and shuddered at the girl's sudden hiss of pain.

"I don't mean to hurt you," he murmured, knowing the Comanche couldn't understand his words. His voice was low, soothing. "But it's the only way to help you. Hold on a little longer."

With Jessie assisting him, he cleansed the wound and bound it with clean cloth. When he was finished, he dipped a cloth in water and began to sponge the blood and dirt from the girl's face and arms.

Throughout the entire ordeal, the girl had spoken not a word, nor had she permitted herself to display any outward sign of suffering. Now, as Danny gently sponged her body, she watched him through a veil of dark lashes.

He brought the damp cloth across her forehead and down the slope of her cheek. His touch was easy and gentle as he followed the contour of her jaw to her lips. When he moved the cloth lower to her throat, he saw her swallow and wished he could swallow the lump in his own throat. He looked into her eyes and saw himself reflected there. Without realizing it, his own gaze softened. A tear trickled from the corner of her eye, and she tried to blink back the remaining tears. Instantly he touched a finger to the moisture. Her eyes widened in surprise before she turned her face away in shame, avoiding any further eye contact.

"Untie her, Cole." Danny's tone was harsher than he'd intended.

"She'll just run the first chance she gets."

"Untie her." Danny wiped his knife on his pants and noted idly that her blood was the same color as the bloodstains left by Cole's wound. There was no difference. Their blood was the same, their pain the same. "She needs sleep and plenty of it if she's going to recover from what she's been through. Our job now is to make her as comfortable as possible."

"She'll run, I tell you."

"I'll keep watch." Danny's voice held a thread of icy determination. Without waiting for Cole's response, he bent and cut the ropes holding the girl. Though her eyes were wide and watchful, they showed absolutely no emotion. "I don't want her to wake up and find herself tied like a prisoner."

Cole studied the boy for long minutes, then turned to watch the girl. Her gaze never left Danny's face.

Cole nodded. "I'll take the first watch. You grab some sleep."

He glanced at the Indian girl, who was still watching Danny as she struggled to tie the amulet about her neck once more. Seeing the effort it cost her, Danny took the leather strips from her hand and tied them about her neck. Her hand closed possessively around the copper disk.

"Rest now," Danny muttered, wishing the girl could understand him. Because he wanted to reassure her, he added, "We'll hold off the evil spirits until you're strong enough to fight them yourself."

Jessie watched her brother flip through the pages of the book until he came to the information he was seeking. Head bent, he digested the knowledge. But when the Comanche girl moaned, all Danny's attention became focused on her. With gentle touch and soothing words, he sought to calm her fears.

They had lingered two days here in the high country. So far the girl had endured fever and chills and a persistent infection that would not give up its hold on her. Though they all took turns sitting with her, Danny was never far from her side. Day or night, at the slightest sigh or moan, he was beside her, whispering words of comfort, administering what little he had to fight her pain.

He had used an entire bottle of Cole's whiskey and had made poultices of herbs and cactus. He had washed the wound with Jessie's lye soap, and slowly the pain and swelling had subsided. Though the girl still cried out in her sleep, the worst was behind them. There was no doubt she would live. But the ordeal had left her too weak to travel.

Danny knew how eager the others were to be back on the trail. When he wasn't worried about the Indian girl, his mind was troubled by thoughts of his pa, alone and hurt somewhere in this vast wilderness. But his first duty was to his patient. Until she could safely travel, Danny had no intention of leaving her here alone.

''Good morning.'' As always, he greeted her softly before tending to her wounds.

And as always her dark eyes watched his every move. Although she refused to speak a single word, she stilled whenever he touched her. There were times he thought she could read his mind.

Danny knelt beside the girl and gently removed the dressings. After examining the wound, he bathed it with lye soap and heard her quick intake of breath at the stinging pain.

''Sorry.'' He gave her what he hoped was a reassuring smile. ''I know this hurts, but it's important to keep this wound clean. Clean,'' he repeated, showing her the glob of yellow soap.

She gave no indication that she understood. Her dark gaze was wary, watchful.

Danny probed the wound and was relieved to find the swelling down considerably. ''Good.''

At his single word, her gaze lifted to his eyes. So unlike any eyes she had ever seen. The color of waving prairie grass in spring. The color of water that lay in rock pools in the high country.

The hands that moved across her flesh were as gentle as the touch of the medicine man whose healing powers were legend among her people. This white man, though barely old enough to be a warrior, was a healer of ills.

As Danny applied fresh dressings to her wound, his fingertips tingled when they came in contact with her skin. He swallowed convulsively, and his Adam's apple bobbed in his throat, nearly choking him.

What was the matter with him? He'd tended every member of his family at one time or another. But never had he felt as awkward and clumsy as he did with this girl.

He tied the last dressing and gave her an encouraging smile.

"You're doing just fine. By tomorrow, you'll probably be strong enough to travel."

She studied him in silence.

"Cole," Danny called. "Explain to her that she will be free to travel with us tomorrow, or head out on her own."

When Cole repeated Danny's words in her own tongue, the girl kept her gaze firmly on Danny's face. She gave no response to the words.

"Does she understand?"

Cole shrugged. "Maybe. Maybe not. The Comanches think it is beneath them to converse with a white."

Danny thought he saw the beginnings of a smile tug at the corner of her lips. But before he could be certain, she regally turned her head away and closed her eyes.

He stood for a minute watching her, then strode away. He ought to be relieved that his patient was healing and would be able to take care of herself. But the truth was, now that the danger had passed, he enjoyed caring for this Indian girl. There was something special about her, something noble. And though she firmly rejected all offers of friendship, he sensed that she trusted him.

These days of enforced inactivity had given Danny time to read his precious medical book. Now he began to keep a journal of the wounds he'd treated. If anything happened to him along the way, he reasoned, it would be good for Jessie and Thad to know how to treat any injuries sustained.

Danny awoke and lay quietly, listening to the deathly silence that lay between darkness and dawn. It was as if the whole world lay hushed, waiting for morning.

It had been his turn to keep watch, and he had fallen asleep. But even though Cole still refused to trust the Comanche in their camp, Danny was convinced that she would not harm them while they slept.

A soft skittering sound broke the stillness, and he tensed before turning toward the movement. The Comanche girl walked slowly from the direction of the creek. Danny was startled by the sight of her ethereal beauty.

While she had been recovering from her wounds, Jessie had washed the girl's clothing and had insisted upon dressing her in one of her clean shirts.

Now the girl wore her native dress, fawn-colored buckskin that molded her young figure and fell in soft folds to just above her ankles.

Danny watched as the girl bent and placed the freshly washed shirt beside his sister's bedroll. Jessie didn't stir.

Next the girl walked to her own bedroll and sat cross-legged, combing her fingers through the damp strands of her hair.

Danny caught his breath at the sight of the raven tresses that fell below her waist. The girl parted the hair neatly and began braiding it. Danny lay quietly, drinking in the sight of the girl in her first spontaneous, relaxed pose. Though she was small and slender, she had the soft, rounded contours of a woman. His heart tripped over itself as he thought of the times his hands had nearly touched the gentle swell of her breast when he changed her dressings.

Without thinking, he sat up in order to better see her.

At his movement she looked across the glowing embers of the camp fire and met his gaze. For the space of a heartbeat, he watched as she studied him without emotion. Then she tossed her head, sending the silken strands dancing like a dark veil about her shoulders. With quick, practiced movements she finished braiding her hair, then stood and walked toward him.

Kneeling before him, she took his hands in hers. He was so stunned he could only stare silently at her.

In perfect English she said, "My life is now yours. If you wish me to be your slave, it shall be as you command."

"Slave?" Danny was astounded not only by her command of his language but by the words she spoke.

Collecting his thoughts, he stammered, "Why didn't you tell us you could understand what we were saying?"

"It is as your chief said. It is not the way of the Comanche to speak to a white man in his language."

Chief. So she recognized Cole as their leader. "Then why are you speaking to me now?"

"You saved my life. You held away the evil spirits." She lifted his hand to her heart, and his blood raced at the contact with her breasts. "My life is now yours."

"That isn't the way of my people," Danny said when he could find his voice. "I doctored you so you could be strong enough to return to your home."

Her eyes widened as if she could not believe what he was saying. "You do not wish to keep Morning Light as your woman?"

"Morning Light." Danny spoke her name as reverently as a prayer.

"I have seen in your eyes that you do not find me repulsive."

"Repulsive?" Danny nearly choked on the word. "I think you're the prettiest girl I've ever seen."

"Then Morning Light will be your woman."

Danny gently shook his head. "I have things I have to do before I—take a woman. And you have to return to your people. They'll be worried about you."

"You do not ask how I come to be out here alone and bleeding."

"Will you tell me?"

She nodded her head and said softly, "I was taken by two white men to a cabin." She pointed to a tall distant ridge of craggy cliffs barely visible in the distance. "When I tried to run they shot me, then left me for dead."

"How long have you been away from your people?"

"The new moon has appeared for a second time," she said softly.

"Over a month."

"I knew my brother and his warriors would find me if I could stay alive long enough. But when I saw your horses, I hoped to steal one and tie myself to the pony until I was found by my people.''

Danny thought of the tremendous courage it would take to chance such a thing in her condition.

"How long did you track us?''

She held up three fingers.

"Three days? How could you keep up?''

"I did not sleep when you did. I took rest only when it was impossible to go on.''

"Will you stay with us, or must you leave now to find your people?''

She released his hands and touched a finger to his cheek. Danny sucked in his breath and tentatively touched a hand to her face. She did not flinch or back away.

"I must leave you,'' she said softly. "If you do not want me as your woman, I must go to my people.''

"How will you find them?''

She gave him a secret, knowing smile. "I will follow the arc of the sun and they will find me.''

Danny pulled the hunting knife from his waist and held it out to her. "You'll need this.''

"How do you know I will not use it on you?'' She gave him that mysterious smile.

"I guess I'll just have to trust you.''

"Trust? Between a white man and a Comanche?'' Her smile grew.

"It's possible, isn't it?''

Her dark eyes settled on his cool green ones for long seconds. Lifting the amulet from around her neck, she gently placed it around Danny's neck. Then she startled him by touching her cheek to his. Before he could react, she jumped up and backed away from him.

"Safe journey, Da-nee,'' she said before turning away.

Danny stood and watched as she bolted through the slowly lifting shadows of dawn. Within minutes she was out of sight.

Da-nee. The sound of his name on her lips did strange things to his insides.

He turned and noticed for the first time that Cole was awake and watching him.

"Morning Light is gone."

"So I see." Cole had seen—and heard—a great deal more than he'd intended.

"I gave her my knife," Danny said simply.

Cole stood and began rolling up his blankets. If Danny was expecting an argument from Cole, he was even more surprised by his casual response. Over his shoulder he said, "That's good. She'll probably be needing it."

"You're not mad? You don't mind that I just let her go?"

"Why should I mind?"

"You didn't want me to help her in the first place." Danny waited before he said with sudden knowledge. "You knew, didn't you? You knew that if I saved a Comanche's life, she'd offer to be my slave."

Cole shrugged. "I figured you'd have to make your own decision about that."

"I told her no," Danny said softly.

"I noticed." Chuckling, Cole dropped an arm about the young boy's shoulders and said, "Let's grab a bath in the creek before your sister wakes up."

As they walked away from camp, Danny asked, "What would you have done, Cole, if a Comanche offered to be your slave?"

Cole thought about the tender scene he'd just witnessed between Morning Light and the boy who was almost a man. And then he thought about the damnably obstinate little woman who was driving him mad with desire. And about the foolish promise he'd made to her brother. A promise that would likely prove to be the most painful one he'd ever keep.

"I'd have probably done the same thing you just did, son." He chuckled, and the warmth of his laughter lifted the last burden from Danny's young shoulders. "Sometimes the only thing a man can do is walk away from that much treasure, before he finds himself getting too greedy."

As Danny dropped his clothes onto the sand, his fingers

touched the Comanche amulet around his neck. He walked toward the water with his hand closed around the disk. It was still warm from the touch of Morning Light's skin. With a light heart he stepped into the icy water.

He was glad now that he'd insisted on helping her. Because of him, she had at least a fighting chance to return to her people. And because of her, he had found a wealth of emotions that he had never before experienced.

Chapter Twelve

On the trail once more, they made good time. Cole and Jessie had used the time of Morning Light's recovery to hunt, and their game bags were swollen with meat. Thad had used the time to pamper their mounts. Sleek and rested, the horses took to the trail with renewed strength.

Jessie noticed that Danny seemed at times to draw into himself. Though he had always been the quiet, thoughtful one, she noticed something new in his silence. From time to time she saw him watching her as she rode beside Cole. Her brother wore a watchful, knowing expression that puzzled her.

Danny found himself looking at Cole Matthews through new eyes. Was it possible that this hardened gunman felt the same sort of tenderness for Jessie that he felt toward Morning Light? Did all men feel this gentleness, this need to protect? Or was he experiencing something so special, so wonderful, that no one in the world could feel quite the same way?

It didn't seem possible that a tough man like Cole Matthews could feel anything this fine about Jessie. After all, Danny had seen the way Cole had boldly taken her into his arms and kissed her with a kind of savage hunger. Such actions didn't speak of tenderness. Still, underneath the tender feelings that had curled in the pit of Danny's stomach, there had been a primitive yearning to pull the Comanche maiden close and press his lips to hers. Maybe if he was as old and experienced as Cole, he would have found the courage to do just that.

In the evening as they sat around the camp fire, sipping the last of the coffee, Danny began to notice the way Cole's gaze followed Jessie's every move. When she bent to stoke the fire or to clear away their evening meal, Cole's opaque eyes narrowed in concentration.

Danny thought about the promise he'd exacted from Cole after their fight. Something told him that despite the fact that Cole was a gunman on the run, he was also a man who would keep his promise. No matter what it cost him.

"You're awfully quiet, Danny." Jessie looked up from the blanket she was mending.

"Just thinking."

"About anything special?"

He frowned. "Naw." He stood. "Think I'll check the horses."

"I just checked them before supper," Thad chirped.

"I'll check them again."

As he strolled away, Jessie watched him with a puzzled look. "What's wrong with Danny lately?"

"Leave him be," Cole growled. "He's just growing up."

"How about me?" Thad climbed into his blankets. "Don't you think I'm growing up, too?"

"You sure are, Half-pint. I'll bet you've grown at least an inch since I first saw you."

The little boy's face was wreathed with smiles as he settled in for the night.

Jessie kissed her little brother and heard his prayers for their safety and that of their pa.

Though he pretended to be busy with a frayed stirrup, Cole found himself grinning at the little boy's fervent words.

When Thad was carefully tucked in for the night, Jessie returned to her mending. "That doesn't answer my question, Cole. Do you know why Danny has become so moody?"

"He'll be fine. He just has a lot on his mind."

From his tone, Jessie knew that Cole had no intention of

discussing her brother any further. With a little snort of disgust, she bit the end of the thread and tucked her precious spool and needle into her saddlebag. Then she crawled between the blankets beside Thad. She was too tired and saddle weary to give another thought to Danny's growing pains.

The tall grasses of the Texas Plains came up nearly to the horses' bellies. As far as the eye could see, the land undulated with waves of green, brown, russet. For the past two days the furnacelike air of early autumn had been heavy, almost suffocating.

As they topped a ridge of prairie grass, Jessie noticed a strange odor. She reined in her mount and searched for a sign of Cole. He had ridden ahead to scout the trail. Her horse, normally surefooted and obedient, suddenly threw his head, nearly tossing her from the saddle. It took all her skill to bring the skittish animal under control. For long minutes she soothed him, stroking his neck, speaking softly, until he stopped fighting her. But even when the horse had stilled, his nostrils flared and his head tossed as he trembled beneath her hands.

Standing in the stirrups, Jessie saw Cole far ahead, moving toward them at a fast clip. She relaxed then, knowing that if there was any trouble, Cole would be the first to spot it. If the trouble were immediate, they had a prearranged signal. Cole would fire a single shot that was meant to send them racing in the opposite direction.

She wiped a sleeve across her brow and replaced the hat that was already damp with sweat. Would there be no relief from the oppressive heat? Glancing skyward, she was surprised to note a dark cloud approaching from the north. Even while she watched, the cloud turned inky black, its outer edges taking on a greenish cast. In front of it rolled what appeared to be a blue mist of smoke.

She heard Cole's shouts. "Take cover. Quick. Find some rocks."

Without waiting to ask questions, Jessie turned her mount

and raced back to where Danny and Thad were slowly following her trail.

"Quickly," she shouted, turning her horse from the trail
toward an outcropping of rocks. "There's some sort of trouble.
This way."

The two boys spurred their mounts to follow. By the time
they dismounted, Jessie had discovered a small low cave
carved in the rocks. With luck, there might be just enough
room to allow the horses to enter.

A minute later Cole reined in his horse. "We have no time
to waste," he shouted, sliding from the saddle. "Find as many
logs and tree branches as you can. Haul them into the shelter
of these rocks."

"What is it?" Jessie asked. "What's happening?"

"Blue norther," he called over his shoulder before scurrying among the boulders.

Jessie froze in her tracks. All her life she had heard stories
about the terrible storms the Texans called the blue norther.
With no warning, frigid arctic winds would blow across the
plains, freezing everything in their path. Men and cattle froze
to death before the winds blew themselves out, leaving a path
of death and destruction for hundreds of miles across the
Texas Plains.

While Thad led their horses inside the small cave Jessie,
Danny and Cole hurried among the rocks, searching for every
piece of firewood they could find.

Within minutes the sky was as black as night. By the time
the first icy winds struck, Cole ordered Danny into the cave.

"Where's Jessie?" Cole stared around the gloom of the
cave.

Danny dumped a load of firewood on the floor of the cave
and brushed his hands on the seat of his pants. "Still getting
wood, I guess."

Cole bit back the torrent of oaths that sprang to his lips. "I
thought she was in here with Thad. Don't either of you leave
this place," he bellowed. "No matter what!" Before they
could protest, he was gone.

The sky was so dark Cole could barely make out the shape of the trees that swayed in the wind.

"Jessie!" Cupping his hands to his mouth, Cole shouted into the wind and swore violently when he realized that his words were being whipped away as soon as they were out of his mouth. Taking his pistol from its holster, he fired and stood very still, listening to the report echo and reecho across the hills.

The wind picked up, bending the trees nearly to the ground. Just when he began to despair of ever finding her, he heard the sound of a gunshot. He turned and began running in the direction of the sound.

"Jessie!" Again and again he called her name, then stopped in his tracks. Had he heard something? He called again and fired his pistol a second time.

Closer now, he heard another gunshot. With his heart pounding in his chest, he stepped to the edge of a ravine and peered through the blackness.

"Jessie, are you down there?"

"Yes. Oh, Cole. Thank God, you're here. I slipped and fell."

As he strained through the darkness, he could see that she was lying on a narrow rock ledge.

"Are you hurt?" His heart actually stopped beating until he heard her feeble response.

"No. I just had the wind knocked out of me. But there's no way to get back up."

"Don't move. Stay right there. I'll think of something." He had no idea what he would do. In the darkness he stumbled around, fighting the wind and the terrible cold that seemed to engulf him like a tomb of ice.

He nearly stumbled over the tree limb, then bent and tested its strength. Lowering it, he shouted, "Are you able to stand?"

The wait for her reply seemed like an eternity. But at last Jessie's voice could be heard above the thundering wind. "I think I can. It's pretty narrow down here, but I think there's room to stand."

"Can you hold on to this branch?"

At last he felt a tug on the limb and knew that Jessie had found it in the darkness. "Yes. I have it."

"Don't try to climb it. Just hold on and I'll pull you up."

With all his might, Cole strained against the weight of the tree limb and the slender girl who clung to it. Though the wind tore at him and the cold bit into him, he ignored his protesting muscles and never stopped until he saw Jessie's head inch above the ravine. With renewed vigor he pulled her to safety. Setting down the heavy burden, he ran to her and pulled her to her feet.

"Are you all right? Have you broken any bones?"

How dare she scare the hell out of him like that? He wanted to shake her until her teeth rattled. He wanted to strangle her by her pretty little throat.

He wanted to hold her.

He pulled her roughly into his arms and held her in a fierce embrace.

For long minutes Jessie's head swam, and she clung to him as though her very life depended on it. "If it weren't for you..." She couldn't go on. Her voice died in her throat.

"Are you really all right?" His tone was tender as his hands moved along her back. He had a desperate need to reassure himself that she was truly safe.

"I'm fine." She tried to laugh, but it came out as a sob.

"Fine?" All the emotions he'd kept bottled up inside exploded. "Do you realize you could have been killed? Why in hell did you wander so far from the cave? You knew what was blowing up out here. Didn't you hear me tell everyone to get in out of the storm? How many times am I supposed to save your hide before you learn some common sense?"

He hadn't meant to shout and swear. But in his fear and frustration, the words tumbled out. When he was finished with his tirade, Jessie stared at him with a look of pain and outrage, then pushed stiffly from his arms.

"How dare you scream such words at me." As he reached

for her, she slapped at his hand and twisted free. "Keep your hands off me, Cole Matthews. I can take care of myself."

His words were clipped. "So I've noticed. Just don't fall off any more cliffs before you reach the cave, or I swear I'll leave you to freeze to death until this storm blows over."

She strode away. He followed, watching as she struggled against the winds that threatened to blow both of them away. By the time they reached the safety of the cave, they were numb with cold.

Inside a hollowed-out log Cole started a small flickering flame. Forcing the horses to their knees, he hobbled them so they couldn't stand and run.

"Why are you being so mean to the horses, Cole?" Thad cried.

"Their only chance against the storm is to remain around the fire. If they were to spook and run, they would freeze in their tracks before we could find them." He shot a meaningful glance at Jessie, who stood brooding beside the fire. "Sometimes it's necessary to be cruel in order to save lives."

She turned away, refusing to meet his eyes.

Searching the saddlebags, he handed out all the food and clothing available. "Put everything on that you can wear."

"Everything?" Danny stared at him as if he were mad.

"You've never felt cold like this," Cole said simply. "Stash the meat under your bodies."

"Meat under us? Are you serious?"

Again Cole shot Jessie an angry look before explaining, "Everything in this cave might freeze if the fire goes out. Unless you can keep the food from freezing, you could starve to death before the storm blows over. Now," he added, "press the saddles and saddlebags around you, to ward off the wind. Huddle close together for body heat." He glanced at Jessie's face and wished now that there had been time to apologize for his angry outburst, to offer her a measure of comfort. "Remember," he said with a low growl of command, "the only time you leave your blankets is to keep the fire going. And then, only if I can no longer do it for you."

Jessie's earlier anger suddenly disappeared. She felt her heart contract. Was he suggesting that some of them wouldn't survive? That he might die before them?

"Cole." Thad's tiny frightened voice could barely be heard above the fury of the wind.

"Yes."

"I'm afraid."

Jessie watched as Cole clenched his teeth against the bite of the wind. He helped them into the common bedroll and climbed in beside them. With unusual tenderness he drew the little boy against his chest. "So am I, Half-pint. So am I."

The storm hit with a fury that was staggering. The winds howled and raged, uprooting trees, sending boulders crashing down upon one another with the force of a freight train.

Inside the cave, huddled together, the four slept fitfully, then awoke to find their little space freezing. Cole would stoke the fire, and in time they would drift once more into sleep. It was impossible to tell day from night, but from the hours they lay shuddering in their bedrolls, Jessie thought that at least two days and nights had passed.

When hunger gnawed at them, they broke off hunks of raw meat and stale biscuits and chewed until their hunger was abated. Jessie was grateful that Cole had had enough sense to think of the essentials before the storm had broken upon them in earnest.

The sky was so black, the only thing visible was the small flicker of flame as Cole continued to feed wood to the fire that was contained inside the hollowed-out log. So many times, as the wind raged against their small cave, they watched the tiny flame flicker and almost die. Their hearts would constrict in fear. Without the warmth of the fire, they would surely freeze to death. But each time the howling wind subsided, gathering force for the next assault, they would see the tiny flame leap back to life to fan and grow into precious warmth.

Cole added more wood to the fire and felt his fingers go stiff from the brief exposure to the frigid air. He had never felt such cold. It went deep into the bones, leaving a body numb.

As he climbed gratefully into the blankets, his hand encountered the softness of Jessie's body. She had shifted Thad to the inside section of the blanket, where his small body could absorb the most warmth. On the far side of Thad lay Danny, his back to the fire, his arms snugly around his little brother.

"You all right, Jessie?" Cole's voice was barely a whisper.

She nodded and felt the sudden chill as his hand touched her shoulder. She took his hands in hers to share the warmth. "You're freezing."

At her touch he felt as if he'd just taken a blow to the midsection. "Damn close to it. That's a wicked wind out there."

She marveled at the strength in his hands. Such big powerful hands. "How long can one of these storms last?"

She felt him shrug beside her. It felt so good to be touching her he had to resist an almost overpowering urge to wrap his arms around her and draw her close against him. He could think of a wonderful way to stay warm. "A couple of days. A week, maybe."

"How are the horses?"

He didn't want to talk about horses. Or about anything. He just wanted to lie here with her and kiss her until she was weak and clinging to him. "Surviving. I gave them enough prairie grass to keep them from starving. But there's nothing else I can do until the storm blows over." He drew closer to her, and she felt a shudder pass through him. Sweet Heaven. He was going mad with wanting her. "We're lucky the horses had time to rest and grow fat while Morning Light was recovering. Without that extra fat, they wouldn't make it."

The winds pounded the cave until the very rocks beneath them shuddered and shifted. Jessie's voice was low with fear. "Have you ever been in one of these before?"

She felt the movement as he nodded his head. "I was a boy no bigger than Thad," he said, remembering. Without realizing it, he touched his hand to her cheek. "My father had dug a small root cellar beneath one end of our sod shack. When the wind blew our house over, we crawled down into the root cellar and huddled together for five days. We existed on a few raw carrots and some seed potatoes.''

Jessie felt warmth spread through her and couldn't decide if it was merely his touch, or the warm feelings his words had caused. She was surprised to think of Cole being part of a family. Until now, she had merely thought of him as a gunman. A picture of a young boy with father and mother and maybe brothers and sisters was a sharp contrast to the man who lay beside her.

"Did everyone survive?" She shivered as his warm breath fanned a strand of hair at her temple.

"My father said it would take more than a Texas norther to destroy the Matthews family."

"Your pa sounds like a proud man."

"He was."

Was. Jessie heard the pain in that single word and felt a comradeship with Cole that she hadn't felt before. He would understand her desperate need to find her pa. He would sense the agony of not knowing whether Pa was alive or... Some day, when this storm was over, and they had all survived, she would ask him how his pa died. But now with the wind keening through the rocks and raging against their tiny cave, she closed her eyes and held on to the knowledge that they were together in this. Cole had survived a norther before; he would survive this one, as well. They would all survive. And when it was over, they would find Pa. With his hand soft upon her cheek, she slept.

Jessie awoke to the eerie sounds of silence. For long minutes she lay unmoving, waiting for the familiar sound of the wind outside their cave. When at last it dawned on her that the storm was over, she reached over to share the good news with Cole. With a sting of disappointment, she discovered that his blanket was empty. The covers were warm where they still bore the imprint of his body.

She climbed from her blankets and strode to the entrance of the cave, which was covered by a saddle blanket to keep out the cold.

Behind her, Thad and Danny sat up rubbing their eyes.

"Where's Cole?" Danny asked.

Jessie shrugged. "Outside, I guess."

The horses, she noted, were gone, but there were fresh droppings on the floor of the cave. They had only been gone for a short time.

With Thad and Danny trailing her, she emerged from the cave to a spectacular sight. The vast Texas Plains were now a frozen wasteland. Sunlight glinted off ice-encrusted trees and rocks. Waves of grass were frozen in motion, glittering under a layer of ice.

"Hellfire and damnation," Danny said, then, at Jessie's stern look, instantly regretted his imitation of Cole. "Did you ever see anything like that, Jess?"

"Never." She peered around, then took several tentative steps onto the icy trail.

"The sunlight hurts my eyes, Jessie."

She turned toward her little brother. "I know, Tadpole. But isn't it beautiful?"

The little boy shielded his eyes and stared around with a look of awe. Never, Jessie thought, would Thad forget the blue norther that had struck with so much fury. "When you're an old man, Tadpole, you'll be telling your grandchildren about this."

"I will?"

She nodded. "And bragging about how wise you were. And how brave."

The three of them shared a laugh and turned to watch as Cole led the horses up the steep embankment. For one long moment his gaze held Jessie's, and she wondered if he was remembering the way she had fallen asleep practically in his arms.

"Looks like the animals will have to wait until the ice melts to fill their bellies,'' he said. ''All the grass is frozen under a layer of ice too thick to break.''

''How will we travel?''

''That sun ought to melt everything by late afternoon. But I think we'd better stay here in the cave until morning. It'll give us a chance to feed the horses. Not to mention ourselves.'' He grinned, and Jessie thought how wonderful his eyes looked when he smiled. ''I'm a little tired of raw meat. I think I'd like to try it cooked for a change.''

Jessie nodded, feeling a lightness around her heart. ''If you get a good fire going, I'll make us a real supper for a change.''

''That's fair.'' Cole handed the reins of the horses to Danny and Thad. ''What do you boys think of our ice castle?''

They turned to study the cave. At its highest point several rocks were welded together like turrets beneath a glittering dome of ice. On either side of the cave were giant boulders glinting with an icy sheen. In the blinding sunlight, the entire structure seemed to be carved from ice.

''It doesn't seem real,'' Jessie breathed. ''But none of this seems real. I still can't believe we've survived a norther.''

Cole's tone was grim. ''I've heard cattlemen say it's the worst storm ever invented by nature.''

''And we survived it,'' Thad said proudly.

''That's right, Half-pint.'' Cole tousled the boy's hair and grinned. ''And that's practically a miracle.''

''What's a miracle?''

Danny shot his sister a grin. ''Remember the Bible verse Jessie always reads?''

''You mean about walking on the water?''

Danny nodded. ''Yeah. Cole means that surviving the norther was like walking on the water.''

''Do you, Cole?'' The little boy turned an innocent face to the gunman.

Cole touched a hand to the boy's shoulder and squeezed. ''I guess I do.'' He found himself uneasy without knowing why. ''Now get busy with those horses.''

When they walked away, Cole turned to study the girl who

was heading toward the cave. "Back off," he warned himself. First she had him feeling guilty every time he swore in front of her or her brothers. Now he'd discovered that she read to her brothers from the Bible. She wasn't the kind of girl a man could have and then walk away from. She was the kind of girl a man could easily begin to think about spending a lifetime with. A girl like Jessie could never be anything but trouble to a man like him.

Chapter Thirteen

The day took on a festive air. All the pent-up fears and emotions the four had experienced during the storm suddenly found release.

The sun rose hot and hazy. By midday most of the ice had melted, leaving clumps of frozen, blackened grass. To the starving horses, it was a feast.

Danny and Thad engaged in an ice battle, tossing clumps of slush at each other until they were soaked and weary from their play. Afterward Jessie insisted that they wash their soggy clothes and lay them on low-hanging bushes to dry. While their clothes dried, they splashed in the swollen creek like two frolicking pups.

When the cave had been cleaned and their bedrolls spread out for airing on nearby rocks, Jessie sat on shore, enjoying her brothers' antics. The thing she and her brothers had always enjoyed most were moments of real playtime. In their harsh environment, such moments had been rare.

Danny swam up behind his little brother. "Better watch out."

Catching him unawares, Danny pushed Thad under the water and laughed when the little boy came up sputtering.

"No fair, Danny. You're bigger'n me."

"Size doesn't matter in the water."

"Is that true?" Thad called to his sister.

"I don't know. But there's one way to find out."

Jessie, unable to resist the challenge, pulled off her boots, then slipped off her shirt and britches. Dressed only in a chemise that barely covered her from breasts to hips, she ran into the creek until the water was up to her shoulders. With sure, even strokes she swam toward her brothers.

"You'll be sorry, Jess. I'm going to get you." Danny swam toward her, meeting her in the deepest part of the creek. When he reached out to grab her, she ducked and came up behind him, catching him by the shoulders. Before he could twist free, she rose up out of the water and pressed with all her might. Though he struggled, she managed to push him beneath the waves. When she let go, he came up sputtering and laughing.

"See, Tadpole," she called to her giggling little brother, "even though he's taller, I was able to sink Danny with no trouble. It isn't who's bigger. It's who's quicker."

"Is that so?"

At the sound of Cole's deep laughter, the three of them turned. He paddled leisurely a few feet away.

"Think you can sink me, Jessie? Or are you only quicker with someone younger than yourself?"

Cole saw the way her eyes lit with an inner fire. He had known that she would be unable to resist his taunt.

"I can sink all three of you." At her brothers' hoots of laughter she added, "Just so I get to take you on one at a time. No fair ganging up on me."

"You'll have to take me on first." Cole's voice was deep with challenge.

"I'll be on your side, Jessie," Thad called.

"All right, Tadpole. Your job is to keep Danny away from me until I've managed to sink Cole."

The two boys began wrestling in the water.

As she turned, she saw Cole standing in waist-deep water. She was stunned by the feelings aroused by the mere sight of him. A mat of dark hair covered his chest and fell in a deep V to below the water at his waist. As he reached deeper water and began to swim toward her, his hands cut through the water with powerful strokes. For a moment she was mesmerized by the sight of his glistening arms and shoulders. Up close his dark hair glittered. His eyes were warm and crinkled with laughter.

"Think you're going to be able to sink me as easily as you did Danny?"

"You'll be even easier." Though she knew better, she enjoyed taunting him.

When he moved within reach, she knew she would have to make good her threat. How could she get the better of a strong man like Cole?

"Better close your mouth, Jessie," he teased. "You're about to swallow half the creek."

When he reached out for her, she surprised him by ducking beneath the water. Before he could react, she caught him by the ankle and tugged with all her might. Danny and Thad howled with laughter when Cole disappeared beneath the waves. A moment later he came up sputtering.

"Very clever." As Jessie tried to swim away, he caught her roughly by the arm and lifted her out of the water, then tossed her like a sack of grain.

She landed with a giant splash, much to the amusement of her brothers. As she sank beneath the water, she caught sight of Cole's legs just a few feet away. Catching him around the waist, she dragged him down until his head was beneath the water, then released him and swam hard and fast toward shore.

She wasn't nearly quick enough. With powerful strokes he caught her and pressed her head under the waves.

Cole surfaced. Tossing water from his head, he swiveled around searching for Jessie. She would have to surface, and when she did, he would be waiting for one more chance at revenge. For long moments he waited. When she didn't break water, he became concerned.

"Where's Jess?" Danny shouted.

Cole's heart stopped beating. He forgot to breathe. Dear God. Jessie. He dove deeply and peered through the water for some sign of her. When he broke the surface, he felt a hand at his shoulder. Before he could turn, he felt a terrible pressure as Jessie shoved with all her might, forcing his head beneath the water once more.

This time when he surfaced he wasn't laughing. "What the hell do you think you're doing?"

"Sinking you," she said innocently.

"You scared the hell out of me, woman. I thought you'd drowned." His hand snaked out, catching her roughly by the arm. For a moment he was too moved to speak. Her antics had shaken him to the core.

"You're just mad because I won."

Cole took a long deep breath and cautioned himself not to show the emotions that were causing such turmoil inside him. He gave an evil grin and pulled her closer. "You always have to win, don't you, Jessie?"

"Yes."

He drew her even closer until their bodies were touching.

Dear heaven, he wasn't wearing anything. She jumped like a scared jackrabbit. As she tried to push away, his legs wrapped around hers, pinning her against the length of him.

"Now what are you going to do, Jessie?"

She saw the teasing laughter in his eyes and knew that he could see the betraying blush that colored her throat and cheeks.

"Let me go, Cole."

"And miss the chance to see you get out of this by your own wits?" The warmth of his laughter washed over her. "Not on your life."

"Duck her," Danny cried.

"Go ahead, Cole," Thad shouted. "Duck Jessie."

"Hey, Tadpole. Aren't you supposed to be on my side?"

"Oh, yeah. I forgot." The little boy was laughing so hard he forgot to be sorry for changing his alliance from his sister to Cole. "Come on, Cole. Duck Jessie again."

"Looks like the vote is three against one," he said, pressing his hands on her head and ducking her beneath the water. This time, though, he refused to let go of her. She wasn't going to

frighten him again. When he pulled her above the water, he
drew her even closer until his arms were firmly around her.

"Had enough?"

She would never have enough of Cole's arms around her.
Even while she laughed and nodded her head, she felt a delicious tingle somewhere deep inside her. As his legs wound
around hers, and his hands held her firmly against the length
of him, she shivered.

"Cold?"

"No. Are you?"

He glanced over to where her two brothers frolicked. Lowering his voice so they couldn't hear, he murmured against her
temple. "Woman, I'm so hot right now, it's a good thing I'm
in this creek."

She laughed and tried to push away, but he held her fast.

"Don't fight it, Jessie. Just let me hold you for a minute
longer."

The laughter died in her throat. The gentle motion of the
water soothed even as it excited. Held firmly against his chest,
Jessie tilted her head to study the spill of dark hair glittering
with droplets of water. As he lowered his face to her, she
studied the way his eyes gleamed in the sunlight reflected off
the water.

He thought of the shock that had gone through him at the
sight of her removing her clothes. In that one brief moment
when she paused on the shore, wearing only a sheer garment
that displayed more than it covered, he had felt as if all the
breath had been knocked from him. He had watched her walk
through the water, had watched as the filmy garment became
wet and clingy, and had felt a tightness in his throat.

Now her hair floated gently around her, forming a halo of
glistening gold. Her skin was so soft, so cool to the touch.
Just below the water he could see the swell of her breasts. The
thought of taking a wet slick nipple into his mouth brought
on a wave of desperate desire. His legs tangled with hers,
drawing her lower torso tightly to him. Having her this close
and not being able to take her was the sweetest torment he'd

ever experienced. Hell. This little woman was driving him mad.

"You're frowning." She touched a finger to the little line that furrowed his forehead.

"It's you."

"I make you frown?"

His voice was rough. "You make me crazy."

"Ah." The way she said that single word told him that despite her innocence, she knew instinctively the ways of a woman and man and sensed just how aroused he had become.

The thought pleased yet frightened her. She wasn't at all certain how to act. Should she let Cole know how much she enjoyed being held in his strong arms? Or would he think she was a wicked woman? She bit her lip, wishing she knew more about men and women. It would be so pleasant to just relax in his arms, to know how to please him, how to tease him.

Cole studied the way she looked, so fresh, so clean, so innocent. When she bit her lip he felt a rush of desire, and had to use all his willpower to keep from lowering his mouth to hers.

Confused, Jessie placed both hands against his chest and pushed. "I think I'd better get out of the creek now."

"Why?" He continued to hold her despite her efforts.

"If we're going to have supper, I'd better start a fire."

"You've already started a fire." When she glanced up into his eyes with a look of surprise, he added fiercely, "In me. And I don't know what it will take to put it out."

The imp inside the young woman took over. "Water," she laughed, splashing him. "Water will put out the fire every time."

Before he could stop her, she brought her hand flat against the water, sending a spray into his face. He blinked and grabbed for her. She backed away and splashed him again, then turned and began swimming as fast as she could.

By the time she reached the shore, Cole was right behind her.

In a taunting voice she called, "You can't follow me out of the water."

"Why can't I?"

"Because you aren't wearing anything."

"And why should that stop me?"

Jessie shot him a horrified look and tried to scramble up the bank of the creek. Seeing another battle of wills, Danny and Thad laughed and cheered.

"It's time you learned you can't always win," Cole said, grabbing her by the ankle just as she was about to sprint away. She landed in the grass before being lifted in his strong arms. With absolutely no concern for his nakedness, he walked to the very edge of the creek. "This time, woman, I win."

Cole tossed her high in the air and watched as she landed in the middle of the creek with a tremendous splash. Moments later she came up laughing and sputtering. Wiping water from her eyes, she shook her head, sending a spray of water dancing in the air before her hair settled to float around her on the waves.

Cole dried himself and slipped into his buckskin pants. From his vantage point on shore, he thought she was the most beautiful creature he'd ever seen. He stood very still, savoring the sight of Jessie swimming toward him. When she stood at the edge of the creek, he watched the way the wet fabric clung to her like a second skin clearly following every line and curve of her slender body. As he reached out a hand to help her up the grassy bank, he felt the heat grow once more.

Her teasing laughter broke the spell. "You win this time. But don't get used to it. I'll see that it doesn't happen again." Before he could respond, she added with a smile, "Now I'll make supper. You boys have yourselves a good time."

Before he could see what she was up to, she tugged on his hand and watched as he stumbled forward into the creek. She calmly walked away while behind her he unleashed a string of oaths.

Supper was a glorious affair. Jessie had cooked venison until it was so tender it nearly fell apart. From her meager supply of flour she made biscuits so flaky they melted on the tongue. The aroma of strong coffee drifted on the fresh evening breeze.

The four sat around the camp fire, refreshed, replete.

"I think you outdid yourself, Jessie." Cole lounged against a saddle, his gaze lifted to the star-filled sky. "That was just about the best meal I've ever tasted."

"I think so, too." Danny polished off the last biscuit and washed it down with clear cold water from the creek.

Jessie basked in the glow of their compliments. It was the first time she could ever remember Danny saying anything good about her cooking. Her skills had always been compared unfavorably with her ma's. As for Cole, she found it rare praise indeed. Usually he preferred to tease her.

"More coffee?" She lifted the blackened pot from the fire and filled Cole's cup.

He gave her a warm smile before once more raising his head to scan the heavens.

"Did you have brothers or sisters, Cole?" Thad asked.

Jessie turned to glance at the little boy and noticed that Thad was resting his back against a saddle. Was Cole aware that Thad was imitating him? Did he have any idea how much he was influencing her two brothers? First she had caught Danny practically swearing; now Thad was adopting Cole's mannerisms.

"I had a younger sister and brother."

"Do they live with you?" Danny asked.

Though Jessie pretended to be busy washing their tin plates in a bucket of hot water, she glanced up at the soft tone of Cole's voice.

"They both died of cholera, along with my mother."

She was surprised at the feelings that washed over her at his words.

"What's cholera?" Thad sipped lukewarm coffee from a tin cup in the same way Cole did.

"I read about it. It's a bad sickness," Danny said. "It kills a lot of people."

"Did you get it, too?" Thad asked.

Cole nodded.

"How come you didn't die?"

Cole stared down into his cup, frowning. "I've asked myself that. I don't have the answer. Maybe I was stronger than they were. Maybe I just didn't get as sick as they did." He shrugged and looked away. "Whatever the reason, I was the lucky one." The tone of his voice said that he still hadn't forgiven himself for being the one to live.

"What about your pa?" Thad asked. "Did he get the sickness, too?"

Cole shook his head. "My father was the strongest man I've ever known. He was never sick a day in his life."

"That's how my pa is," Thad said proudly. "Isn't he, Jessie?"

"Yes." She dried her hands and indicated the bedrolls spread out beside the fire. "I think you'd better get some sleep now. We have a lot of miles to make up."

Thad yawned and moved reluctantly toward the blankets. Tomorrow he would have to face long hours in the saddle. But at least he'd had a special day today. With more warmth than usual, he hugged his sister as she tucked him into bed.

Danny and Cole sat talking quietly about cholera and its treatment for nearly an hour before Danny yawned, stretched and climbed wearily into his bedroll.

Jessie knew she should be tired. Swimming in the creek had tested muscles she hadn't even known she had. But she was reluctant to end this special day.

She filled Cole's cup with more coffee and poured the last of it into a cup for herself. For long minutes they drank in companionable silence, enjoying the night sounds.

"It sounds like your family was close-knit."

He nodded. "I grew up hearing stories about my grandfather. He was a legend in my house."

"Why? What did he do?"

"It was how he died that set him apart from other men."

"How did your grandfather die, Cole?"

She watched him drain his cup and set it down, then roll a cigarette. He pulled a flaming stick from the fire and held it to the tip. Inhaling, he blew the smoke out in a stream before speaking.

"He died March 6, 1836."

Jessie went very still. Every man, woman and child in Texas knew the date. It had been imprinted on their minds from the time they could speak and understand. "The Alamo." Her voice was hushed with wonder. "He died trying to save the Alamo."

Cole nodded and drew smoke into his lungs. "My father said there were one hundred thirty-eight men who died at the Alamo. And only seven were native Texans. But that day, they all became Texas heroes. Their deed will live on for as long as there is a Texas."

She heard the note of pride in his voice and felt a lump in her throat. "Your pa must have been very proud of him."

"He was. I never knew my grandfather. But my father saw to it that his memory was kept alive for all of us."

Their sudden easy comradeship gave her the courage to ask the question she'd wondered about earlier. "How did your pa die?"

His tone roughened with emotion. "He was shot in the back by a coward."

"Oh, Cole. How terrible. Did they hang the man who did it?"

He stubbed out the cigarette and got to his feet. Before he turned away, Jessie saw the look that came into Cole's eyes. That hard feral glint she had seen on the first night, when he had been forced to kill the men who had captured her. The eyes of a hunter.

"Hanging's too good for a coward. I want him to answer to me."

Chapter Fourteen

For the next five days their odyssey took the travelers on a northerly course across Texas. The tracks of thousands of cattle were deeply imprinted in the soil. This was the trail of gold for cattlemen—the Chisholm Trail, leading to the stockyards in Abilene and the Kansas Pacific Railroad.

Jessie studied the line of horses ahead of her. Danny rode in front, with Thad following. She felt a surge of pride in her brothers. Though both boys were often weary of the trail, they never complained. And though most nights they fell into their bedrolls as soon as they had eaten an evening meal, they never asked to stop.

Directly ahead of her rode Cole. As her thoughts drifted, she realized how much she had begun to care about the gunman. What would she and her brothers do if Cole was forced to leave them to escape his nameless, faceless enemy? Jessie turned in the saddle to scan the far horizon. Someone could be out there right now watching their every move. She rubbed at the stiffness in her shoulders. Would they ever feel safe? Would they find Pa? Questions. Unending questions. They made her weary. She brushed away such worrisome thoughts.

Throughout the long journey, Cole had said little about himself except to answer specific questions put to him by Danny or Thad. Jessie was careful to ask nothing, sensing his discomfort when the attention centered on him. But from the

things Cole told them, she had a clearer picture of the boyhood
he had lived in this wild primitive land called Texas.

He had grown up in a loving, affectionate family. But the
death of his mother and sister had left him and his father
without the softening influence of a woman. It was obvious
that Cole Matthews was a man accustomed to taking care of
himself. He was a man who lived life by his own rules. When
she complained about his swearing, which to her sensitive ears
had not improved one bit, he would go off in search of game.
Or in search of solitude, she thought, gritting her teeth.

As Cole scanned the countryside, he found his thoughts
drifting to Jessie. Damn her. Even when he should be concentrating on staying alive, she was there distracting him. He had
kept his promise to Danny. He forced himself not to touch her
or even get close to her. It took every ounce of his willpower
to keep his distance. Sometimes in the small hours of the
morning when her brothers were sound asleep, he lay in his
bedroll thinking about what it would be like to lie with her,
to love her. The thought of her long slender fingers touching
him, brushing his naked flesh, made him quiver with desire.
And the thought of her tempting lips on his brought a rush of
heat that even a dip in an icy creek could not dispel.

He wanted her. Sometimes he wanted her so badly his only
defense was to leave without an explanation, without a backward glance. And when he had worked off his frustration by
stalking the barren Texas wilderness in search of game, he
would return to face another day of unending hunger for an
obstinate little woman who could drive him mad without even
trying.

Cole nudged his horse, and Jessie trailed along at a leisurely
pace. She saw the frown that often furrowed his brow and
wondered where he went in his mind when he looked so fierce.
She sighed and wished they could share their thoughts. But
Cole was a loner. And she and her brothers were an unwel-
come burden to a man like him.

They plodded on throughout the long day. Though the sun
was hot, there was enough growth to keep the dust down.

The land was covered with dense thickets of prickly pear, chaparral and low brush, making progress slow. But though the horses were hampered by the underbrush and the boys complained about the slower pace, Cole had reminded them that they would find an abundance of game.

By late afternoon Cole topped a ridge and saw the glimmer of sunlight on water. He turned in the saddle and called to Jessie, "Looks like a creek. That water's clear and the horses are tired. Let's make camp here."

Cole urged his horse into a gallop until he caught up with Danny and Thad, who were far ahead. By the time the three arrived at the sheltered campsite, Jessie had already begun a fire.

She looked up with a little frown as they approached. "We're down to the last of the venison. After supper we'd better do a little tracking."

Cole swung from the saddle and handed the reins to Thad. "If you don't need me, I'll see what game I can scare up right now."

As Cole turned away, Danny reached for his sister's rifle, eager to follow along. "Here, Thad," he said, turning over the reins to his little brother. "We'll be back in time for supper."

Jessie watched as the two strode away. Ever since Danny had managed to bring down a buffalo, it was taken for granted that he would bag his share of game. And with each success, his self-esteem grew. Perhaps she shouldn't be so eager to scold Cole, she warned herself. Some of the things he had taught Danny were worth more than a lifetime of schooling.

Jessie watched as Thad led the horses to the water and patiently waited while they drank their fill. Then he led them back to camp and began the tedious task of unsaddling the animals and rubbing each one down. The horses, lathered from a day of hard riding, were eager to be turned loose in the lush grass growing near the creek.

Jessie made a batch of biscuit dough and set it on a warm rock to rise. When it was ready, she kneaded it, then began cutting it. While she worked, she found herself humming a tune her mother used to hum when Jessie was a little girl.

"I got all my chores done," Thad said proudly.

Jessie barely looked up from her work.

"Think I'll head into that thicket and look for Danny and Cole."

Jessie nodded and said absently, "Don't go too far, Tadpole. Supper will be ready in an hour or so."

As the boy walked away, Jessie found herself struggling to remember the words to the song that played in her mind. How long ago had it been since she'd heard her ma sing that song? Eight years ago? Eight years, and the words were lost to her. With a little frown she started again, trying to hold on to the fleeting image of her beautiful young mother and the songs she had sung to her children.

Cole and Danny spotted the buck at the same moment. Both of them froze, then lifted their rifles to their shoulders. Glancing at Danny, Cole motioned for him to take the first shot. If the boy missed, Cole was ready to back him up.

As Danny took careful aim, a second deer appeared in the clearing. Cole turned slightly, adjusting his sight to the newcomer. Cole and Danny shared a grin of satisfaction. With two deer there would be enough meat for the next hundred miles. As if on cue the two fired simultaneously. The sound of gunfire echoed like thunder through the hills. As they watched, both deer leaped in a death dance, toppled and fell to the ground.

Working side by side, Cole and Danny tossed aside their rifles and drew out their knives. With great skill they bled the animals and began the long process of skinning and gutting them.

"Cole. Danny."

Both looked up at the sound of Thad's distant high-pitched shout.

"Over here, Half-pint."

Cole mopped at the sweat that beaded his forehead and bent once more to his task.

"Where are you?" The small voice sounded farther away than it had a minute ago.

"Damn." Leaving the knife in the flesh of the deer, Cole stood and started toward the sound of Thad's voice. "I'll fetch your brother before he gets himself lost in these woods."

Danny nodded and continued skinning his buck.

Cole picked his way through the thicket of prickly pear, absently wiping blood on his pants. Up ahead through a maze of trees, he could make out the form of the little boy.

"Come on, Half-pint. We have a lot of work to do before…" The words died in Cole's throat.

At the sound of snarling and thrashing in the thicket behind him, Thad turned in the direction that Cole was staring. Charging through the brush toward him was the meanest looking animal he had ever seen. It was about sixty pounds, with a mane of long black hair. The grizzled snout faintly resembled that of a wild boar.

Thad let out a bloodcurdling scream. Fear left him paralyzed. He wanted to run, but his feet would not respond to his wishes. Instead he stood rooted to the spot, staring as if mesmerized as the animal charged nearer.

"Thad." Cole felt a surge of helpless frustration. In his haste to find the boy, he had left both his rifle and knife behind. And now, unarmed and helpless, he found himself facing the most dangerous animal in all of Texas. A breed of wild boar with teeth as deadly as razors. A dreaded and feared javelina.

Cole noted that when the boy froze in his tracks, the animal had slowed its charge. It now stood watching and sniffing. Within minutes, though, the javelina would attack in all its fury. And when it did, there would be no stopping it.

"Don't move." Cole inched his way toward the boy, praying for enough time to reach him.

The animal snorted and Cole knew it was about to charge again. The javelina was the most ferocious game animal in

Texas. Its razorlike teeth could take off a man's leg with one
bite. He had no doubt what the animal's teeth would do to a
boy the size of Thad.

"Dear God." Cole was not a praying man, but as he
watched the animal make menacing advances toward little
Thad, he realized just how much he loved the boy. He would
let nothing in this world harm Thad. He had to save the boy.
Had to. Even if it meant he would die trying. As he reached
Thad's side, Cole hugged the boy to him and felt the wild
beating in his heart. He wrapped his arms around Thad and
held him closer, striving desperately to share his own strength
with the boy.

As the javelina stomped the ground and snorted, it began
to charge forward with furious speed. With no thought to his
own life, Cole grasped Thad by the shoulders and thrust the
lad behind him, out of the way of attack. He did not fear death.
His only thought now was saving Jessie's little brother. Unarmed, he planted his feet firmly and waited for the animal's
final deadly lunge.

At the sound of Thad's scream, Jessie looked up from the
fire and whirled toward the rifle, which she kept in the boot
of her saddle. The horses were tethered near the stream, but
the saddles had been set in a semicircle around the camp fire.
The boot of her saddle was empty. Danny had taken her rifle.
She turned toward his saddle. In quick strides she removed
Pa's buffalo rifle and began running toward the thicket where
she had last seen her brother.

Gunshots. Hadn't she heard gunshots a few minutes before
his screams? God in heaven. Had he been shot? Why hadn't
she paid more attention to Thad? Why hadn't she kept him
with her until Cole and Danny returned? How many dangers
could await an unsuspecting child in the wilderness? As she
ran through the thicket, unmindful of the low-hanging
branches that snagged at her britches and tore at her hair, she
berated herself for her carelessness. Thad. Sweet little Thad.

He had needed some attention from her, and she had failed him. Again. Why was she always so careless?

The silence, that terrible deadly silence, frightened her more than Thad's single scream. Why were there no more sounds? Even the insects had stopped their buzzing, as if awaiting some fatal climax.

Tearing through the brush and undergrowth, she topped a rise and came to a skidding halt. Just below her stood Cole and Thad. And facing them was the most vicious animal Jessie had ever seen.

It took her a moment to figure out what was wrong with the scene before her. Cole ought to be holding his rifle at the ready. But his hands, she noted, were empty. Where was his rifle? His hunting knife?

As she stood watching, Cole, with deadly calm, shoved Thad behind him and turned to face the animal. In that instant she realized that Cole was about to sacrifice his own life for Thad's. With no weapon and no way to defend himself against the deadly attack, he would surely lose his life in order to save her little brother.

''Greater love hath no man...'' The familiar words of the Bible flashed through her mind. Love. The thought left her stunned and reeling. Love. Tears misted her eyes, and she brushed them away furiously with the back of her hand. Cole loved Thad so much he was willing to do anything in order to save him. And she knew in that same instant that she loved Cole Matthews. Loved him as she had never loved anyone before. It no longer mattered who he was or what he was. She loved him. Loved him with a fierceness that gave her renewed strength. She would never love any other man in quite the same way again.

As those thoughts imprinted themselves on her mind, she watched in horrified fascination as the animal, snorting and slathering, charged toward Cole. From the corner of her eye she saw Danny running from the opposite direction.

Her fingers felt stiff and awkward on the trigger of her pa's gun. If this was her own rifle, she would at least have a chance.

But this buffalo rifle of Pa's was too unfamiliar to her. She
had never even fired it before. And now, when she had just
come to realize how much she loved Cole, she was not going
to be denied the chance to tell him. He couldn't die. Not now
when there was so much to live for. She knew that if she tried
to shoot the animal, she risked killing Cole, as well. Already
their images ran together into one wild, twisted shape.

Through a blur of tears, she watched as Cole leaped ahead
to meet the charge in order to keep the animal from reaching
her brother. Just as the animal streaked through the air toward
Cole's outstretched arms, she reacted instinctively. No matter
what the cost, she had to try to save him. She squeezed the
trigger and heard a tremendous explosion rumble across the
land. The report sent her pitching backward. She heard a heart-
wrenching scream and couldn't tell if it was Thad's voice or
her own. It sounded strange and high-pitched and far, far
away. And then she was drifting, sliding along a dark tunnel.
As wave after wave of pain crashed through her brain, she
slipped into blessed unconsciousness.

Chapter Fifteen

"Hey, Jess. Wake up. What's wrong with you?"

Through layers of sound and shadow Jessie struggled to respond to Danny's voice. But her mind couldn't seem to focus.

"Jessie." Strong arms wrapped around her, and she buried her face against a scratchy shirt and hung on, feeling oddly safe and happy.

"Jessie. Are you all right?"

At the sound of Cole's deep voice, she nodded and sighed, wishing they could remain like this until she could pull her scrambled thoughts together. As if reading her mind, Cole lifted her in his arms and began carrying her back to their campsite, all the while cradling her against his chest.

She found herself weeping and didn't know why. But when he whispered words of comfort, she only cried harder until, concerned, he knelt down and set her on her bedroll.

"Are you hurt?"

She shook her head and looked away, embarrassed to be caught blubbering like a baby.

"Then what is it?"

"I thought I'd killed you."

He smiled then, and she thought her heart would burst from the sweet pain that smile caused.

"I'm still alive." He placed her small hand in his as if to

prove that he wasn't just her imagination playing tricks.
"Without a scratch, thanks to you." His voice sounded oddly
gruff. "You saved my life, Jessie."

"But I was almost too late. I thought…" She was mortified
to realize she was crying again.

"Hey, Jessie. Are you crying?" Little Thad looked concerned.

"Of course not." She wiped furiously at her tears with the
back of her hand. "I never cry."

"Did you see what you shot?" Thad was standing over her,
a smile splitting his face from ear to ear. "Cole says it's a
javelina." In imitation of Cole he gave it the Mexican pro-
nunciation, *havaleena.* "Cole said that's like a wild pig, only
meaner."

Jessie watched numbly as Thad pointed toward the carcass
of the dead animal, which he and Danny had struggled to carry
back to their camp.

"That was some shooting, Jess." Danny knelt beside her,
his eyes wide with respect. "I never thought you could handle
Pa's rifle like that."

She gave a weak laugh. "Neither did I."

Cole continued to study her closely, noting the pallor that
left her skin the color of pale alabaster.

"What your sister needs right now is some rest." When she
made a move to protest, he placed a hand on her shoulder,
holding her still. "You lie here. We'll bring you some supper."

She fell back against the blanket and watched as Cole filled
her plate. Danny poured coffee and trailed behind Cole. Not
wanting to be left out, Thad broke off a hot biscuit and carried
it to her.

She ate in silence while the others relished their supper.
Thad recounted every moment of his brush with the dangerous
javelina, his voice high with excitement. Now that the danger
had passed, he went over each little detail of the adventure.

Every now and then she noticed that Cole was watching
her. But though Thad and Danny tried to get him to talk about

the terrible experience, he merely nodded occasionally while they did all the talking.

At last they seemed to have talked themselves out. Their thoughts turned inward.

"Would he have killed you, Cole?" Thad asked after long moments of contemplation.

"Maybe." Cole finished his supper and sipped hot strong coffee.

"You were going to take him on rather than let him hurt Thad, weren't you?" Danny's voice lowered.

"I was going to try."

"But he'd have killed you."

Cole rolled a cigarette and held a flaming stick to the tip.

"Didn't you think about that?" Danny persisted.

"There wasn't time to think." Cole drew deeply, filling his lungs with smoke.

"I wasn't thinking about anything except how scared I was," Thad said. He turned to his sister, and she saw the sudden knowledge in them. "But you weren't scared, were you, Cole?"

"Sure I was, Half-pint."

"But you didn't cry or run away. You stayed and faced him."

"Sometimes that's the only choice a man has," Cole said simply.

Danny's voice took on a new edge of respect. Suddenly the excitement and the drama of the day faded with the knowledge of what this man had really done. "You were going to die before you'd let him hurt Thad."

Cole tossed the cigarette into the fire and stood. "That's enough talk. I think we've all had our fill of excitement for one night. Time for bed."

Danny stood and walked closer, then extended his hand. "Thanks, Cole."

Cole studied the boy in the firelight and accepted his handshake. "You're welcome. Good night, Danny."

As Danny turned away, Jessie was surprised to see Thad

walk to Cole and extend his hand as his brother had done. Cole took the pudgy fingers in a firm handshake, resisting the urge to hug the boy to his chest as he had earlier.

"Thank you, Cole." Even Thad's high voice seemed changed by what had happened this day. His tone was tinged with awe. "You saved my life."

"Your sister did that. Be sure you thank her."

"I will. Good night."

"Night, Half-pint."

Both boys kissed their sister before climbing into their bedrolls.

In the darkness Cole asked, "More coffee, Jessie?"

"Thanks." She accepted the cup and sipped, feeling the warmth of the liquid and the heat of the fire. But the warmth that was growing within her had nothing to do with the coffee or the fire. It was the knowledge that Cole was alive. Alive and here with her. It no longer mattered how long he stayed. For now, for this night, he was safe.

"You're quiet, Jessie. Are you sure you're all right?"

"I'm fine. Just—shaken by what happened."

"You saved my life. For that I'm grateful."

"I'm the one who's grateful. I saw what you did out there."

He gave her a sideways glance and sipped his coffee in silence, wishing there was some way to say all the things he was thinking. The thought of seeing little Thad ripped apart by the vicious animal had left him shaken to the core. Even the value of his own life had paled beside that of Thad. The two boys who had once been a burden were now very important in his life. Though he hadn't taken the time to figure out why.

When the prolonged silence became awkward, he stood. "Guess I'll go down to the creek and wash this blood off."

Jessie watched as he strode away. For long minutes she sat staring at the flickering flames of the fire. Then she smiled a mysterious woman's smile. She got to her feet, still draped in her blanket. Checking to see that her brothers were fast asleep, she stepped away from the fire and into the shadows and silently made her way to the creek.

Cole looked up at the robed specter standing alongside the bank of the creek. "You startled me, Jessie. What the hell are you doing here?"

"I came to help you wash."

"What?"

She dropped the blanket and held out the cake of fragrant soap. "After what you did today, I think you deserve something besides that old lye soap."

Before he could speak, she began unbuttoning her shirt.

"Now what are you doing?"

She smiled and hoped he wouldn't notice that her hands were shaking. "I just told you. I'm going to join you in the creek."

"Go away, Jessie. I'm too tired for this."

When she continued unbuttoning her shirt, he let out a sigh of frustration. "I suppose you expect me to turn around out of respect for your privacy."

She slipped off her shirt and reached for the buttons of her britches. Even in her nervousness she had to smile. "I expect you'll want to watch me."

She glanced over in time to see his look of surprise.

When she had stepped out of her britches, she began to untie the ribbons at the shoulder of her chemise.

Cole stood very still, cursing the cloud that crossed the moon, blotting out her image for a moment. When the cloud passed, Jessie was bathed in streams of golden moonlight. He caught his breath at the sight of her. She was more beautiful than he could have ever imagined. So young, so slender, with narrow hips and high rounded breasts. Her skin looked cool and pale and untouchable.

She picked up the soap and began to walk through the shallows. He watched as the water lapped at her thighs, then higher to cover her hips, and higher still until only her head and shoulders were above the water. When she was a few feet from him she paused.

"Turn around."

Wordlessly he obeyed. She began moving the soap across his shoulders and along his back, marveling at the muscled strength of him. As she moved the soap to his waist, she felt him tense. Before she could stop him, he turned and caught her in an iron grip.

"Now what is this game you're playing, Jessie?" His voice was rougher than he'd intended.

"I told you. I came here to help you bathe. You saved my brother's life today. It's the least I can do."

He felt a wave of fresh frustration that left him trembling. His voice was harsh. "I don't want you to think you owe me anything for today. I did what I had to do. Nothing more."

"I'm not here to pay you back."

"Then why are you here?"

She ran her tongue over dry lips and fought to keep her tone casual. "I discovered something amazing today."

He waited, watching the way the moonlight played across her cheekbones, giving her a dark mysterious look that was intriguing.

"I discovered that I love you."

He went very still, letting her words wash over him. He could not have heard her. This couldn't be happening. "What the hell are you talking about?"

"I love you, Cole. When I saw you willing to sacrifice yourself for Thad today, I realized how noble you are. And I realize, too, that you almost died without ever knowing that I love you."

His eyes narrowed. "So now that I'm still alive, you think you'd better tell me fast, before I get myself killed. Is that it?"

She smiled and he felt a tightening deep inside. "Something like that. Knowing that I love you is so wonderful, I want to share it with you."

He kept his hands firmly at his sides. There was no way he

could risk touching her now. There were too many feelings rushing through him, leaving him reeling. ''All right. You've told me. Now what?''

She felt a swift stab of pain at his cold, cutting tone. Her own voice lost some of its enthusiasm. ''Nothing more, I guess. This was the only way I could think of to show you how I felt.''

As she turned away, he caught her by the shoulder and spun her around to face him. ''By washing me?''

She shrugged. How could she tell him that she hadn't thought this thing through? That she had acted on impulse and had no idea where it would lead? She had wanted to be a temptress but didn't quite know how. ''I didn't know what else to do. Whenever we start to become friends, you always seem to turn away from me.''

When she refused to meet his gaze, Cole caught her by the chin, forcing her to look up at him. ''Is that what you think? That I don't want to be close to you?''

She hoped he couldn't see the betraying blush that colored her cheeks.

His tone grew soft. ''I think you should know something. Your brother and I fought one night.''

''You and Danny?'' She knew they would have been badly mismatched. ''Danny would dare to fight you? Why?''

She heard the unspoken laughter in his voice. ''It was over you.''

''I don't understand.''

''He accused me of treating you with disrespect because he saw me kissing you.''

''Oh.'' She felt a wave of embarrassment at the knowledge that Danny had seen them together. And then a wave of tenderness for a young brother who would be willing to fight a tough gunman like Cole because of her honor.

''And after that fight he demanded a promise from me.''

Jessie waited, feeling her cheeks grow hotter.

''I promised your brother that I wouldn't touch you again.''

''I see.'' She paused then glanced up at him through a veil

of lashes. "And you're a man who always keeps your promises."

"I am." He bit back the laughter that welled up inside him at the look of bitter disappointment on her face. "But there was one provision added to that promise."

She swallowed and waited to hear the rest.

"I agreed not to touch you unless it was what you wanted. If it was what you wanted, the deal was off."

Jessie remained very still.

"Now," he said, still fighting the laughter. "If it's what you want, would you like to wash my back?"

The smile returned to her eyes. As she lifted her soap-filled hand, he caught it and pulled her close. His voice was low with emotion. "One more thing. This isn't a game we're playing, Jessie. If you stay here with me, I won't be able to walk away after one kiss."

"I—I know that."

"Do you? Do you really know what you're doing?"

"No. But I'm sure that I love you, Cole. And I want to stay."

His voice was barely a whisper. "You stay at your own risk."

"I'm good at taking risks."

"Too damn good."

He saw her blink away the little flicker of fear in her eyes and knew that she had no idea what she was getting into. For that matter, neither did he. He knew only that he could no more send her away than walk on this water. It would take a miracle to send her away now. And he was no miracle worker.

He motioned to the soap still held in her hand. Then he turned away from her. Over his shoulder he drawled, "It's been a long time since I had a woman scrub my back. I think I'm going to enjoy this."

With halting, awkward strokes Jessie moved the soap across his shoulders and down the column of his spine. She felt him tremble slightly as her hand traced his waist and across his hipbones. Sensing his reaction, she grew bolder, bringing the soap up one side of his body and down the other. But when he turned to face her she found all her courage fleeing.

"That felt good, Jessie. Seems I told you that once before, when you bathed my gunshot wounds. You have a nice gentle touch."

He saw the way her cheeks reddened at his words, and he couldn't resist teasing her a little more.

"If you'd like, you can start at my shoulders and work your way down."

With his dark eyes watching her, she found her hands were trembling again. Clutching the soap, she moved along one shoulder, then the other. As her fingertips came in contact with the mat of hair on his chest, she experienced a strange tingling sensation deep inside.

"Oh, Jessie," he breathed. "Do you have any idea what your touch is doing to me?"

It was impossible to speak. She could think of nothing to say. Instead she moved her hand lower across his rib cage to the flat planes of his stomach.

He stood very still, waiting to see what she would do now. Though Jessie had every intention of moving her hand lower, she found she couldn't.

"Now what?" Cole asked in a voice tinged with unspoken humor.

She swallowed. "I—thought I'd wash your hair."

"My hair?" He laughed then, and it was such a joyous sound she forgot to be embarrassed.

Lifting her hands to his head, she began to lather. As her fingertips caressed his scalp, Cole sighed and felt himself begin to relax.

"I don't think I've ever had my hair washed by someone else. It feels good."

Growing bolder, Jessie scooped a handful of water over his head and began lathering it harder. Her fingers were gentle as they moved through his hair, kneading his scalp. He felt a curling sensation all the way to his toes.

"Now duck under the water and I'll help you rinse it," she ordered.

He did as he was told, and Jessie massaged his head while he held his breath. When he came up for air, his dark hair glistened in the moonlight.

"Now it's my turn," he said, taking the soap from her.

Before she could protest, he began lathering her hair. His fingers were strong and firm as they moved through the tangles, massaging her scalp, her neck, her temples. With a little sigh she gave up any further protest and gave in to his tender ministrations. When her hair was thoroughly soaped, he whispered, "Hold your breath."

He pushed her gently beneath the waves and watched as the soap floated free, leaving her hair shimmering in the moonlight.

She laughed and tossed her head, sending a spray of water high into the air. Her hair floated behind her like a golden veil.

Before she could move away, Cole began running the soap across her shoulders and down her back. And then with a little gasp she felt his hands move across the slope of her hips to her stomach, then higher to her ribs, and higher still until they stroked her breasts. Instantly she felt her nipples harden and wondered if he had felt it, too. She chanced a glance at his eyes and saw them narrow with sudden knowledge.

He drew her close until their bodies were touching. The water swirled around them, but even its coolness couldn't chill the heat that flowed between them. The weightlessness was a pleasant sensation as Jessie floated in Cole's arms.

With unhurried movements they touched each other's faces, arms, throats, rinsing away soap, kissing away tiny droplets of water.

"Jessie." His gaze fastened on her mouth, and she felt the blood rush to her temples.

All her life, Jessie had hated her name. It was, she thought, a boy's name. And Pa had wanted lots of sons to help him with the ranch chores. But suddenly, hearing Cole say it, she thought it was the most beautiful sound she'd ever heard. "Oh,

Cole," she murmured. "Say my name again. Just that way. Soft and husky. Like a whisper on the breeze."

"Jessie. Jessie. Jessie." He drew her even closer until he could feel her heartbeat thundering inside his own chest. And then he lowered his mouth until it hovered just above hers.

"Say you want this, Jessie. I need to know it's what you want."

"I want…" She could barely get the words out. Her throat was so clogged with fear and desire she thought she might choke on the words. "I want you, Cole."

His mouth closed over hers, absorbing the words. The kiss was hot, hungry, by turns giving, then demanding, until she felt drained by it. His tongue traced the fullness of her lips until she ached for his lips on hers. Instead he held her close and pressed moist kisses to her temple, her eyelids, her cheek. She lifted her lips to him and waited, waited until she thought she would go mad from wanting his kiss. And when at last his lips covered hers, the kiss was savage, desperate, filled with a hunger that left them both gasping.

She wrapped her arms around his neck and pressed herself to him. He caught her breath and shuddered at the contact.

He let out a long savage oath and caught her by the shoulders. "Do you want us to drown?"

She laughed low and husky, sending shivers along his spine. "You'd never let anything happen to me."

"You're too trusting."

"Only with you."

He lifted her easily in his arms and strode from the water. On shore he laid her on the blanket and stretched out beside her. Before she could even wrap her arms around him, he pulled her close and covered her mouth with his. His tongue parted her lips and invaded the sweetness of her mouth, tasting all the wonders that were hers alone. The fragrance of crushed roses was all around her—on her skin, in her hair, fueling his desire.

Boldly she followed his lead, allowing herself to explore the intimacies of his mouth. He tasted dark and mysterious, with just a hint of tobacco on his tongue. His lips still held the coolness of the creek, but his flesh was warm wherever she touched.

Cole wanted her. Wanted her desperately. But he forced himself to bank his needs. This was her first time, and he would make it as gentle, as easy as possible. With only lips and tongue he roamed her face, exploring her eyelids, her ear, her mouth. He ran openmouthed kisses along the column of her throat and felt her tremble. As his lips moved lower, they probed the swell of her breast. And when his mouth closed over one moist nipple, he felt her gasp and arch against him. With slow teasing kisses he thrilled at her moans of delight and frustration. And while his mouth fed at her breasts, his hands moved lower, touching, exploring.

His fingers found her and brought her to peak after peak of sensations. Dazed and breathless, she tried to stop him, but he gave her no time to stop, to think.

Of their own volition her hands moved over him, discovering rippled muscles along his shoulders and back. Her fingertips skimmed his stomach and moved lower until she felt him shudder at her touch.

As she reached another peak, her hands clutched at his shoulders. With a groan he covered her mouth in a savage, desperate kiss and lowered himself to her.

Still he hesitated. "Tell me," he whispered into her mouth. "Tell me you want me."

Her words were a low guttural moan of desperation. "I—want—you—to—love—me."

Hadn't he already told her he loved her? He couldn't remember. He couldn't think. Needs, raw, pulsing needs drove him over the brink.

He took her then, forcing himself to go slowly, urging himself to be gentle. But as she moved with him, he forgot to be gentle. Passion, so long suppressed, exploded. In a frenzy they took each other on a journey beyond madness.

Chapter Sixteen

In the stillness of predawn, Cole lifted himself on one elbow and stared down at the beautiful creature in his arms. Her pale golden hair spilled about the dark blanket like a scattering of moon dust. Her skin was white and as soft as a newborn foal's muzzle. Long spikey lashes created shadows on her high cheekbones. She had pulled a corner of the blanket over her, and he found himself mesmerized by the dark shadowy cleft between her breasts.

What she had given him last night had been a very special gift. She had given him herself, her love, without question, without conditions. A slow smile touched his lips. When had the little tomboy learned to be a wild, tempting seductress? When had the girl become so much woman? It was obvious that she had never before been with a man. And yet, for all her innocence, no woman had ever made him ache with such desperation.

All night they had loved, slept fitfully, then loved again. Each time they came together, they discovered new and wonderful things about each other. Each time she had taken him higher. And each time he had wanted her more. He would never have enough of this woman. She had bewitched him. From this moment on, his life was forever tied to hers.

He watched her stir and felt a tiny pinprick of fear. Such

an alien feeling for him. But this small creature had the ability to terrify him.

What if, in the cold light of morning, she regretted her actions? It was one thing to mistake gratitude for love. And under the intimate cover of darkness, it was a natural thing to give in to the passions that flowed. But now that dawn was approaching, would she feel shame or regret at what they had shared?

As her eyelids flickered, he forgot to breathe. His heart forgot to beat.

For a second Jessie held off the moment when she would come fully awake. Instead she lay quietly, savoring the warmth of the body beside hers. She knew him, knew his scent, knew his touch and the warmth of his breath. And she knew him in a way she would never know any other man.

Love. It enveloped her in its warmth. So this was what it felt like to be loved. To awaken to the touch of a lover's hands, to be enfolded in strong arms was a very special feeling.

"Good morning." She yawned, stretched. With a smile touching her lips, she wrapped her arms around his neck and drew him down for a sweet feather-like kiss.

The moment his lips found hers, he felt his heart begin to beat once more. Heat flowed through him, warming the chill that had settled around his heart.

"I was afraid you might not like what you see," he murmured against her lips.

"Umm." For long moments she appeared to be half-asleep. Then she startled him by her sudden catlike action. Rolling on top of him, she peered down into his face. As her hair swirled around him, she ran a finger across his scratchy stubble of beard. "And what do I see? Looks like a trail bum," she said in a husky voice. "Or maybe a horse thief. You definitely can't be the man I went to sleep with last night."

"And why not?" He wound a strand of her hair around his finger and pulled her head down until her lips hovered a fraction above his.

"The man I was with last night was handsome and smooth shaven. And you look more like a shaggy mule than a man."

"Do I now?" He drew her head even lower and kissed the tip of her nose.

"I know a foolproof way to determine if you're the same man." She wriggled about, aware that her movements aroused him. "Kiss me. If you are Cole Matthews, I'll know by your kiss."

He fought back the wild surge of desire. How was it possible to want her again so soon? "Thank you, miss." His eyes glinted with humor. "And where would you like me to kiss you?"

"Oh, you do manage to kiss me in the nicest places."

"So do you, as I recall."

She felt a thrill at the intimacy of his tone. With a little laugh she ran her hand down his side until she felt him tremble, arousing him further. "Nervous, stranger?"

"You're driving me crazy, Jessie."

"Good. You're far too serious. You need to be a little crazy."

"Serious, am I?" Without warning, he rolled them both over, pinning her beneath him. "What I'm about to do to you is very serious. So pay attention."

He covered her mouth with his and kissed her until she was breathless.

As his hands began to work their magic, she whispered, "I knew all along it was you, Cole." He had left his fingerprints on her body, her soul, her heart. "I'd know you even in the dark."

"Stop talking, Jessie," he breathed against her mouth. "We have serious business to take care of."

And then there was no need for words. They were lost in a world of feelings. A world of wild, primitive sensations. A world of love.

Cole lathered his face and began removing his beard with a straight razor. All the while, Jessie watched in fascination, running her fingers along his smooth skin, distracting him until he managed to cut himself. When he swore low and fierce, she reminded him that he was in the presence of a lady. Minutes later she was peering into his chipped mirror from behind him, making faces that left him weak with laughter.

"I can't shave and watch you making monkey faces at the same time."

"Then I suggest you do one or the other. But hurry," she added, slipping the blanket from her naked shoulders.

He finished shaving in minutes, then wiped the lather from his face before following her into the creek. Together they frolicked like two children. They teased, splashed and came together with soft, intimate touches. When they emerged, they dressed quickly to ward off the morning chill.

While Cole rolled their blanket, Jessie started breakfast. By the time Danny and Thad awoke, venison snapped and sizzled in a skillet and coffee boiled over hot coals. The last of yesterday's rolls were heated, giving off the wonderful aroma of baking bread.

An hour later they prepared to break camp and take to the trail once more.

"You're awfully happy this morning, Jessie," Thad observed. "What happened to you last night?"

"Nothing." She felt herself blush as Cole turned to give her a knowing look.

As Jessie checked her saddlebags, Cole pressed something into her hand. Glancing down, she saw that it was the precious rose-scented soap.

"Better not forget this," Cole murmured.

"Where did you find it?"

"On the bank of the creek." He bent low, murmuring for her ears alone, "I look forward to having my back scrubbed with this again tonight."

She gave a low throaty laugh that whispered over his senses, making him wish it was already evening. "And what if my brothers don't cooperate and go to sleep early enough?"

"I'll wait all night if I have to. Sooner or later they have to fall asleep."

"And what if I fall asleep first?"

The laughter died in her throat when she glanced up, catching the simmering look in his eyes. "Believe me, woman, I'll find a way to wake you."

She watched as he strode away, then pulled herself into the saddle. When she turned, she was dismayed to see Danny watching her with an odd look on his face. Before she could study him further, he wheeled his mount and took the lead.

They had been in the saddle for hours, and Cole found himself constantly looking over his shoulder. Although he had seen nothing out of the ordinary, he had the distinct feeling that they were once again being watched.

As the sun rose higher, Cole saw Danny veer off from the lead position. The lad spoke to Thad, then to Jessie, before urging his horse toward the spot where Cole followed at a slower pace.

"Sun's so hot we're practically cooked," Danny called as he reined in his mount. "Why don't we head up toward those rock cliffs? There'd be some protection from the heat."

"Maybe you're right." Cole shielded the sun from his eyes and tried to ignore the prickly feeling that had persisted for hours. "But let's stay close together." At Danny's arched brow he added, "Never know what we might be heading into."

"Right." Danny squinted against the glare and wondered why Cole was being so skittish. Had he seen something suspicious? Or was it, as Danny suspected, because Cole was distracted by thoughts of his sister? Something had happened between them. Cole and Jessie seemed so aware of each other today. All morning he had seen the looks passing between these two. And even on the trail he had seen the way Jessie turned in the saddle from time to time to glance at the man who took up the rear position. "I'll keep Thad close to me. You keep an eye on Jessie."

Cole nodded and waited while Danny rode ahead to tell the others about their plans.

Within minutes they had turned their horses toward the outcropping of rocks that rimmed the trail. At Cole's command Jessie rode close to him. Beside her, Danny and Thad rode side by side.

As they neared the cliffs, Cole heard the shrill cry of a hawk. He glanced skyward, then cursed his stupidity as the realization dawned. Though it was a perfect imitation of a hawk, it wasn't a bird at all. It was a signal.

"Comanche. Hit the dust."

Even while he slid from the saddle and reached for his gun, Cole's gaze was scanning the other three to make certain that they followed his terse command. Crouched behind his horse, he turned his full attention to the cliffs.

Within seconds, dozens of Indians came streaming over rocks and boulders, brandishing bows and arrows or holding aloft glittering knives. Their blood curdling battle cries were enough to cause terror in the hearts of those who faced them. There was no way of knowing how many more Indians were still concealed behind the rocks.

A tall Indian grabbed little Thad by the arms and tossed him high in the air, then caught him and pinned him in an iron grip. Immediately Danny aimed his buffalo rifle at his brother's captor.

"Let my little brother go or I'll blow you apart," he warned.

The Indian let out a whoop of laughter as three warriors knocked Danny to the ground and wrestled the rifle from his hands. They pinned his arms behind him, forcing him to watch helplessly as Jessie and Cole continued to fight for their lives.

Three Comanche caught Jessie. Though she kicked and bit, she was no match for their strength. And when Cole tried to come to her aid, he found himself surrounded by fierce warriors whose slashing knives and singing arrows quickly disabled him. His gun and rifle lay in the dust, kicked out of reach by moccasin-clad feet. His arms were pinned behind him in a painful, wrenching grip while blood oozed from half a dozen wounds.

When all four had been subdued, they were forced to watch helplessly as the Indians taunted and threatened.

Into their midst rode the Comanche chief astride a spotted Indian pony. In perfect English he called, "Woman-With-Hair-Like-The-Sun."

At Jessie's little gasp, Cole strained to see clearly the figure bathed in blinding sunlight. He felt a chill curl along his spine. The Indian sat tall and straight on his pony, his dark hair falling in two braids to his waist. His shoulders were wide, the arms heavily muscled. His head was lifted in a proud tilt, the eyes dark and probing, the nostrils flared in contempt. In his hand was a lance decorated with eagle feathers. Cole had no doubt about the Indian's identity. Two Moons. Fierce warrior. Chief of the Comanche nation.

"Why are you here?" Jessie called. "We've done nothing to you."

"I have been following you. Have you forgotten that you are under my protection?" the Comanche chief asked sternly. "You are to be my woman."

"She'll never be your woman."

Despite the strong arms that held him, Cole nearly twisted free before being subdued once more by the warriors. For the first time, the Comanche chief turned his full attention from Jessie.

Two Moons studied Cole with grave intensity, noting the finely honed muscles of his shoulders and upper arms, the powerful thighs. Because of this white man's barely contained rage, it took four warriors to hold him back. But it was the man's eyes that arrested the Comanche's gaze. This man had the narrowed, unblinking stare of a seasoned gunman. With this man there would be no hesitation, no backing away from a fight. And the chief was angry enough to enjoy a fight. But there was no time for such pleasures.

With calculated disdain, Two Moons shifted his gaze back to Jessie.

"You must give up this foolish journey. I have been patient long enough. Your father has joined the spirits of the dead. You will come with Two Moons and be his woman."

"She's my woman." Cole's words were spoken with deadly calm.

Jessie saw the Comanche chief's eyes narrow fractionally. At a single command from Two Moons, a Comanche warrior caught Cole in a stranglehold about the neck and brought his knife to Cole's throat, prepared to kill the white man who would defy his chief.

"No." Jessie's eyes were wide and pleading. "Please. Don't hurt him." Her voice trembled. "Or my brothers."

The chief hesitated, watching Jessie's eyes.

"If you let him live, I'll..." She swallowed, knowing that once the words were spoken there was no way to take them back. "I'll go with you and be your woman."

"So." Two Moons studied her closely. "Your father rejected my offer of two-and-ten ponies for you. Though he knew it was more than the Comanche had ever offered for a woman. And now you would give yourself to me for only the life of these two puny boys?"

"And the man," she said quickly.

Her words brought a scowl to the chief's face. "The man. Does this white man speak the truth? Has he made you his woman?"

Jessie could feel the tension as everyone awaited her reply. If she told the truth, Cole would surely die for touching the woman Two Moons had singled out as his own. But even if she lied, there was no guarantee the Comanche wouldn't kill Cole, and kill her brothers, as well.

She took a deep breath and decided to risk everything. "He speaks the truth. I am his."

Both Danny and Thad stared in openmouthed surprise at Jessie's admission.

The Comanche chief's eyes darkened with fury. As he began to lift his hand in signal for the warriors to kill, a girl's voice broke the stillness.

"These are the white men who saved my life."

Morning Light stumbled out from behind the shelter of a boulder. The man who had been trying to subdue her cast a terrified look toward his chief before hanging his head in shame.

"It is not for you to speak," Two Moons shouted. "This is between Two Moons and the white woman."

"These are the ones who saved me. He was their medicine man," she said, pointing toward Danny. "And the woman and man assisted him. Without them I would surely have died before reaching our people."

Two Moons turned toward Jessie. "Does my sister speak the truth?"

"Your sister?" Jessie's gaze shifted to the lovely young woman whose proud features were unmistakably the same as that of the man astride the pony.

"Did she not tell you? Morning Light is sister to Two Moons, chief of the Comanche."

Jessie swallowed back the knot of fear. She had seen how disdainfully the girl's words had been received. Still, it was their only hope. She would try anything to save the people she loved. And if she failed, it would no longer matter what happened to her.

She met the chief's burning gaze without flinching. "We helped Morning Light, though we did not know she was your sister, Two Moons."

The Comanche studied Jessie for long moments before turning toward the Indian girl. "This is true? You did not tell them?"

"The white woman speaks the truth."

Two Moons mulled over the unexpected kindness. He saw the way his sister studied the white boy.

Turning toward Morning Light, he asked, "This is the medicine man?"

At his sister's slight nod, he turned back to Danny and waved off the hand of the warrior who held him prisoner. "Your life shall be spared. You saved the sister of the Comanche chief from the evil spirits. She speaks of your good medicine. You will always be welcome among my people.''

Danny swallowed and rubbed his throat that had been nearly crushed by the Indian's grip. As he did, his fingers brushed the amulet. ''I'm—I'm not a doctor yet. But some day I hope to be. And when I am I'd be proud to take my medicine among your people.''

Two Moons saw the shy smile that passed between the white boy and his sister. With obvious anger he spoke to her in their language and watched as she meekly made her way back to the side of the Indian whose duty it was to protect her.

Danny watched as she was forcibly led behind the boulder. In his eyes was a bleak look of longing that did not go unnoticed by the others.

Two Moons turned his attention to Jessie. For long minutes the Indian studied the young woman who stood beside the white man. When at last he spoke, his voice sounded not so much weary as resigned. ''So that you will know that the Comanche owes no debt, I will leave you to this white man. And the word will go out to all Comanches that you are to be afforded safe passage through our land.''

''You will let my little brother go,'' she said with more boldness than she felt.

Immediately Two Moons spoke to the warrior who held Thad imprisoned in his arms. When the little boy was free, he ran to Danny's outstretched arms. Both boys hurried to stand beside their sister, who hugged them fiercely and forced herself not to cry. There must be no show of weakness in front of this arrogant chief.

Jessie turned to glance at Cole and saw that his hands were still clenched tightly at his sides, while a warrior kept his arm firmly about his throat, brandishing a knife inches from his flesh. The Comanche chief followed the direction of her gaze before he turned his attention back to Jessie.

Two Moons allowed his gaze to roam the young woman's face, her hair, her slender frame encased in her brother's britches and faded shirt. With a slight nudge of his heels, his pony started forward until it reached Jessie's side. Two Moons leaned down and caught a handful of silken yellow hair and watched as it sifted through his fingers.

Behind him Cole sucked in his breath and felt the cold steel of the Comanche blade.

Two Moons came very close to smiling for the first time. Still holding her hair, he jerked Jessie's head upward, forcing her to meet his steady gaze. The hint of a smile lingered on his lips. ''This white man will be a poor substitute for the chief of the Comanche. Two Moons would have given the Woman-With-Hair-Like-The-Sun fine Comanche warriors.''

''Please let him go.'' Jessie's words were barely more than a whisper.

The Indian absorbed the warmth of her breath, the deep resonance of her trembling words, before releasing her. With a look of disdain for Cole, Two Moons straightened and gave a signal to his warriors.

The Indian holding Cole stepped away.

Two Moons nudged his horse into a trot. With head held high, he rode away from them without a backward glance.

The Comanche warriors slowly disappeared behind rocks and boulders. A few minutes later they were seen moving silently astride their ponies toward the hills that loomed in the distance.

For the first time, Cole's hand relaxed and dropped to his side. Jessie turned toward her younger brothers, expecting to see fear or even tears of relief at the departure of the Indians. Instead Thad's mouth hung open. In his eyes was a mixture of astonishment and admiration.

Danny continued to stare at the Indians until they were no more than a blur among the rocks and brush. On his face was a look of sorrow at something precious that had been found and then lost, a look of longing so intense Jessie felt her heart go out to him. But when she made a move toward Danny, he twisted away, ashamed of his display of emotion.

Jessie turned and fell into Cole's arms. For long minutes

she clung to him, needing to absorb his strength. As she started to push away, he drew her firmly to him.

Against her temple he muttered, "When Two Moons touched you, I wanted to kill him."

He released her, turned on his heel and grabbed the horses' reins, leading them toward the rocks. He needed to be busy to work off his anger and frustration.

For long minutes Jessie watched him, reeling at what he had just revealed. Jealous? Cole? She felt an almost uncontrollable urge to laugh. And then without warning she found herself weeping instead. She had prepared herself for the death of all those she held dear. Her brothers, who were more important than life to her. And Cole, who had become equally important. Weighed against that, her own fate had not mattered.

Chapter Seventeen

The warm evening was dusted with just a hint of cool breeze, the distant peaks of mountains ran red with the bleeding sun. Along the banks of the river, where they had made camp for the night, insects chirped and hummed. This hazy, restful place seemed a million miles away from the simple sod shack they had left so long ago.

The horses were fed and rested. Supper had been a fine meal of venison and sourdough biscuits. Everyone had taken a long soothing bath in the river, and their clothes were spread over low-hanging bushes to dry. Cole rolled a cigarette and lifted a flaming stick to the tip. He filled his lungs with smoke and watched while Jessie sat beside the fire, wrapped in a blanket, pressing water from her freshly washed hair.

She and Cole had long ago stopped hiding their affection for each other. It was not unusual for her to touch a hand to Cole's cheek in passing or for Cole to press a light kiss on the tip of her nose when she was scolding him for swearing. When the boys were sound asleep for the night, she and Cole would slip away to a quiet place to love.

Thad and Danny had accepted this new aspect of their relationship with more ease than Jessie had expected. At first she had been hesitant to let them see her true feelings for Cole. But when she managed to overcome her shyness, she realized that her brothers had been aware of the situation almost from the beginning.

"You like him, don't you, Jess?" Danny asked one morning as they saddled their horses in preparation for breaking camp.

"Yes. Is that all right with you?" She wasn't even aware that she was holding her breath until her brother made his response.

"I guess so. As long as it's what you want."

"It's what I want," she said simply.

"It doesn't bother you that Cole's a gunman?"

She bit her lip, reluctant to admit that the thought often bothered her. "I know that he's a man on the run, and that he can't promise me a future. I'll just have to settle for whatever time we have. I can't help the way I feel about him."

Danny nodded his understanding. "I know. I can't help liking him, too. He's saved my hide more times than I care to count. If I'm ever in a fight, I want him on my side."

Little Thad's approval was evident in the way he hung on Cole's every word. The little boy had found a hero, who was gradually becoming a substitute for the father he so badly missed.

"Would you have fought Two Moons for Jessie?" Thad asked innocently as he climbed into his bedroll for the night.

Cole's hand, smoothing the blankets over the boy, paused in midair. He cast a speculative look at Thad and replied, "I guess I'd have had no choice."

"You could have let him take her."

"Would you?"

Thad's eyes were wide with innocence. "Course not. But that's different. She's my sister. She doesn't mean anything to you."

Cole's response was immediate. "She means everything to me, Half-pint."

"She does?"

Cole tousled the boy's hair and tucked the blankets under his chin. "Yep." He saw Jessie glance at him from across the fire and grinned. ''Who else can make biscuits that melt in your mouth? And who else would see to it that we take a bath regularly?''

Thad's high-pitched laughter danced in the night air. ''Did your mom make you take baths when you were little?''

''She sure did. My father and I had to go out to the creek and haul in buckets of water every Saturday night.''

''That's the way Jessie was with me and Danny and Pa,'' Thad said in awe. ''Did your ma make you go to church every Sunday?''

''Yep.'' Cole chuckled and stretched out beside the boy, resting his back against the trunk of a gnarled tree. ''We had to drive the buckboard nearly twenty miles to the nearest town every Sunday to hear the preacher talk about fire and brimstone.''

''Yeah.'' Thad cushioned his head on his arms just the way Cole did and stared up at the sky alight with a million winking stars.

''But you know something, Half-pint? I didn't really mind. In fact, I liked going to church and meeting all the other families from miles around. It was a good feeling, taking the morning off from chores, and eating big picnic lunches in the churchyard afterward.''

''Yeah.'' The little boy closed his eyes, picturing the way it might have been if his mother hadn't died, if his father hadn't given up on the town and the church. ''Jessie tried to make Pa take us to church, but he wouldn't. And once in a while Jessie took us, but most of the time there were too many chores around the ranch. Pa used to get real mad if we didn't get everything done before dark.''

Cole glanced at the young woman who'd been forced to grow up so soon. Her head was bent over her mending. The dancing flames of the fire turned her hair to a curtain of red gold. It couldn't have been easy for her, but he'd never heard her complain.

''What was your ranch house like, Cole?'' Thad asked, his voice thick with sleep.

"It was actually two wooden buildings, with a dogtrot between. In one end we all slept, and in the other there was a big kitchen. At roundup time my mother and sister used to cook for nearly thirty men every night until the herd was taken for slaughter."

"You must have had a big ranch."

"It was big, even by Texas standards."

"Did you get to ride with the herd?"

Cole smiled as memories washed over him. "My first time was when I was nine. We rode up the Shawnee Trail through Dallas, crossed the Red River near Preston, past Fort Gibson, and entered the southeastern corner of Kansas near Baxter Springs. We had a herd of over five thousand head of cattle, with twenty-two men and me. Those steers were only worth about eight dollars a head in Texas, but in Kansas they brought thirty dollars each. And," he added proudly, "our Texas longhorns hardly lost any weight at all on the long trek."

"Five thousand cattle," Thad said, stifling a yawn. "I've never seen more than a hundred steers at a time."

"It's quite a sight." Cole stared at the sky, tracking the path of a shooting star. "They stretch out for miles." He settled himself more comfortably and added, "There's something special about being on the trail. The sound of cattle lowing all through the night. The smell of coffee and grits and flapjacks cooking before it's even light out."

"Sounds like some of Jessie's breakfasts, doesn't it?"

Cole flashed a smile in the darkness. "Your sister's one hell of a cook."

"We're sort of like a family now, aren't we?"

At Thad's innocent question, Cole went very still. "What do you mean?"

"Oh, you know. Jessie's the only ma I've ever known. And now that you and Jessie like each other, I feel almost as good as if Pa were along. I feel safe with you, Cole."

The man beside him grew silent. Strange. He'd been thinking the same thing about feeling like a family. This was the closest he'd come to having a family in a long time. He loved

these two boys as much as if they were his own. And there
was no denying his feelings for Jessie. But safe? He shook his
head, denying the little thread of fear that insinuated itself into
his mind. If only he could keep them safe. He hoped his presence among them wouldn't bring them harm. He'd been witness to enough violent death. He couldn't bear to involve
them.

At the sound of soft even breathing, he glanced down at the
little boy and realized that he was already asleep. With a rare
display of tenderness he bent his lips to the pale blond head.
When he strode toward the creek, he wasn't even aware of the
gangly youth who stood in the shadows and watched. But
Danny felt himself echoing the sentiments of his little brother.
Something had happened along the trail. Something he hadn't
quite figured out yet. Maybe they weren't quite a family, but
they were definitely not the same people who had started out
on their quest so many long miles ago.

Cole wrapped a blanket around Jessie's shoulders and lifted
her into his arms. With a muffled laugh he carried her off to
a hill overlooking their camp.

When he set her on her feet, he took the blanket from her
and spread it on the grass. Taking her hand, he drew her firmly
into his arms and lowered his mouth to hers.

"I've thought of nothing but this all evening," he muttered
against her lips. He absorbed the first jolt of heat at their contact.

"Really? And I thought the only thing that interested you
was that frayed old saddle of Danny's that you worked on for
hours."

He framed her face with his big hands and cut off her words
with a quick hard kiss.

"That poor kid was going to find himself sitting in the dust
in another day or so. He needs a sturdier saddle."

"It's all we had."

"Jessie." He caught her and turned her into his embrace.
"I wasn't being critical. I just meant that this journey has been

hard on the horses and equipment. Not to mention the people involved.'' He nuzzled her lips until he felt them warm and soften beneath his.

The familiar tingle began low in her stomach and continued to build. She sighed and gave herself up to the kiss before murmuring, ''We've gone so far, Cole. And still there's been no sign of Pa. What if we've done all this for nothing?''

''Nothing?'' He reached for the buttons of her shirt and eased it from her shoulders. Lowering his mouth, he ran moist kisses across her shoulder to the sensitive column of her throat and thrilled to her shuddering response. ''Without this journey I'd have never met you. Think how empty my life would have been.''

His lips moved lower until they captured her breast. With a little gasp she clutched his head as she felt the passion begin to pulse through her. Passion that was fueled anew each time he touched her. Just as she felt her legs weaken and tremble, he caught her in his arms and lowered her to the blanket. With hurried movements they shed their clothes and lay together flesh to flesh, heartbeat to heartbeat.

Desire quickly became need. A hard driving need that had their pulses racing, their hearts hammering.

Cole knew now that he would never have enough of her. A hundred times, a thousand times would never satisfy him. He wanted her always. His woman. His mate.

How natural it seemed to love this woman. He hadn't felt this young, this carefree in years.

''I've never thought I was a man who needed much, but I wish...''

''What do you wish for?'' She touched her lips to his throat.

''I wish, just for tonight, I could give you a fine big ranch house with a soft feather bed. And gowns of satin and lace, and all those things women yearn for.''

As she started to protest, he added bitterly, ''Hell, I can't even tell you about myself. Who I am, where I'm headed. I can't promise you a future. I can't even promise you tomorrow.''

"You've given me something better," she whispered against his lips. "We have cool green grass and a sky full of diamonds. We have this night. And best of all, we have each other. And as for who you are, what you are—" she smiled and he felt his heart ache at the sweetness of her, "I know all I need to know about you. You're strong and good and decent. And whatever happened before I met you doesn't matter. All that matters is that we have each other now."

His mouth covered hers in a hot, hungry kiss that spoke of his desperate need to make this night of loving last forever. As he lost himself in her, he felt a wave of gratitude to the Fates that had brought them together.

Above them, millions of stars glittered in a black velvet sky, and a pale yellow moon seemed to cast its golden rays of benediction upon the lovers.

"You did a good job, Half-pint." Cole examined the horse's foreleg. The swelling of the past two days was nearly gone. "Whatever you did, it worked."

"Aw. It was just a salve made of cactus juice and creek mud that my pa taught me."

"You're one fine horseman. I know a lot of ranchers who would give their best stud bull to know what you know."

As Cole walked away, the little boy beamed with pride. Nearby Jessie felt her heart swell. Did Cole have any idea what his kindness did for her little brother's self-esteem?

"Cole."

On his way to the creek, Cole turned at the sound of Danny's hushed voice.

"Cole? Could I talk to you?"

"Sure, Danny." He paused beside the gnarled sun-bleached tree limb where Danny was sitting. Setting down his bucket, he propped a foot on the branch and rested both hands on his knee. "What about?"

"It's about—" Danny's Adam's apple bobbed as he swallowed and tried again. "—Morning Light."

Cole felt a wave of compassion for the lad in his first throes of lovesickness. At least now he understood the look on Danny's face. "Sure. What would you like to know?"

"Will Two Moons choose a husband for his sister? Is that the way it's done?"

Cole shrugged. "Sometimes a husband is chosen, especially if the girl has no suitors." He fought back the smile that threatened. "When a maiden is as pretty as Morning Light, there will probably be plenty of braves hoping for her favors."

Danny's face became bleak. "She is pretty, isn't she?"

"But she has grit, as well," Cole added quickly, sensing Danny's sense of despair. "I don't think Morning Light would take a husband unless he was the one she wanted."

A spark of hope glinted in Danny's eyes. "What if she refuses to choose a brave? Will the chief allow her to wait for the man she loves?"

Cole dropped a hand on the boy's shoulder. "The chief would be a fool to try and force a girl like Morning Light to marry against her will." Cole's voice lowered. "Two Moons is a smart man and a fair one. Besides, he loves his sister. I think he'll at least try to respect her wishes."

Danny nodded, wanting desperately to believe what had just been said by a man whose wisdom he respected.

As Cole stood, he asked in a rush, "How long does it take a man to become a doctor?"

Cole shook his head. "I don't really know, Danny. I guess it depends on how smart a man is, and how much he wants to learn. There are a lot of things a man can only learn by doing."

"Yeah." Danny seemed to weigh Cole's words before he stood and extended his hand. "Thanks, Cole. I've had a lot on my mind that's been troubling me. It's good to be able to talk to a man. I'd never be able to talk to Jessie about things like this." He gave a sheepish grin. "You understand."

"Sure I do. Sometimes it's not such a nice feeling to find yourself caring about a woman. Then you find yourself taking on her troubles, as well as your own."

"Yeah." With new insight Danny glanced up at Cole. "Is that how it is with you and Jessie?"

Cole nodded. "I wish more than anything in the world I could find your pa for her, so things could be easier for her than they are now."

"Things were never easy for Jessie," Danny said in a remarkable display of wisdom. "Pa wanted a son when he got Jessie. And she's tried to be one for him ever since."

"Instead he got himself one amazing daughter and two fine sons."

Danny met Cole's gaze and felt a lightness around his heart where only minutes ago there had been a heaviness. "Well. I think I'll get some sleep now."

As Cole watched, the young lad strolled back toward the camp fire. His shoulders were straight, his head high. And when he walked, there was a jaunty air to his steps.

If only, Cole thought, taking up the bucket and heading toward the creek, every problem in life could be solved so easily.

As he entered the shadows, the prickly feeling returned. Things had gone smoothly for too long. He glanced up at the full moon and watched the clouds scudding past. He hated to see only the dark side of things, but something told him the trail was about to get bumpy once more.

Chapter Eighteen

"I know you've seen lots of small towns since you left your home," Cole said. "But you've never seen anything to compare with Fort Worth."

"Is it as big as Little Creek?" Thad asked.

Cole swallowed back his laughter. "Bigger."

"Bigger'n Little Creek?" Thad glanced at Danny and saw the look of expectancy.

On their journey they had stopped in several small towns. Most of them looked alike, with a main street consisting of a scattering of wooden buildings that housed a general store, a church or schoolhouse, a saloon and sometimes a hotel above, and at the end of the street a blacksmith and stable. Each time they visited a town, they stocked up on necessary supplies. In every store, saloon and stable they inquired about Big Jack Conway. Each time, they received the same reply. No one had seen a man matching his description, though many had witnessed large herds of cattle being driven through the territory.

"We ought to be coming up on Fort Worth before the day is through," Cole cautioned. "I think we'd better plan on taking a day there before we head out. It'll give us a chance to take on supplies before we hit more wilderness. Besides, I think you three will be goggle-eyed by all you'll see."

"Huh." Jessie felt a rush of annoyance at the look on her

brothers' faces. "It's just another town. The only reason I'm willing to stop is to see if anyone spotted Pa."

"I don't think one man would be remembered in a town like Forth Worth."

"Are you telling me the town is so big they wouldn't notice a man like my pa?"

"I guess you'll just have to see for yourself, Jessie."

Cole urged his mount forward and the others followed suit.

"I don't believe what I'm seeing."

Jessie sat astride her horse and stared at the town spread out before her. Her brothers' eyes were as big as saucers trying to take in the amazing sight.

Fort Worth was situated on a broad plateau. The Chisholm Trail had made Forth Worth a booming cow town filled with saloons, gambling casinos, variety theaters and dance halls. Wooden buildings had sprung up everywhere to accommodate the tired, dusty drovers on their way to Abilene.

"Come on," Cole said, taking the lead. "We'll stable our horses and get rooms at a hotel."

"A—hotel?" Jessie thought about the meager funds left in her saddlebag. "Won't that cost a lot of money?"

"I'll buy."

"We can pay our own way." Jessie's mouth curved down into a frown. Just because she loved him didn't mean she'd stopped taking care of herself and her brothers.

"If you'd like, the boys can bunk with me," Cole said softly, understanding her need for independence. "That way you only need to get one room."

She gave him a weak smile of gratitude and turned to stare as they entered the town.

Cowboys, spurs jingling, six-shooters strapped at the hip, milled about, clogging the dirt streets and wooden walkways. In the doorways of saloons and gambling halls stood women in gaudy dresses, beckoning to the strangers.

"Jessie, look." Thad pointed to the doorway of a variety theater where a thin wiry man juggled pistols. As they spun

crazily in the air, he'd catch one, fire it into the air for attention, then toss it and catch another, following the same routine.
Within minutes a crowd had gathered, and a man began urging
them to step inside and see an even more exciting demonstra-
tion during the show.

"Can we go?" Thad was twitching with eagerness.

"Maybe later," Cole said. "First we have to stable the
horses and get a room for the night."

They stared in fascination as horses and wagons vied for
the right-of-way in the narrow dirt road that was the main
street. Easing through the congestion, they made their way to
the El Paso Hotel, a tall three-story wooden structure.

As Danny began untying his bedroll, Cole stopped him.
"Just bring in your saddlebags. We'll leave the saddles and
bedrolls with the horses at the stable."

All three slung leather saddlebags across their shoulders and
followed Cole inside.

"Yes, sir?" The clerk looked up from his ledger. He wore
a black broadcloth coat and vest to match. Across the vest
draped a gold chain on which was attached a gold watch. He
had shiny black hair neatly parted in the middle, and the ends
of his mustache were waxed to keep them from drooping.

"Two rooms," Cole said.

"That'll be two dollars a room. Fifty cents extra with bath."
The clerk seemed to be taking special notice of the young
woman with pale yellow hair who was wearing men's britches
and a faded shirt. Even in such clothes she was pretty enough
to make a man suck in his stomach and straighten his shoulders.

"We're looking for a man," Jessie said, feeling her cheeks
redden at the insolent way the man studied her. "His name is
Big Jack Conway. He was heading for Abilene with a herd of
longhorns."

The clerk's gaze shifted to a man across the room who had
suddenly stilled at the girl's words. Pushing his way through
a crowd of drovers, the man stood at the other end of the

counter and pretended to be engrossed in watching the crowds of people.

"He's a big man," Jessie said, "with dark curly hair and a mustache and side whiskers."

"He always wears an old leather vest with the initials *JC* carved into it," Danny added. "And his saddle has those same initials carved into the side."

"Do you know how many men pass through this town?" the clerk asked in a bored voice.

"Yes, but—"

"Half the drovers never stay in a hotel anyway," the man went on. "Most of them camp outside of town with their herd and only come in to get drunk or to get—" he glanced up at the scowl on Cole's face, then continued nervously "—some other pleasure."

Cole gave the man a piercing look and slapped his money on the counter. "We'd like our rooms now."

The clerk wisely tore his gaze from Jessie. "This way, please."

"Jessie, you and the boys follow the man to your rooms."

"Where are you going?"

"I'll see to the horses."

Jessie nodded and herded her brothers toward the stairs. As they passed, the stranger studied them carefully, then walked to the clerk's ledger and turned it. Tracing a finger along the names, he halted, read the room numbers and strolled away.

"This is the gentlemen's room," the clerk said, stepping aside as Jessie and her brothers crowded into the neatly furnished room.

There were two wide beds and a wooden dresser. Over the dresser was mounted a mirror. In the corner stood a wooden washstand with a pitcher and basin. Beneath each bed was a covered chamber pot. A window overlooked the main street. Outside the window was a wide balcony that ringed the entire hotel.

"The lady's room is next door," the clerk said.

Jessie and the boys followed him. When they stepped inside the second room, Jessie stared about in silence.

In this room there was a single big bed covered with a plain crocheted coverlet. Being a corner room there was a window on either side, affording a view of nearly all of the town. Fresh white curtains billowed at the open windows. Beyond them was a glimpse of the balcony. The wooden dresser and washstand were identical in size to the pair in the other room. But the pitcher and basin were decorated with a delicate rose pattern. And the oval mirror above the washstand was rimmed with a band of hand-painted roses. To one side of the door, a pair of chairs flanked a small round table. The chairs, Jessie noted, were covered in a rose needlepoint design.

"I hope you'll be comfortable, ma'am."

"Thank you. It's lovely."

"How do we take a bath?" Danny asked.

"The men's bathhouse is next door. For the lady, a tub and water will be brought to the room if requested."

"Yes, please," Jessie said shyly.

"I'll see to it immediately." The clerk turned away with an air of importance.

"A bathhouse." Danny let out a long slow hiss of air when the door had closed behind him. "I wonder what that's like."

"I don't know. But I want you to stay with Thad. The looks of some of those cowboys worried me."

Thad's eyes danced with unconcealed excitement. "Aw, Jessie. After what we've been through on the trail, what could happen to us here in a big civilized town like Fort Worth?"

What indeed? She pushed aside any lingering fears. As the two boys left, she walked around the room, touching a hand almost reverently to the pristine coverlet on the bed. How Ma would have loved a room like this. She crossed the room and touched the basin and pitcher. They seemed too pretty to wash in. She resisted the urge to fill the basin and wash her face and hands. She would wait until her bath. Reaching into the saddlebags, she removed the rose-scented soap and laid out a clean shirt and britches on one chair.

Almost timidly she sat on the edge of the bed and tested the soft mattress. What luxury. Even back at home the bunks had been stuffed with grass. She had never felt anything so soft in her life.

Growing bolder, she stretched out, feeling the mattress sag beneath her weight. Cradling her head was a down-filled pillow so soft it felt as if she were cushioned on air. With a sigh she curled up on her side and closed her eyes. She would only rest a moment. Then she would check on Danny and Thad.

Jessie sprang up, confused, disoriented. Someone was knocking loudly on her door. How long had she been asleep? A glance at the window showed that the sun had long ago drifted across the sky. Early-evening shadows filtered through the gauzy curtains.

When she opened the door, a young boy entered carrying a round washtub. Behind him was a young woman carrying two buckets of steaming water.

"Sorry this took so long," the girl said with a smile. "There were so many requests for water, and we can only heat six buckets at a time on the cookstove."

"That's all right. I didn't even notice the time."

The boy placed a folded blanket on the floor and helped the girl pour the buckets of hot water into the tub.

"The water is still warm," the girl explained as she laid out linen towels. "But by the time we carry it up the stairs and pour it, it's already losing some of its heat and by the time you undress, it will be growing even cooler. Most folks prefer a warm bath when they come in from the trail."

"Thank you." Jessie followed them to the door, threw the lock and began removing her clothes.

When she was naked, she bent over the tub and ran the soap through her long hair, soaping and rinsing until it was thoroughly clean. Wrapping a towel about her head, she dipped a toe into the water. Perfect. She stepped into the tub and sank gratefully into the warm water. She lathered her body and leaned back with a sigh.

At a slight scuffling sound she glanced up to see a black-booted foot slip through her opened window. Just as she was about to scream, a figure in lean black pants and a white linen shirt appeared.

"Cole." She whispered his name on a whoosh of air and found herself studying the way he looked—droplets of water sparkling in his freshly washed hair, crisp new clothes molding his hard lean figure.

"Why are you coming in through the window?"

He gave her a wicked grin. "Since your two brothers are so exhausted from their baths that they're sound asleep on my bed, I thought this might be the best way for a gentleman to call on a lady."

She gave him an appraising look. "In that getup you do look like a gentleman. Where did you get the clothes?"

"The same place I got these." He removed a bundle from beneath his arm and lifted out a gown of ivory gossamer.

Jessie's mouth dropped open. For a moment she couldn't speak. Then, finding the words, she gasped, "Cole, where did you find something so beautiful?"

"You can find anything in this town, if you know where to look." He dropped the gown across a chair and laid a package beside it, then crossed the room and stood beside the tub, staring down at her. "I didn't know I'd find you looking so fetching when I walked in."

In a tone of voice that told him she had learned the art of flirting, she said, "A gentleman shouldn't watch while a lady takes her bath."

"And why not?" He folded his arms and studied her through narrowed lids. "This gentleman has seen you in creeks and rivers, remember? In fact, this gentleman has helped you take your bath. A number of times."

"A gentleman should never tell such things about a lady."

He began unbuttoning his shirt while Jessie stared in surprise.

"What are you doing?"

"You need a little help washing your back."

He removed the rest of his clothes, picked up the soap and knelt beside her. She felt the laughter bubbling up inside her as he began making lazy circles on her stomach. Slowly she felt her skin begin to tingle from his touch. He continued washing her until he felt the subtle change in her. He saw the way her eyes darkened with desire.

Dropping the soap, he started to stand. "Maybe you're right. A gentleman ought to leave a lady alone in the bath."

"Don't you dare." She caught his hand and pulled him down until his face was inches from hers.

"Do you think we can both fit in that little tub?"

She pressed her lips to his throat. "We can certainly try."

Without warning, he lifted her and covered her mouth in a searing kiss. He began carrying her toward the bed.

"Cole, I'm soaking wet."

"Don't worry, love, I'll dry you."

He reached for an embroidered linen towel and wrapped it about her before pulling back the coverlet and laying her gently on the bed.

Surrounded by the softness of down and filled with the fragrance of crushed roses, their lovemaking took on a tenderness they had never before experienced.

"Is it really me?" Jessie twirled about the room and studied her reflection in the oval mirror.

The bodice of her modest gown molded her high firm breasts. The skirt had rows of ruffles that swept the floor, completely covering her worn, dusty boots. At her waist was a sash of pale blue, complementing the blue of her eyes.

Cole's gaze feasted on the vision in white. Never had he seen a more beautiful woman. Her hair had been brushed into soft waves that fell nearly to her waist. Her skin was sun kissed from the long weeks on the trail. Her eyes sparkled as she circled the room, dancing with excitement.

"Jess." At the pounding on her door, both Jessie and Cole looked up. "Hey, Jess. Let us in."

"Sounds like the boys are awake and ready to see the town." Cole strode across the room and threw open the door.

Danny and Thad were dressed in dark blue pants and suspenders. Their shirts were crisp white linen. Their hair had been cut and parted in the middle and slicked back behind their ears.

"Oh, my. Don't you look grand."

"Cole bought these," Thad said proudly.

Danny was speechless, staring at Jessie with a look of surprise and admiration. "Where'd you get that dress?"

"Cole bought it." She twirled. "Like it?"

"Gosh, Jess. You look beautiful. You look—" he swallowed "—just like Ma." Danny's voice was hushed.

For a moment Jessie felt thunderstruck. Knowing her brother's love for their mother, this was the highest compliment he could pay her.

"I don't remember Ma, but you look as pretty as one of those ladies in Ma's books," Thad said.

"Thank you. Thank you both." She bent and hugged her little brother, then brushed a kiss on Danny's cheek.

"Come on," Cole said, breaking the spell. "It's time you saw Fort Worth."

With his arm around Jessie's waist, he led them from the room and down the stairs.

As they passed through the lobby of the hotel, Jessie noticed dozens of cowboys milling about. Several stopped talking when they caught sight of her. She felt Cole's arm tighten at her waist, and she experienced a warm flutter of happiness. Cole's woman, her heart whispered. With Cole she felt warm and safe.

A man across the room was studying Jessie in a way that made Cole want to throttle him. And yet Cole couldn't blame him. In this gown she looked more beautiful than any bride. What man could help but stare at a woman like Jessie? Especially if he'd been out on the trail for weeks or months?

Cole led them across the dusty road and into a large wooden house where they ordered steak, lamb chops, roast beef and pork, all with potatoes, two vegetables, bread and butter, milk and tea, and for dessert, apple turnovers hot from the oven.

All around them were drovers, freshly bathed, in stiff, uncomfortable shirts, their hats and gun belts hanging on pegs about the room. Though some of the cowboys smoked, Jessie noticed that their conversations were muted, and a prominent sign requested no swearing. At her impish grin, Cole turned, noted the sign and burst into a low rumble of laughter.

They ate until, replete, Cole paid the woman twenty cents apiece. They headed toward the noise and tinny music of the casinos.

Behind them a man blended into the shadows, keeping them always in his sight.

Cole felt the prickly feeling of being watched, and he turned to scan the crowds. Although no one seemed to be paying them any special attention the feeling persisted.

At Thad's urging, Cole took them to a variety theater where for a dime they watched a woman sing in a warbly voice about the pleasures and pain of lost love. Several of the cowboys were moved to tears by her words. Then a man in tight-fitting breeches and a woman in a gown of red satin danced to the tinny sounds of a piano. Several cowboys in the audience began booing, and when the rest of the crowd joined in, the couple beat a hasty retreat from the stage.

At last they were treated to the act Thad had wanted to see. The juggler came on stage tossing horseshoes that glinted in the bright glow of lanterns. To much applause he began juggling woven baskets until there were so many in the air they couldn't be counted. He never missed one, and when he had finally caught the last, the crowd roared its approval. Now he brought out his showstopper. He began juggling pistols, catching every third pistol and firing it before tossing it up to join the others. He continued this dazzling display until everyone in the audience was certain his arms would fall off from the exertion. By the time he finished his juggling act, the audience was on its feet, clapping and whistling.

When a fat lady came on stage playing the spoons, Cole

herded them from the theater. "Pretty soon now," he whispered, leading them from the darkened room, "those cowboys are going to grow mean. And when they do, you don't want to be around."

Even before they were outside, they heard the sound of booing and the roar of gunfire. Two sheriff's deputies charged past them to calm the crowd. As Cole watched them, he saw a man duck back into the shadows. For a moment he thought about going back to investigate, but Thad stifled a yawn, distracting him.

"I think we've seen enough for tonight." Cole bent and lifted the boy into his arms. Thad promptly rested his chin on Cole's shoulder and closed his eyes.

At the hotel entrance stood a cowboy who stared up at the balcony, then scratched a match across his boot and held the light to a cigar. As Cole and Jessie brushed past him, he turned toward them with an evil leer. Instinctively Cole dropped a protective arm about Jessie's waist.

As they passed a cluster of strangers, one of the men said, "Mighty fine-looking wife and family, mister."

"Thank you." Cole felt an unexpected surge of pride at the man's words.

Jessie couldn't believe her ears. Cole had made no move to correct the man. It gave her a strange heady feeling to think that she and Cole could be mistaken for husband and wife.

Beside them, Danny stood a little taller. He wondered when he'd be tall enough to look Cole in the eye, man to man.

And though Thad had been nearly asleep, the words had instantly registered in his mind. Someone had mistaken Cole for his pa. He felt a strange lump in his throat and tried to swallow it down. Pa. When were they ever going to find him? He sighed, a sound so sad and haunting that Cole found himself cradling the boy with great tenderness.

They were all smiling dreamily as they made their way to the door of Jessie's room.

"We'll see you safely in first," Cole was saying. "And then we'll turn in."

Still holding little Thad, he opened the door to her room. On the dresser top a lantern cast a yellow glow across the room. And as Jessie stepped further inside, she let out a cry.

The room had been completely torn apart. Bed covers were strewn in a heap in the corner of the room. The soft feather mattress had been slashed. Feathers floated everywhere. Jessie's saddlebags had been rifled, her meager belongings tossed about. Dresser drawers were lying upside down.

Cole set Thad on his feet and strode to the room next door. As he opened the door, a similar sight greeted him. Both rooms had been completely ransacked.

He let out a savage string of oaths. Fool. He had seen all the signs, but he'd been too blinded by thoughts of pleasing Jessie and her brothers to pay attention. And now he had led them straight into danger that could cost them all their lives.

Jessie and the boys stared about the room, taking in the empty drawers, the slashed saddlebags and spilled contents.

In a whispered voice Jessie asked, "Who would do this, Cole? Why?"

His mouth was a tight grim line of anger. "Get your things together. We're leaving. Now."

Jessie watched as the boys began gathering their saddlebags and clothes. "Thad asked how there could possibly be any danger in a civilized town like Fort Worth."

"Civilized?" Cole bent and retrieved the medical book he'd bought for Danny. The pages had been torn from the binding and tossed about like dry leaves. "Not all the wolves are out on the desert, Jessie. Some of them go about masquerading as men."

Chapter Nineteen

All night their horses trudged north while they alternately dozed in the saddle and looked over their shoulders toward the lights of Fort Worth.

The beautiful gossamer gown was rolled into a ball and stuffed into Jessie's saddlebag. Once again she wore her brother's cast-off britches and rough woolen shirt. Danny, Thad and Cole had removed their fine new clothes, as well, replacing them with more rugged pants and heavy shirts.

Cole chose their campsites carefully, scouting for sheltered areas beneath rock ledges that could be approached from only one direction. That way, one of them could sit watch while the others slept. They lingered only long enough to refresh themselves before pushing on. Northward. Always northward. At last they reached Doan's Store, which stood on the banks of the Red River.

"We'll take on supplies here," Cole said, swinging from the saddle.

Jessie noticed that his hand hovered above his gun as he led them inside the general store. He looked around, scanning the face of every man before relaxing.

"This is the last outpost in Texas," Cole explained as they stared about it at the fully stocked shelves. "The drovers know that they won't find anything more until they reach Kansas."

As Jessie eyed the sacks of flour and sugar, he cautioned,

"We want to move fast, Jessie. Take only what we can carry in our saddlebags."

She nodded and began assembling the necessary supplies. Outside they parceled the items among the four horses.

As they mounted, Cole added, "Remember, we're leaving the protection of Texas behind. Where we're about to go, the only law is the law of the Indian."

As they forded the Red River, Jessie turned in the saddle for a final look at the shore. Texas. More than anything, she wanted to return to its shores with Pa. She wouldn't think about the dangers that lay ahead. She would hold only to the thought that somewhere in Abilene she would find her pa. And they would return as a family.

Between Red River and Caldwell, Kansas, lay a stretch of rugged, desolate land that exacted a toll from longhorn and drover alike. Indian Territory. Here the Indian law prevailed for there were no lawmen around. Many of the Indians seeking refuge here had been driven from their ancestral lands by the invasion of whites. White men who crossed Indian Territory did so at their own peril.

As their horses scrambled up the grassy bank of the Red River, Cole checked his rifle and pistol before returning the rifle to its boot. Though it was his nature to anticipate trouble, he was even more cautious now. The incident at Fort Worth had left him more shaken than he cared to admit. He couldn't afford to be careless again.

He glanced at Jessie and saw that she too was checking her pistol and rifle. Beside her, Danny rode with the buffalo gun across his knees. Though Cole knew that might be mistaken for a sign of hostility by the Indians, there was nothing to be done about it.

"Thad," Cole said, pulling his mount beside the boy's. "Have you ever fired a pistol?"

Thad blinked and shook his head. "Pa was going to teach me, but he never found the time."

"Tonight, when we make camp, I'll give you a few lessons."

When he turned away, Jessie muttered, "It isn't fair, Cole. Why can't you let him be a little boy for a while longer?"

"Fair? Who told you life was fair?" He caught her reins and held her horse when she would have turned away. With his face close to hers he said through clenched teeth, "It wasn't my choice to bring him along and expose him to this hell. But if you want him to live to be a man, you'd damned well better teach him how to protect himself."

She saw the anger and frustration in his eyes and sensed that it wasn't directed at her. It was this place. And the terrible helplessness.

Cole released her bridle and waited until she had passed. Taking up the flank position, he squinted against the merciless sun and kept a tense silent vigil.

It didn't take the Indians long to discover the four whites who invaded their territory without a herd. All through the day, clusters of Cheyenne, Kiowa, Cherokee and even Comanche warriors watched from hilltops as the four horses picked their way across the desert. By night, as he sat the first watch, Cole felt the hair at the back of his neck rise and knew that they were being silently observed.

"Cole." At Thad's whispered voice, he swung around.

"What is it, Half-pint?"

"You promised to teach me how to shoot."

"Yeah." He nodded toward the darkness just beyond the glow of their fire. "I don't think our hosts would like to hear the report of gunfire. It might just get them riled up enough to attack. But I can at least show you how to handle a gun."

He picked up his pistol and handed it to Thad. The boy tested its weight a moment, then lifted it, placing his finger on the trigger.

"Firing the gun's the last thing you need to learn," Cole said, holding out his hand. Reluctantly Thad handed it back to him. "The first thing you must know is how to load and unload this gun, even in the dark.'' Very slowly Cole opened the chamber and showed the boy the bullets. ''You load this way,'' he said, shoving a bullet into the chamber. ''The Colt Army .44 is a six-shooter. That means it holds enough bullets to fire one every day and rest on Sunday.''

At his joke, Thad grinned. ''Are you going to let me fire it?''

''Not tonight.'' Again Cole nodded toward the shadows. ''No sense provoking a fight we don't want. But if you know how to load it and aim it, there's nothing to firing it.''

He handed the gun to Thad and watched as the boy unloaded the gun, then carefully loaded it. When the gun was loaded, the boy held it up, pointing it toward the outline of a rock in the darkness.

''Focus until you can see that the barrel of the gun is pointed dead center at your target. After you've fired a few times, you'll learn how to keep your hand steady even though the gun's report nearly blows your fingers off.''

''Will it hurt?''

''You or the one you're aiming at?''

Thad laughed until he realized that Cole wasn't joking.

''This is a weapon of destruction,'' Cole said solemnly. ''Whenever you aim it at someone, you have to be prepared to take his life. That's an awesome responsibility.''

Thad swallowed. He had never really thought about the consequences of firing a gun. As he held the revolver in his small hand, he suddenly had an image of his father. The image was so real, tears stung his eyes. Before he could stop them, the tears began to flow.

''What if someone shot Pa? What if my pa's dead?''

Cole went very still.

''Sometimes I don't think we're ever going to find him.'' Thad looked up at Cole with such desolation it nearly broke his heart. ''What do you think, Cole?''

He touched a hand to Thad's shoulder. ''I know you're doing all you can to find your pa. Maybe that's better than waiting and not knowing.''

"I miss him." Thad's voice quavered and broke. "And sometimes I think I'll never see him again."

As the sobs broke from him, he turned away, ashamed to be caught crying. Cole reached for him but he pushed away, trying vainly to shrug off his touch. "I know I shouldn't cry."

"Why?"

"Pa said a man doesn't cry."

Cole's voice was husky with emotion. "My father was the strongest, bravest man I've ever known. But when my mother and sister and brother died of the cholera, I watched him sob out all the tears he'd stored up for a lifetime. And the only comfort I could offer was to hold him. Hold my big strong father in my arms and let him cry." Cole's voice was low with feeling. "There's no shame in a man crying. The shame would be in not being able to get on with his life after the tears are shed."

For the first time, Thad felt free to release all the fears that had been building over the miles. He fell into Cole's arms and sobbed as though his heart would break. When at last the tears had run their course, he lifted his head. His pale lashes glistened.

"I don't want to be a baby," he sniffed, accepting Cole's handkerchief.

"You're no baby." Cole watched the boy struggle with the last of his tears. "You're a fine son to your father. And you're going to be a fine man someday. One your pa will be proud of."

"You think so?" Thad wiped his face with the back of his hand, unaware that he still held the gun in his other hand.

"I know it. No matter what we find at the end of the trail, I have no doubt that you'll be able to pick yourself up and make something of your life."

Gently Cole took the gun from Thad's hands. "Tomorrow night, if we don't have any unwanted visitors out there, I'll let you fire my pistol. I think you're ready for that responsibility." He caught Thad by the shoulders and firmly turned him in the direction of the bedrolls. "Now you'd better get some sleep. We have a long day in the saddle tomorrow."

Thad nodded and started away, then turned and extended his hand. "Thanks, Cole."

Cole studied the small pudgy hand for a long moment before he enclosed it in his big palm. "You're welcome, Half-pint."

With a light heart the boy crawled into his bedroll and fell into an exhausted sleep.

His back to a rock, Cole tested the weight of his gun. Deep in thought, he closed his hand around the metal and tried to remember a time when he hadn't carried a gun. Too long ago, he thought. A lifetime ago. He returned the gun to his holster.

As the embers of the fire burned low, he rolled a cigarette and thought about Jessie and her brothers. He no longer wondered whether they were fools or heroes. He knew only that he was in for the long haul. He'd see them to Abilene or die trying.

By the second day the Indians grew bolder, sometimes even standing quietly in the path of their approach, staring intently at the little party. At the last minute the Indians would nudge their ponies, stepping aside until the four had passed. At times Jessie counted more than two dozen warriors keeping pace with them, watching, waiting. More Indians, the women and children of the various tribes, kept watch from the protection of rocks and trees.

The Indians said nothing. And at Cole's instruction, their party neither spoke nor acknowledged the Indians in any way. They rode single file with Jessie in the lead and Cole at flank.

Each day as their little party set out, they felt the strain of not knowing what the Indians had in store for them. They were forced to realize that at any time the Indians chose, they could be eliminated with no effort.

"Why can't we speak to them?" Danny demanded as they set up camp for yet another night.

"It's up to them to make the first move." Cole sipped

strong coffee and rubbed at the knot of tension at the back of his neck.

"But maybe if they see that we're friendly, they'll leave us alone."

"I have a feeling they know everything about us." Cole tried not to watch as Jessie bent over the fire. He wanted her. Desperately. But these nights he couldn't afford to let down his guard for even an hour.

"Then why don't they speak?"

"They don't need to. To them, we're unworthy to be addressed."

"How much farther," Thad asked.

"A couple of days." Cole stood and strapped on his holster. "I'll take the first watch. The rest of you get some rest."

He touched a hand to Jessie's hair as he passed her. Damn, he missed holding her.

As he walked away, she drew her arms about herself, trying to maintain the warmth of his touch. She needed his strength, needed the healing power of his touch. But she had no right to lean on him. She had always prided herself on her strength. The day would come, she warned herself, when Cole Matthews would ride out of her life. When that day came, she would have to be strong enough to go on without him.

Without him. The thought was as bleak as the landscape.

The days had become an endless vista of sand and rock and barren hillsides. The Indians continued to watch as the party of four horsemen made its way north.

At times the Indian warriors were close enough to touch. At other times they stayed in the hills, stretched in a line as far as the eye could see. Yet not one of them lifted a hand in greeting. Nor did any lift a hand to halt their progress.

Jessie pulled the cowhide jacket around her to ward off the wind that had grown colder. She was grateful for the buckskins that Cole had given her brothers. Very soon the glorious autumn weather would be chilled by winter. She tried to still the sense of urgency that often rocked her these days. They had come so far, but they could not go home without Pa. Abilene. The word sang in her mind. If Pa was anywhere in Abilene, they would find him.

"Jessie."

She was jolted out of her reverie by Cole's low hiss. Swinging in the saddle, she saw a bronzed, muscled warrior slowly approaching, followed by over a dozen braves.

"There's no sense going for your guns," Cole commanded, seeing Danny's hand tighten around the rifle butt. "From the looks of it, this chief has come to talk."

"Woman-With-Hair-Like-The-Sun."

At the familiar greeting, Jessie could only stare in surprise.

"I am Runs-Like-Antelope, cousin to Two Moons."

At the mention of his name, Cole's hands tightened at the reins. This was the Comanche who had been chased clear across Texas for the massacre of a dozen settlers near Deer Creek. He had a reputation as a ruthless killer of whites. Cole counted the number of warriors and decided he would only further risk their lives if he went for his weapon. From the time they'd entered Indian Territory, they had been aware of the risks. Now their only hope was to hear what this Comanche had to say.

"Two Moons has commanded safe passage for you and these white men," the chief said. "The Comanche honor the word of their chief."

"Thank you."

Before Jessie could say another word, the proud chief turned his mount and galloped away. His warriors followed closely behind, leaving the four in a cloud of dust.

"You mean that's all?" Jessie turned to Cole.

He shrugged. "They are a people of few words. He said what he needed to say."

"Why didn't they tell us this when we entered their territory?" Danny's face was a puzzled frown. "I sure would have slept better knowing they were going to honor Two Moons' promise."

"So would I," Cole said softly. "Come on."

"What's the hurry?" Danny called.

"Nothing against your sister's Comanche friends," Cole said, taking the lead, "but I'd rather not push them to the limits of their patience."

They urged their mounts into an easy canter and watched with a mixture of surprise and disappointment as the Indians who had been dogging their trail for days disappeared for good.

The following morning they learned why.

As they came up over a ridge, Cole let out a string of savage oaths. The others reined in their mounts and caught their breath.

On the branch of a cottonwood, the wind blew a bulky object in slow torturous circles. As they drew closer they realized what the object was. A man. A very dead man dangling from the end of a rope.

Chapter Twenty

"Welcome to Kansas." Cole's lips were compressed into a thin tight line as he urged his horse past the gruesome sight.

"Aren't we going to bury him?" Jessie couldn't tear her gaze from the man's purplish face, the swollen tongue lolling to one side of his mouth.

Overhead buzzards circled lazily, waiting for the strangers to leave. Flies buzzed. The stench of rotting flesh was almost overpowering.

"Cole, we can't leave him like this."

Cole shot Jessie a cold look. "Someone from the town will take care of it. They'll need the space for another hanging."

"You mean this happens often?"

"In Caldwell this is almost a daily occurrence." While he spoke, he deliberately led them away from the grizzly scene in the direction of the town. If he'd known what they would find, he would have found a way to bypass this place and spare them this.

"Caldwell calls itself the Border Queen, since it's the first town along the Chisholm Trail north of Indian Territory. This is the place where the drovers can let down their hair and do all the things they only dreamed about for the last hundred miles. And for some, horse thieves, drunken murderers, this is the end of the line."

"Is it as bad as Fort Worth?" Danny asked.

"Caldwell makes Fort Worth look like a Sunday school. The saloon owners here boast that a marshal's term in office usually lasts about two weeks."

"Are we staying here, Cole?" Danny studied the town up ahead. It was nothing more than a dusty street lined with drab wooden buildings. Though it was now drowsing in the mid-morning sun, he tried to picture it by night with painted women beckoning from doorways and drunken cowboys accepting their invitations. The scene in his mind wasn't a pleasant one. Especially in light of what they had just witnessed.

"We're only staying as long as it takes us to lay in fresh supplies." Cole studied the position of the sun and gave them a lazy smile. "I figure we ought to be back on the trail by noon."

He thought he noticed all three let out a sigh of relief at his words.

"How much farther to Abilene?"

Cole met Jessie's steady look. "Seven or eight days. Six if we ride hard."

"We can ride as hard as it takes," she muttered. "Six days. Let's get those supplies and get started."

Cole cast one last backward glance at the hanging tree and followed them through the town to the general store. He'd breathe a lot easier when he had them safely out of this place.

Cole felt the curious stares of the store owner and the drovers who milled about. It was unusual to see a woman and little boy along the trail. And even more unusual to see a woman dressed like a drover, in sheepskin jacket and faded britches.

When they entered the store, Jessie took the hat from her head and shook the dust from it, unaware that the sight of golden tangles spilling about her face was enough to take some men's breath away. She was stunning. Even in dirty trail clothes, she was the kind of woman a man dreamed about on long lonely nights.

While he lounged in the doorway, Cole studied each man in the store. And while he pretended to be looking over the supplies, Cole was really watching to see that Jessie was not accosted by bold drovers who had spent a little too much time away from their homes.

In less than an hour the supplies were loaded in their saddle-bags, and the four slowly made their way along the road leading out of Caldwell. All four felt as if a weight had been lifted from their shoulders when they were once more on the trail to Abilene.

Abilene. Jessie went to sleep with the word on her lips. She awoke with but one thought. Abilene. The end of the trail. The answer to all her questions.

There was a renewed sense of urgency to her journey. She rode all day without thought to her protesting muscles and woke from sleep ready to hit the trail again.

Within days they passed through Wichita and Newton, spending only enough time in each town to ask about Big Jack Conway. Even the lack of response no longer frightened or angered Jessie. It was as she expected. There had been too many drovers and too many herds. One man, even one as fine as Pa, wouldn't have made an impression on these people. But in Abilene, she promised herself, everything would be different. Someone in Abilene would know where he was. And their family would be whole again.

Abilene! Jessie had feared that it would not live up to her expectations. But seeing the town only made it seem larger than life. Abilene was certainly different from anything they'd seen so far. The town already had five hundred permanent residents, ten saloons, five general stores, two hotels and two so-called hotels where the patrons didn't necessarily stay the night. It also had two distinct personalities. North of the Kansas Pacific tracks was Kansas Abilene; south of the tracks was Texas Abilene, which housed the cattle pens, saloons, houses of pleasure and the hundreds of rowdy cowboys shaking the dust of the trail from their boots. The main thoroughfare in

Texas Abilene was Texas Street. It was choked with so many horses and wagons that it was impossible to move.

"Seems awfully busy for this time of year," Cole said, glancing around at the throngs of cowboys who clogged every inch of space along the walkways. "Must be a big herd in today."

Keeping their mounts firmly in check, the four inched their way along the dusty road until they came to the Merchants Hotel.

Leaving the horses with Thad and Danny, Cole led Jessie inside. When they stepped inside the hotel lobby, they were amazed to find dozens of cowboys milling about.

They stopped at the registration desk. Jessie arched an eyebrow toward a sign that read, All Firearms Are Expected to Be Deposited with the Proprietor. She glanced meaningfully at Cole. "Are you going to turn in your pistol?"

"Why not?" he asked, glancing at the room filled with unarmed men. "If it's the law, I have no choice but obey it. Besides," he said, motioning to the clerk walking toward them, "he looks like he means business."

The clerk was tall, heavily muscled and wearing a six-shooter on each hip. Not even a drunken cowboy would be foolish enough to give him trouble.

"We'd like two rooms," Cole said, slapping his money on the counter.

"We don't have a single room left."

"No rooms? Must be some herd." Cole's glance encompassed the crowded room.

"No herd," the clerk said. "Everybody for miles around is in for the hanging."

"Hanging."

"Isn't that what you folks are here for?"

"I'm afraid not." Cole returned the money to his pocket and picked up his hat as if to leave.

"Can you tell us where to look for a room?" Jessie asked.

The clerk shook his head. "Even the private houses are taking in roomers for the night. This hanging is the biggest event of the year. It's not too often we get to see a cattle rustler hanged.''

Jessie fought back a sense of despair. To have come so far and be denied a place to sleep. ''You mean there's not a single room available in all of Abilcne?''

''I don't think so, miss. Looks like you might have to spend the night at the stables. That is, if they aren't already filled, too.''

''The stables. Thanks,'' Cole said, turning toward the door. He dropped a hand beneath Jessie's elbow and headed toward the entrance. As an afterthought, he asked, ''By the way, who's getting hanged?''

''Fellow named Conway,'' the clerk said.

Jessie froze in her tracks. Very slowly Cole turned. ''Big Jack Conway.''

''Yeah. That's the one. You've heard of him, I see. Hanging's tomorrow morning.''

Cole took Jessie's hand and forcibly led her from the hotel. She stared straight ahead, completely oblivious to the shouts and laughter of the cowboys combing the streets for excitement. She didn't even notice the crowds pushing and shoving their way along the bustling walkways. But when she saw little Thad holding the reins of his horse, she knew that she couldn't fall apart. For Thad's sake, for Danny's sake, she would go to the marshal's office and right this terrible wrong.

''What's wrong with Jessie?'' Thad asked.

''Your sister's had some bad news.''

''About Pa?''

Jessie knelt in the dirt and stared deeply into her little brother's eyes. ''There's been some terrible mistake. I'm going to have to clear it up.''

''Mistake?''

''The marshal's holding a man for rustling. They think it's Pa. We're going to have to get over there and see who this imposter is.''

"Let's go then." As she started to stand, Thad said softly, "Jessie?"

"Yes, Tadpole?"

"What if it is Pa?"

She pressed her forehead against his. "It can't be. We know Pa wouldn't steal cattle."

"Yeah." The little boy handed her the reins of her horse. "Yeah. That couldn't be Pa in jail."

As her brothers pulled themselves into the saddle, Jessie met Cole's dark somber gaze. She looked away quickly, hating what she saw. Pity. And what was worse, knowledge. The knowledge that the man in jail could be her pa. And if so, because of some terrible misunderstanding, he would die in the morning.

They fought their way down Texas Street, clogged with farm wagons, mule trains and horses until they came to the marshal's office. Tying the horses, Jessie caught her brothers' hands and took a deep breath before leading them inside.

A man looked up from behind a desk. His shirt was stained with sweat. The buttons of the shirt were straining under his enormous bulk. Tufts of gray hair were plastered to his head. The butt of a cigar was clamped between yellowed teeth. "Something wrong, miss?"

"No, sir. I mean, yes, sir. Are you the marshal?"

"Marshal Tom Smith is over at the Merchants Hotel having supper. What can I do for you? I'm Deputy Grundy."

The man didn't make a move to stand, and Jessie realized that it would probably be too much effort.

She glanced around and moved closer to the desk. "My brothers and I are here to see the man calling himself Jack Conway."

"You can see him in the morning," the man said, suddenly frowning. "Swinging at the end of a rope."

"You don't understand," Jessie said, beginning to talk faster as she always did when she was nervous. "Our pa is named Jack Conway, and we know he's no cattle thief. So that means that the man in your jail has stolen our pa's name. We want to find out why, and where our pa is.''

The deputy glanced from Jessie to the man who stood behind her. ''You with the lady?''

Cole nodded.

''Then I'll tell all of you. No one gets to see the prisoner. He was found guilty by a federal judge in a court of law, and tomorrow morning he'll hang for his crimes. And until then my orders are to see that no one gets near him.''

''But our pa's been gone for months now. This man might know where he is.''

''I have my orders from Marshal Smith.'' He glanced at the girl, appreciating the way her slim hips were molded in the britches, and dragged his gaze to the boys who stood on either side of her. ''For all I know, you might be bringing him a gun so he can kill himself rather than face hanging.''

''We'll be happy to hand over our weapons to you,'' Cole said quietly.

The deputy stared pointedly at the Colt Army .44 resting at Cole's hip. ''Even without their guns they aren't going to see him, mister. No one is going to see that prisoner until tomorrow when he—''

Cole cut him off sharply. ''Jessie, you and your brothers wait here. I'll go find Marshal Smith.''

''The marshal won't like having his supper disturbed,'' the deputy said with a sly grin. ''And believe me, when the marshal is unhappy, someone usually lands in a jail cell.''

''Don't go, Cole. Don't rile him.'' Jessie thought about all the times Cole had watched over his shoulder. Like a man on the run from the law. ''We'll just wait until he comes back.''

''Marshal isn't coming back until morning,'' the deputy said.

''I have to see this man who's stolen my pa's name.''

''You'll see him.'' Without another word Cole turned and stormed away.

Jessie herded her brothers from the room, unable to bear the way the deputy was looking at them. Outside she led them to a wooden bench and sat down between them, drawing them close to her for comfort.

"Cole will get the marshal to let us in," Danny said with more confidence than he felt.

Jessie felt her heart sinking. What would they do if Cole landed in jail, too?

"Sure he will," Thad echoed. "And when we talk to him, he'll tell us where Pa is. Maybe he's hiding until this hanging is over."

"Why would Pa hide?" Jessie hoped the boys wouldn't notice the slight tremble in her voice.

"'Cause he's innocent and somebody stole his name."

Jessie's mind was whirling with so many fears, so many thoughts, she could no longer sort them out. They sat in the shadows, watching as cowboys staggered from saloons and disappeared into the night. They listened as gunshots echoed in the street. They heard the tinny sounds of a piano and the rough language of the trail bums and the laughter of the women who entertained in the upstairs rooms of the almost-hotels. And as the night wrapped itself around them, they huddled together and waited. Waited for Cole to work a miracle and get them permission to see the imposter. Waited for dawn, when a man would hang for stealing cattle.

The marshal was young—not quite thirty—with slicked-back dark hair beneath a wide-brimmed hat. His neatly trimmed mustache enhanced strong, even features and a slightly cruel mouth. He had a walk that was more a swagger and there was an air of superiority about him. He had, after all, been hired by Mayor Henry to clean up Abilene. And that was what he intended to do. He was paid one hundred twenty-five dollars a month and two dollars for every arrest.

The signs in every public place demanding that firearms be deposited with the proprietor had been his first step in the campaign to clean up this violent town. The public hanging of a cattle thief would be the second. When the cowboys who ran roughshod over the good citizens of this town saw that he meant business, they would obey his laws without question. Or cool their heels in jail until they learned to live by the rules. At two dollars a head he just might become a very rich man.

He would never have given up his supper for any ordinary citizen's request. But the man striding along the dusty street beside him was no ordinary man. Even without the six-shooter at his hip, Cole Matthews would have been a man of impressive authority.

As the two men approached the jail house, Jessie and her brothers scrambled from the wooden bench and stepped from the shadows.

"So. This is the young lady who would like to meet the prisoner." The marshal tried not to stare at the beautiful young woman in men's clothes. As she moved further into the light that streamed from the window of the jail house, his eyes widened. She wasn't just beautiful. She was stunning. Not at all what he'd expected.

"I'm Marshal Tom Smith, ma'am." He touched the brim of his hat. "Mr. Matthews has made me aware of your concern about the prisoner's identity. If you'll follow me, I'm certain we can clear this up in a matter of minutes."

As he led the way, Jessie dropped a protective arm about her brothers. They followed him into the jail house. At the first sight of the marshal, the deputy was on his feet. His mouth gaped in surprise. "Marshal Smith. Didn't expect you back tonight."

"The young lady and her brothers want a look at the prisoner." Taking up a lantern, he opened an inside door and led the way to the cells.

Jessie and the others deposited their guns on his desk and followed.

A tall rangy cowboy jumped up from a bunk and gripped the bars of his cell. "About time, Marshal. I've been expecting my boys to get me out of this manure pile." Seeing Jessie, he added, "Excuse me, miss. Didn't mean to talk like that in front of a lady."

"Sit down, Purdy," the marshal shouted. "I told you you wouldn't be leaving with your drovers in the morning, and I meant it."

"My boys will tear this place down before they'll leave me behind." The cowboy's hands twisted at the bars until his knuckles were white from the effort. "I'm the trail boss. Without me no one gets paid for this drive."

"You should have thought about that before you shot up Morgan's Saloon. In my town, mister, I don't abide drunken behavior from no-good Texas cowboys."

As Jessie followed the marshal toward the next cell, she felt the touch of the cowboy's hand on her hair. Wide-eyed, she turned, only to find sad dark eyes burning into hers. "I have a wife at home in Texas who looks a lot like you," he muttered. "She'll be worried sick when I don't return with my boys."

"I'm sorry." With nothing more she could say or do, Jessie hurried past.

The marshal stopped at the second cell and held up the lantern. Jessie saw a tall broad-shouldered figure turn from the high narrow window where he'd been staring into the night.

"Got a visitor, Conway. This young lady and her brothers think you stole their father's name."

Jessie stepped closer while her brothers crowded around beside her. The man's face was in shadow. He crossed the narrow cell. As the marshal lifted the lantern even higher, illuminating the handsome Irish face covered by a bristly beard, Jessie let out a cry.

"Oh, dear God in heaven. Pa! It's you. Pa."

Chapter Twenty-One

"Jessie. Oh, honey." The man stared at her as if seeing a vision. He was rooted to the spot, unable to move. "How'd you get here, girl?"

"I—" she tried to swallow the lump that was stuck in her throat. "—just kept looking until I found you."

"All the way from home? All alone?"

"I had some company." She moved aside to reveal Thad, who was clinging to her pocket, and Danny, who was partially hidden behind her. "We've been searching for you for so long."

Jack Conway's eyes widened. "Danny. And Thad." Tears glistened on his lashes and he didn't bother to wipe them. In a voice choked with emotion, he whispered, "My babies. My babies came clear to Abilene to find me. And you find me here in this stinking jail on the last day of my life."

"No." Danny grabbed at the bars and his fingers tangled with his father's. "You're not going to die. We're not going to let them hang you, Pa."

The man's voice grew tender. "Look how tall you grew, son. Why, I think we can practically look each other right in the eye."

"You listen to me, Pa. They're not going to hang you." Danny's tone sounded sterner than anyone had ever heard.

234 *Texas Heart*

"We won't let them. We'll explain that this is some terrible mistake."

"There's no mistake," Marshal Smith said calmly. "There's already been a trial. A witness identified Jack Conway as the cattle thief. And a federal judge has ordered him to be hanged."

"Who was this witness?" Jessie demanded.

"A very respected man in this town. Mr. Y. A. Pierce, who is one of the biggest trailing contractors in Abilene."

"A trailing contractor?" Cole's eyes narrowed fractionally.

"Mr. Pierce runs cattle for small ranchers who can't afford to pay men for the months it might take to drive a small herd to Abilene for shipment."

"Isn't he the man who talked you into joining his cattle drive, Pa?"

Jack Conway nodded at his daughter's question.

"For a fee," the marshal explained, "he puts together drives that total several thousand head. He supplies the drovers, the chuck wagon, cook and food, and here in Abilene, the pens and storage until the cattle can be sold and shipped." Marshal Smith spoke in tones that left no doubt that he greatly admired Y. A. Pierce. "Some day Mr. Pierce will be a giant in the cattle industry."

"Mr. Y. A. Pierce is a damned liar," Jack Conway growled.

"The words of a convicted cattle rustler hold no weight with me." The marshal made a move to shepherd them from the room.

"Marshal Smith," Cole said in a dangerously low voice, "I suggest we leave this family alone for a private visit. They've come a long way to find their father."

"A dangerous criminal can't be…" The marshal's words died in his throat when he saw the icy look in Cole's eyes. He cleared his throat. "I suppose a few minutes can't hurt."

He set the lantern on the floor and led the way back to the front office. With a last glance at Jessie and her family, Cole followed.

As soon as they were alone, Jessie, Danny and Thad reached

through the bars to touch their father. With tears streaming down his face, he gripped their hands, stroked their faces and drank in the sight of them as only a condemned man could do.

"What happened, Pa?" Jessie's voice was barely more than a whisper.

"Pierce is the biggest thief I've ever met." Jack Conway's voice was filled with contempt. "But the marshal was right about one thing. Someday Mr. Pierce will be a giant in the cattle industry. He persuades poor dumb ranchers like me to entrust their cattle to him, then he robs them blind and gives them less than half what their cattle earned. And expects us to thank him."

"You mean he's stealing from everybody?"

Conway nodded his head. "Pierce controls the market here. If the buyers don't offer him top price for the beef, he stores them until the price is driven higher. He charges the poor ranchers not only for the drovers, but for the price of feeding the cattle until they bring the higher price. And he keeps the high price and pays back the lower one. If he bothers to pay at all."

"You mean some ranchers don't get paid?"

"If there's enough profit to be made, he'll see that the rancher meets with an 'accident' rather than share the wealth."

She felt a chill along her spine. "Why did he accuse you of rustling?"

Jack Conway lowered his voice and motioned for his children to draw closer. "I found out about the money box."

"What money box?" Jessie drew an arm about her little brother and felt him clutching at her for support.

"Mr. Y. A. Pierce had thousands of dollars in a strongbox. When I happened across him counting it, he lied and said it was going to be used for wages the drovers had earned. But when we reached Abilene, he told us he had no money to pay us. He told us we could go home and wait for him to pay us later, or stay in Abilene until he got enough money from the sale of the herd."

"You mean he expected the ranchers to go home without their pay?"

"He knew we couldn't afford to. But we couldn't afford to stay, either. We didn't even have the price of a room or a meal."

"What happened to the money box, Pa?"

"I stole it."

"What?" Jessie sucked in her breath. "Why?"

"Because it was the only way to prove that he was lying. He was never going to reveal that money, and I knew it."

"Where is it now, Pa?"

He lowered his head and whispered, "Where Pierce can't find it. That's why he framed me for cattle rustling."

"How did he frame you, Pa?"

"He arranged to have some of the cattle moved, then accused me of stealing them. The rest of the drovers knew how many head we'd brought in, and they counted nearly two hundred head of cattle missing. They never would have guessed that he stole his own cattle."

"Didn't you tell the judge the truth? Didn't you tell him about the strongbox?"

"The federal judge was only interested in stopping the large-scale stealing that's been going on for the past two years. Like most folks, he thinks that a man like Y. A. Pierce is too rich to need to steal. And as for Marshal Smith." He gave a snort of disgust. "The marshal knows that this hanging will make him a legend in the West."

Jessie saw his lips tremble for a moment before he went on. "I guess I did only one thing right in this world. I raised some pretty fine children, didn't I? And if I have to hang for a crime I didn't commit, then I figure the three of you are going to get rich from the crime I did commit."

"No, Pa. We aren't taking that money chest," Jessie said, anticipating what her father had in mind.

"With no pa and ma, you're going to need all the help you can get."

''The Bible says 'Thou shalt not steal,' Pa,'' Jessie hissed. ''And nothing good will ever come from it.''

With a thoughtful look Jack Conway tousled Thad's hair, so like Jessie's, so like his dead wife's, and felt a hard lump settle in his throat. In a whisper he said, ''My baby rode over six hundred miles. I guess that means you aren't a baby anymore.'' He lifted a hand to Danny's shoulder and felt the solid muscles beneath his hand. ''A man. You've become a man while I was away.'' With a bittersweet smile touching his lips, he reached a callused finger to Jessie's cheek. ''Soft. So soft. When did you become as pretty as your ma?''

Guilt over what he had done warred with the need to secure his children's future. When he spoke, Jack Conway's voice held a note of resignation. ''I want you kids to leave tonight. I don't want you anywhere near here tomorrow when they hang me. They're going to make a celebration out of my hanging, and I want to die knowing my kids were spared.''

''We're not going,'' Jessie said with a sudden vehemence.

''Don't you get ornery with me, girl.'' Jack Conway's voice took on the old familiar tone of authority. ''You may be tough enough to watch your old man swing from a tree, but you're not putting your little brothers through a thing like that.''

''You don't understand,'' Jessie said quietly. ''I have no intention of watching them hang you.''

''Then get out of this town. Tonight.''

''No.'' He saw the way her jaw set. Hadn't she inherited that obstinate streak from him?

''Damn it, Jessie. You listen to me.''

''No, Pa. You listen to me. We're not running away. And you're not hanging in the morning.''

''You got a plan, Jess?'' Danny felt a sudden urge of adrenaline. He'd seen that look in his sister's eyes a thousand times before. And always it meant that Jessie was about to dig in her heels.

''Not yet. But I'll think of something. I've got to get out of here, Pa. I need a place to think.''

She pressed close to the bars and strained to place her lips

on her father's bearded cheek. He bent close and touched callused fingers to her face. Danny and Thad caught their father's
hands and felt his fingers dig into their flesh.

"We'll be back, Pa. Before dawn. And when we return,
we're not leaving without you." As she opened the door to
the marshal's office, Jessie heard Cole's voice, low, insistent.

"...willing to testify, if the federal judge wants to hear me."

Jessie motioned for her brothers to be quiet. Keeping the
door open a crack, she watched and listened. Cole was facing
the marshal. His features were grim.

"Good. That's good." Marshal Smith had his back to Jessie. But she could almost see the grin on those cruel lips.
"We've been wanting to stop this rustling operation for two
years. And if what you say is true, and we have the big man
right here in our clutches, the judge will be more than happy
to listen to a federal marshal of your reputation."

At his words, Jessie sucked in her breath. This didn't make
sense. Cole, a federal marshal?

Through the maze of questions that whirled in her mind,
she forced herself to listen to Marshal Smith's next words, "It
was lucky for all of us that you teamed up with those kids
when you did."

"Yeah. Lucky." Cole's voice was devoid of all emotion.

Jessie closed the door and pressed her back against it, feeling a wave of nausea. Shock wave after shock wave rolled
through her, leaving her numb. Lies. Everything Cole had ever
said and done. Lies. All the kindnesses to her brothers. All the
things he'd whispered. All the love they'd shared. All lies. All
just an opportunity to find her father.

Tears stung her eyes, but she blinked them away. Never
would she allow herself to cry over a liar and a cheat. Cole
Matthews was as good as dead to her. He had broken her heart.
But he wouldn't win. She would see to that.

"What's wrong, Jess?" Danny studied the whiteness about
her lips and feared that she was about to collapse. Maybe the
long journey and the shock of their father's conviction was
too much for her. Never had he seen her look so fragile.

"It's—Cole." She could barely bring herself to speak his name. It hurt. Oh, how it hurt. "He's a federal marshal."

"Marshal? He's a gunman, Jess. A man on the run."

"Don't you see? That was all just an act. He's been lying to us so he could find Pa."

"No!" Danny started toward the door, but Jessie caught him by the shoulder. "Let me go, Jess. I'm going to tell him what I think of his lies."

"I have a better idea." Her tone was low, angry.

"What?" Both Danny and Thad watched her closely.

"We'll pretend to think he's still our friend. And whatever we decide to do about Pa, we'll have to keep from Cole. We can no longer trust him." She remembered what Pa used to say about not trusting fast women or men who wore badges. How right he'd been.

She pulled open the door and led her two brothers into the marshal's office. Immediately Cole and Marshal Smith stopped speaking.

"You ready to go?" Cole asked.

Jessie couldn't bring herself to look at him. If she did, she knew he'd read the pain in her eyes. And the fury. Instead she kept her gaze firmly fixed on the floor. "We thought we'd take the horses to the stable and see if we can sleep there."

"Good idea." Cole noted her pallor and wished he could comfort her. What a shock it must be to find, at the end of a torturous journey, that the father she had sacrificed everything for was about to hang for cattle rustling. "I'll join you there when I've finished up here. I have some important things to do first."

Jessie took up their guns, then dropped an arm around her little brother's shoulders and led him from the jail. Behind her, Danny cast a long speculative look at Cole before turning away.

When they left, the marshal took a gold watch from his pocket. "We're going to be cutting this close. Think there's time?"

Time. Cole thought with a sinking heart. If only there were more time. Time to get this untangled. Time to work it all out.

"There has to be," he said, swinging away. "We'll make every minute count."

As soon as they left the marshal's office, Jessie drew her brothers into the shadows.

"Now what, Jess?"

"I don't know. Let me think a minute." She paced back and forth, back and forth. From somewhere beyond, in the darkness behind the jail, she could hear the low hum of voices. Moving deeper into the shadows, she rounded the corner of the jail. There were two small windows set high in the building. One of them, she knew, was in Pa's cell. The other would be above Mr. Purdy's.

Purdy. What had he said to the marshal? A thought flitted through her mind. The beginnings of a plan.

Nearby she heard the shout of a drunken cowboy and the report of gunfire. It was just another cowboy letting off steam, but someone had to investigate. Within minutes she heard the deputy shuffle away from the jail.

A harness jingled as someone hitched a team. She strained in the darkness to make out the shapes. A mule team, she determined. Ten mules. The plan became clearer. Without taking the time to think it through, she whirled and headed toward the saloon. Danny and Thad had to run to keep up with her.

"Where are we going, Jess?"

"To Morgan's Saloon. And when we get inside, we're going to ask if anyone is from Mr. Purdy's crew."

"Why?"

"Because we need to find his cowboys if we're going to help Pa."

"I don't understand." Danny caught her arm, but she kept on going. "What do Purdy's men have to do with Pa?"

"You'll see." She pushed open the swinging doors and strode inside. Behind her trailed Danny and Thad.

At a table in the corner of the room, half a dozen men were

playing cards. At the bar several women dressed in gaudy gowns were talking to the customers and drinking watered-down whiskey. One of the women spotted Thad and sauntered over, hands on hips, a teasing smile curling the corners of her painted lips.

"A little bit young, aren't you?" She grinned as the men around the bar began to laugh.

"Yes, ma'am." Thad snatched his hat from his head as he'd been taught by Jessie.

"You looking for a good time?" the woman said to Danny, running a hand suggestively along his arm.

He blushed and drew his arm away. "No, ma'am. We're looking for Mr. Purdy's men."

One of the men from the poker game looked up at the mention of his boss.

"You're looking in the wrong place for Purdy. He's in jail."

"We're looking for his men," Jessie said, feeling her cheeks redden as several men turned to study her.

"You're looking at them." The man discarded a card and accepted another from the dealer. "What do you want with us?"

Jessie glanced around and realized that almost everyone in the saloon was watching and listening.

"I—I can't tell you here. But I have a message from your trail boss. And if you're interested in hearing it, meet me behind the stable in five minutes."

"Five minutes?" A man on the stairs paused with his arm about the waist of a smiling woman. "Hell, honey, I can't finish my business in five minutes."

Jessie blushed clear to her toes as the room erupted in laughter. Then she said angrily, "Five minutes. Anyone interested had better be there."

Motioning to Danny and Thad, she spun around and ran in her eagerness to get away from this horrible place. Outside she continued running until she reached the stables. Once there she whispered her plan to her brothers. Before she had even

finished, there were a dozen armed men standing quietly behind her, waiting for her to speak.

These men weren't laughing and making rough jokes now.
They were scowling. And watching her with such intensity
that Jessie felt tiny beads of sweat form on her forehead. Whatever her plan was, it had better be good. If these men didn't
cooperate, there wouldn't be time for a second plan. In fact,
if she didn't quickly persuade these men, she and her brothers
might find themselves at the wrong end of a gun.

Chapter Twenty-Two

"You want us to tear down the jail?"

The men who had crowded around her so eagerly now stepped back a pace as if to better study this strange little creature.

"What were you doing talking to Purdy?"

"I was in the jail...visiting the marshal," she lied.

"And right in front of the marshal, Mr. Purdy suggested a jailbreak?"

"Of course not." Jessie tried her sweetest smile. "I found myself alone with him for a minute, and he whispered his plan."

"Sounds like the ravings of a drunken cowboy," one of them said.

Several joined in the nervous laughter.

"Fine. If you want to go home without your pay and wait until your trail boss gets free, go ahead. But if you'd like to buy your wives some pretty dresses before you get home, I think you'd better listen to me."

When she saw their smiles fade, Jessie began to speak quickly before she lost them.

"That old jail is just made of rocks and dried mud. One good team would bring it down." She paused to study their faces and went on, "I happened to see a mule team down the street. Freshly hitched and ready to go, if a man was willing to chance it.''

"I can drive a team better'n anyone here," one of the drovers said with pride. "You just tie a rope to the windows of that jail, and I'll make that team move like they've never moved before."

Jessie shot a knowing glance at her brothers. "We'll do the tying," she said. "We'll need some of you to cause a commotion at the other end of town in order to distract the marshal. Think you can handle it?"

The men grinned. "Have you ever seen a bunch of thirsty cowboys who didn't know how to cause a commotion?"

"You'll need a fast horse for Mr. Purdy," Jessie added. "Once that jail comes down, the marshal will be hot on our trail."

"I'll take care of his horse," one of the men said.

"Then I guess we're all set. Let's move."

"Just a minute," one of the men said, shoving his way to stand in front of Jessie. "What's in this for you, girlie?"

She swallowed and decided to gamble with the truth. "My pa's in jail with Mr. Purdy. We aim to break him out, too."

The man studied her for long silent minutes. Nodding, he turned to the others. "What're we waiting for?"

Jessie let out the breath she'd been holding and dropped an arm around her little brother. "Thad," she whispered, "it's up to you to have our horses ready."

"I'll have them."

"Good boy. We'll see you at the jail in a few minutes."

She hugged the young boy close, then touched Danny's sleeve. "Come on. We have work to do."

At the sound of gunshots from the far end of town, the marshal's door opened. From their hiding place in the shadows, Jessie and Danny watched as Marshal Smith and Cole strode from the jail and ran toward the commotion.

"Come on."

Moving quickly through the shadows, Danny hoisted Jessie

on his shoulders while she tied a sturdy rope around the bars of Pa's upper window.

"What the hell are you doing?" came a whispered voice from within.

"We're breaking you out of here, Pa," she called. "When this wall comes down, be ready to ride."

"Are you crazy? You'll have us all shot."

"That's better than being hanged, isn't it? At least this way you'll have a fighting chance."

"I won't have my babies risking their lives." Jack Conway reached as high as he could and twisted his fingers around the bars as if to stop her.

"We're not babies, Pa." Her voice faded as she leaped from Danny's shoulders to the ground. "And it's our decision."

He heard the slight muffling sounds outside, as well as his daughter's lowered voice at the window above Purdy's cell.

"Who's there?" Purdy called out.

"Jessie Conway. Stand away from the window, Mr. Purdy. We're about to haul this wall down. And when we do, you and your men had better ride like the wind. 'Cause Marshal Smith is going to be as mad as a hornet."

Jessie knotted the rope around the bars and gave it a quick tug. Leaping once more from her brother's shoulders, she and Danny watched as the drover led the mule team toward the jail.

"Oh, no." Danny gave a low moan as the sounds of gunfire began moving closer toward them. "The commotion is coming this way. Hurry."

As the sounds moved even closer, Jessie and Danny fumbled with the ropes, struggling to secure them despite fingers that were awkward with nervousness. When they were finished, they nodded to the drover.

"You know what this makes us, Jess?" Danny gave his sister a final solemn look.

"I know. Criminals. Jailbreak is a serious offense. If we're caught, we could all hang."

"Are you scared, Jess?"

She threw her arms around his neck and hugged him fiercely. "I'm scared to death. But we have to save Pa."

"I know," he breathed against her temple. "I know, Jess. I'm with you."

They drew apart and watched as Thad approached on horseback, leading three horses.

"Where'd you find Pa's horse?" Danny called.

"In the stable. They were probably going to sell him after the hanging," Thad whispered. "His saddle, bridle and saddlebags were still in the stall. So I helped myself to them."

"Good boy." Jessie hauled herself into the saddle and gave him a trembling smile.

The drover lifted a whip to the team. For one terrible moment they held their breaths as the team strained against its burden. Then, with the sound of mortar cracking and rocks tumbling, the entire wall of the jail crumbled and fell. Within minutes the roof of the jail house caved in on itself. In the dust and confusion, Big Jack Conway stumbled forward, wiping his eyes as if unable to believe what had happened.

"Pa. Over here." As he staggered about, unable to get his bearings, Jessie grabbed the reins of his horse and hurried forward.

"Come on, Pa. We have to ride."

The gunshots were now directly in front of the jail house. There were shouts and curses, and Jessie knew that the marshal had discovered the jailbreak.

As her father pulled himself into the saddle, Jessie saw Mr. Purdy mount and join the crowd of drovers who were racing out of town, scrambling for safety.

"Thad, you take the lead," she called.

The little boy leaned low over his horse's head. Behind him, Danny cradled the buffalo rifle in his arms and followed. Jessie waited until her father passed her safely, then took up the rear.

For a few confused minutes the gunshots faded as the marshal and his deputy, along with Cole, assessed the situation.

Cole took a moment to study the cloud of dust that still swirled around the pile of rubble that had been the jail. The mule skinner whose team had been used in the jailbreak was hopping around, swearing a blue streak and examining his animals for injuries. A crowd had begun to form as cowboys and saloon girls joined the townspeople from nearby houses, murmuring among themselves about the brazen trail crew who could pull off such a bold jailbreak.

Realizing that they were losing their prisoners, the marshal and his deputy leaped on their horses and began a hasty pursuit.

Deep in thought, Cole hesitated a minute longer. It was true that Purdy's men were the ones to cause the ruckus at the other end of the town. And there was no doubt who had handled the team. It would take a damned good drover to drive a mule team of that size. But there was more to this than a couple of drunken cowboys freeing their boss. Purdy was only going to spend a couple of weeks in the jail, until the marshal was satisfied that he'd learned his lesson about getting drunk in Abilene. Jack Conway, on the other hand, was about to be hanged in the morning. And he was gone, too. Conway and his family. Without a trace. With a string of oaths, Cole realized that Jessie had outsmarted him. Once again, he hadn't counted on her determination. Somehow in that devious little mind of hers, she had come up with a way to use Purdy's men to her advantage.

At the sound of gunfire, he came out of his reverie with a start. Jessie. She could be killed before he could intervene.

Cursing to himself, he leaped onto his horse and raced toward the sound of gunshots.

Marshal Tom Smith was mad. He'd staked his reputation on this hanging. And now everything was going wrong. As he rode, he nursed an unreasonable sense of frustration.

He was furious with Cole Matthews, the most feared man in Texas, for barging in and stealing his thunder. He was furious with Purdy for making him look foolish in front of the entire town. And he was furious with Big Jack Conway and his family for ever having lived.

Purdy's men had wisely separated, breaking into clusters of three or four and taking different paths. That way, the marshal would have to decide which group to follow. In the confusion, Smith knew most of them would manage to escape. Most, but not all. He was still marshal of this town. And someone, by thunder, would pay for this humiliation.

Up ahead he spotted four horsemen. Turning his mount, he raced along, straining to keep them in sight.

"Halt," he shouted. Above the sound of thundering hooves, his words were lost. "Stop or I'll shoot."

The horses in front of him continued their frantic pace without even pausing. He aimed his gun and fired, then emptied his gun in the darkness.

Ahead of him Jessie flattened herself in the saddle and urged her mount to go even faster. At the sound of gunshots she saw her father jolt and crouch low in the saddle. As they entered a thicket, Jessie ignored the little stabs of pain as tree branches snagged at her hair and clothes. Ride, her heart cried. Ride until they were free of this place forever. Ride until they could put this nightmare behind and return to their beloved home.

The way Jessie figured it, they had five hours before daylight. If they were to make good their escape, they had to keep riding until then. And by the first light of day they would have to find a place to hide until darkness could cover their trail once more.

They raced through the dry flat land of Kansas, keeping well away from marked trails. Occasionally they heard the shout of a rider or the crack of gunfire, but they were able to keep to the shadows and avoid being seen. Once the marshal and his deputy passed so closely Jessie could hear what they were saying, could actually smell the sweat and leather and horseflesh. But the trees and rocks blended into the shadows, affording them perfect cover. When the lawmen were far enough away that the clatter of hoofbeats couldn't be overheard, Jessie motioned for the others to follow.

Whenever they could, they rode flat out, running the horses

until their energy began to flag. Then they would walk them until their breathing became easier. By pushing hard, they managed to pass by Newton while the residents of that sleepy cow town were still in bed.

At a creek they watered the horses and filled their canteens.

"Are you all right, Thad?" Jessie asked.

"I'm fine."

"We won't be able to stop until morning." She gave him a worried look. He was so young to have to face up to such a grueling journey. With this act, she had placed his life in jeopardy.

"I'm not tired, Jessie. I just want to get Pa home."

"I know." She drew Thad close, and both glanced at their father, slumped in the saddle, accepting a drink from Danny's canteen.

"Let's move," he called hoarsely.

Jessie helped her little brother mount and pulled herself wearily into the saddle. There was only another hour of darkness left. And then they would seek shelter for the day.

The farmhouse built into the slope of a hill had long since been deserted, an apparent victim of fire and neglect. The only thing left standing was a stone chimney. The single outbuilding was no better. Though it had escaped the fire, the roof had collapsed, crushing the walls inward, leaning at drunken angles toward each other.

"There's no shelter to be found here, Jess." Danny surveyed the scene with a rising sense of panic. Already the sky was light. If they were being followed, they would be easy prey in this wretched landscape.

"We can't go on." Jessie slid from the saddle and led her horse, kicking at the debris.

"We can't stay here." Danny glanced at his father, expecting him to agree. Instead Jack Conway leaned forward in the saddle, his face nearly buried in the horse's mane. His eyes were closed, his breathing labored.

"This was once a working farm. There must be…" Jessie

stopped and studied the tangle of vines on the far side of what was once the big sturdy house. Stooping, she began frantically pulling at the vines.

"Here. Danny." At her words, he ran to her side and stared. Beneath the vines was a wooden door. Both Jessie and Danny pulled on it with all their might. Though the hinges protested, the door slowly opened, revealing a musty root cellar. Jessie tied a rag to a stick and from her precious store of matches lit it. Holding the torch aloft, she entered the cellar and peered around.

The dank, musty odor of rotted fruit and moldy earth pervaded the air. Cobwebs hung from rafters. Forest creatures had obviously discovered the treasures hidden here, and their tracks were visible in the earthen floor.

"There's room for us and the horses," Danny said behind her, "but what about food? We didn't even think to load our saddlebags with anything."

"I'll hunt a rabbit before going to sleep," she assured him. "You make a small fire inside. We can let it simmer all day while we sleep. By the time we're ready to move out, we'll have enough food cooked for the next two or three days."

Danny nodded. "I'll go get Pa and Thad."

Jessie watched as he strode away. Minutes later she heard his frantic cry. "Jess. Come quick."

With her gun in her hand she dashed from the cellar. For a moment she gazed around in consternation. There wasn't a rider in sight.

"What is it? What's got you so upset?"

"It's Pa, Jess."

She glanced at the figure in the saddle. "Pa?" Moving closer, she reached a hand to him. "Pa? What's wrong?"

As she touched his shoulder, he toppled from the saddle and lay unmoving in the grass. Rolling him over, Jessie touched a hand to the dark stain covering the front of his cowhide jacket.

"God in heaven. Pa's been shot."

And from the amount of blood that had soaked through his clothes, he'd been bleeding profusely all night.

Chapter Twenty-Three

They rolled their father's big frame onto a blanket, and with the three of them pulling, pushing and dragging, they managed to get him into the musty cellar.

Once he was safely hidden, they hurried outside to cover their tracks. Mindful that they were being followed, Jessie took pains to sweep away every sign that the dust and debris of the old house had ever been disturbed. She scattered dirt over the trail left by the heavily burdened blanket. She replaced pieces of chimney stone and charred wood until at last satisfied, the three hurried inside to see to their father's needs. While Jessie cut away his jacket and shirt, Danny prepared the necessary supplies. Rummaging through their saddlebags, he found soap and an old shirt that could be torn into strips. In his father's saddlebag he located half a bottle of precious whiskey.

At the sound of horses' hooves above them, Jessie looked up. "Horsemen. Coming this way." Her eyes reflected the fear and dread she felt.

She hurried to the cellar door, opened it a crack and grasped a handful of vines, shaking them so that they would drift down over the door, then closed it carefully.

For long minutes the horses could be heard moving across the space where only a short time ago they had dragged their unconscious father's body. Jessie clung to Thad's hand and found herself wondering if they had managed to erase all their

tracks. What if the horsemen could see the trail they had made
with the blanket and its heavy burden? What if someone saw
a sign that the debris had been disturbed? Worse, what if
someone spotted the cellar door and decided to take a closer
look?

They heard muffled voices, but were unable to make out
the words. Was one of the riders Cole? He had been the one
to teach them everything they knew about erasing any trace
of their presence. With his trained eye he would spot even the
smallest detail out of the ordinary. Jessie strained to identify
the voices. The deeper pitched voice had to belong to Marshal
Smith. The other was higher pitched. His deputy, she thought.
There were several other men cursing and shouting. None of
them was Cole. Of that she was certain. Had he gone on ahead
to scout the terrain? Or was he following with a second band
of men? She fought to shake off the terrible sense of loss.

Jessie glanced at Danny. Though he had to be aware of the
danger of being discovered, he continued to bind his father's
wounds. The lantern she had found on a shelf in the cellar
cast flickering shadows on the earthen walls, magnifying and
distorting each of Danny's movements. She felt a welling of
emotion. He was so brave, this brother who had the gift of
healing. And somewhere along the trail he had become a man.
A man who could forsake his own needs to see to the needs
of others.

She patted Thad's arm and walked back to assist Danny.
Picking up a rag, she mopped at the beads of moisture dotting
her father's brow and was grateful that he had lapsed into
unconsciousness. He made no sound that might give away
their presence in this underground shelter and alert the men
who searched just a few feet above them.

When at last the sound of hoofbeats faded into the distance,
Jessie threw open the door of the cellar and allowed the fresh
clean air to enter the musty dwelling.

As bright morning sunlight penetrated the gloom, she studied the figure of her father. The blanket upon which he lay
was soaked with his own blood. His skin was a sickly gray.

His breathing was labored, and as she bent closer she could hear the rattle of fluid in his lungs. The fear that sliced her was sharper than any razor.

In a muted whisper she said, "You've done all you can, Danny. Now you and Thad must sleep."

"What about you, Jess?"

"I'll find something for our supper. Then I'll join you."

"I'll start a fire." Though he made a move to help, Jessie noted that Danny's movements were slow and awkward.

"No. You've done enough. Sleep. Without it, we're all lost."

She watched as Danny and Thad curled up beside their father. Within minutes they were asleep.

Picking up the rifle, she made her way to the thicket in search of game.

When at last rabbit meat simmered in a pot over hot coals, Jessie climbed into her bedroll beside her father and gave in to the overwhelming weariness that enveloped her. Before she drifted off to sleep, her last thoughts were of Cole. Cole. Jessie's heart contracted. She had loved him, truly loved him. But he was a lawman sworn to do his duty, no matter what. And she had chosen the other side of the law. They were forever divided. There would be no going back now. He was lost to her forever.

The sun hovered on the horizon, casting ribbons of fire across the land. The air was still, with no breeze to stir the leaves. Jessie watched as her father struggled to sit up.

"You'll tear open that wound if you move, Pa," she scolded.

"We're leaving," he said through gritted teeth. "If we stay here another day, they'll find us."

"If you try to ride, you'll bleed to death."

"I'd rather bleed to death in Texas than die in this godforsaken hole. You heard me, girl. We're riding."

She glanced helplessly at Danny and saw him shake his head. They both knew the danger of trying to travel before the wound had healed. But Pa knew it, too. And he was willing to risk dying rather than stay here another night. If there was one thing she was sure of, it was that none of them would win in an argument with Pa. He was the most stubborn man ever born.

"All right, Pa," she said grudgingly. "We'll ride. But as soon as you start to bleed, we stop. Agreed?"

He nodded and bit down on the pain as he struggled to stand. Jessie saw him blanch before pulling himself to his feet.

She packed their food into saddlebags and helped Thad saddle the horses. When everything was ready, their father, leaning heavily on Danny's arm, came slowly from the cellar and pulled himself into the saddle. Jessie saw him wince and knew what it was costing him to attempt to ride. Though she wanted to cry out in protest, she kept her silence. Texas. Home. It was the one thing that kept Pa going. It was what kept all of them going.

With Danny leading, they headed out into the darkness.

They rode by night and slept by day, using any shelter they could find.

Each night Danny tended his father's wound. And though her brother said little, Jessie knew that the wound was not healing properly. Without prolonged rest Jack Conway's body couldn't fight the infection. The strain of hours in the saddle caused the wound to bleed anew each night. And the loss of so much blood was draining the once vigorous body. But though he suffered unbearable pain, they never once heard their father complain or ask to rest.

At Caldwell they spotted a fresh body hanging from the tree. Jessie felt her skin crawl as they rode past the gruesome sight. Seeing it renewed her determination. They had done the right thing for her father, she knew. The only thing.

Leaving Caldwell behind, they plunged into Indian Territory.

By dawn, Jack Conway was too weak to sit in the saddle. When they stopped in the shelter of a rock ledge for the day, they found that he had dug his hands into the horse's mane and held on by sheer willpower alone. As soon as the horses halted, he fell to the ground and lay motionless.

"Pa." Danny leaned close with his ear to his father's chest. At Jessie's worried look, he nodded his head to indicate that he had found a pulse. It was faint and thready, but still there. "Pa. Can you hear me?"

"Don't...stop." Jack Conway began coughing, and Jessie watched with horror as a fresh trickle of blood oozed through his shirt.

"We have to stop, Pa," Jessie said, kneeling beside him. "It's daylight. We have to rest here until dark."

Her father's hand found hers and grasped it painfully. Despite his wound there was surprising strength there.

"Promise me," he whispered, "that we won't stop until we reach Texas."

"You need to rest, Pa." Jessie knew she was close to tears, but she couldn't seem to control her emotions. "If you don't give yourself time to heal, you'll never see Texas."

"I'll...see...Texas." The hand holding hers went slack. She realized that once again he had slipped into blessed unconsciousness.

The sun hovered on the horizon, a brilliant orange globe that seemed to ignite the sands. Jessie shifted and sat up, rubbing her eyes. Beside her, Danny and Thad were still asleep. They had slept the entire day. As she turned to study the figure of her father, she caught a sudden movement out of the corner of her eye. Instantly she reached for her gun, then froze.

A Comanche sat astride a spotted pony. Beside him two braves struggled to fasten something to her father's horse.

"Runs-Like-Antelope." She stood facing the cousin to Two Moons, who had given them safe passage on their earlier trek through Indian Territory.

Immediately Danny and Thad awoke and sat up. Beside them their father stirred and tried to rise. Wincing in pain, he fell back and was forced to listen helplessly.

"You must move quickly," the Comanche chief said. "The white men who follow you are not far behind."

"My father is gravely ill."

He nodded towards the poles covered with hides that were being affixed to her father's horse. "It will carry him."

She stepped closer. "Thank you. I can't give you anything in payment."

"I know of your kindness to one of The People. Morning Light is daughter to my father's brother. There are no debts between us."

She felt the sting of tears at his kindness. "We'll leave as soon as it's dark."

"No." Runs-Like-Antelope held up his hand. "You must travel by day, as well as night."

"The men following us will find us."

"My people will see to it that no trace of your tracks remain."

She watched as the Indians moved away and disappeared beyond a ridge of rock.

As quickly as possible, she and her brothers settled their father on the travois, covering him with a hide. Pulling himself into the saddle, Danny took the lead. Thad caught the reins of their father's horse and led him behind his own mount. Jessie took up the rear, keeping an anxious eye on her father while she rode. Though he was in obvious pain he made no sound of protest.

She clung to the tiny thread of hope. Within days they would be back in Texas.

What had started out as a fine misty rain in the morning had become a drenching downpour. They rode all day, pulling their cowhide jackets around them, wearing wide-brimmed hats to keep the rain from their eyes.

Jessie had tucked the hides firmly about her father, covering even his head, so that the only parts of him exposed to the rain were his eyes and nose.

They reached the Red River in late afternoon. At Jessie's

orders they steered a wide berth around Doan's Store, keeping far enough away so that any drovers there wouldn't see them as they crossed into Texas. Because of the rain, the water was swirling as high as their horses' bellies.

Danny cast a worried look at Pa, then at his sister. "What'll we do now, Jess?"

"I—can—ride." They heard Pa's voice, muffled beneath the hides.

Danny shook his head emphatically and waited for Jessie to do the arguing. Instead she merely nodded. "There's no other way."

"He can't do it, Jess."

"He can. He will." Wearily she climbed from the saddle and began unfastening the hides that secured their father. "Come on, Danny, Thad. Give me a hand."

Big Jack Conway leaned heavily on his children as he struggled to pull himself into the saddle. As his horse waded into the river, the others mounted and rode beside him. As soon as they were on the other side, he slid from the saddle and slumped to the ground. Immediately Jessie knelt by his side.

"Listen," Pa whispered to Jessie so the others wouldn't hear. "The gold is buried in a grave in Abilene. The tombstone reads *J. Conway, 1870.*" At Jessie's little gasp he chuckled. "They buried a rustler who had no name. At least none they knew of. So I gave him my name. And my gold, when everyone was gone."

"Why are you telling me this now?"

"Because the day may come when you'll need that gold. It'll still be there a year from now. Or ten years. If you change your mind and want it, it's yours for the taking."

"I don't want it, Pa. I'll never want it. I'll help you back to the travois." Jessie began to stand.

Pa held up a hand. "No more."

"We're in Texas now, Pa. We're halfway home."

"No." As Danny and Thad looked on in dismay, he took a fit of coughing. When it was over, fresh blood oozed through his jacket. His voice was little more than a raspy whisper. "I've gone as far as I can go. But at least I'll die in Texas."

"Don't talk like that." Danny took a step closer and touched a hand to his father's forehead. His skin was on fire. Danny pulled his hand away as if he'd been burned.

"Dying's not so bad," Pa whispered. "At least I'll finally be with your ma again." He closed his eyes. "I've missed her. Missed her so much." His eyes blinked open, and for a moment he couldn't seem to comprehend the three strangers who stood watching him. Then a look of recognition flickered in his eyes.

"Jessie," he whispered, "you're just like me, girl. Too tough and ornery for your own good. But you look like your ma. Like an angel."

Jessie felt the beginnings of a lump in her throat and swallowed.

"Danny." Pa reached out a hand to his older son and felt the strength as Danny grasped his palm. "You have a special gift, boy. Use it to heal."

"Gift." Danny's voice was rough with emotion. "If I can't save my own father, what good is it?"

"You don't understand, do you, son?"

At Danny's questioning look he whispered, "I don't want to live anymore. It hurts too much. Let me go, son. You have to learn to let go sometimes. But never stop using your gift for others."

He turned his head slightly to study the little boy who stood back, his eyes round with fear. "Thad." Reaching out a hand, Pa grasped the boy's pudgy fingers and drew him close. "You're so young to be without parents. But you've got Jessie and Danny. I know they'll take good care of you, Thad."

"Yes, Pa." The little boy's voice trembled with unshed tears.

"You're mighty good with horses, boy. But there are other things in life. Take the time to get to know people. I'm afraid I kept you to myself too much."

"No, you didn't, Pa."

"I was selfish, boy. I was afraid, after losing your ma, that I might lose you, too. All three of you," he added, gazing at the three faces who were watching him with such concern.

"I was too hard on you, Jessie," he said, reaching out for her hand. Instantly she grasped his hand and squeezed. "I leaned on you, girl. And you never let me down. Not once." For a moment his eyes closed, and Jessie shot a worried glance toward Danny. But before the boy could search for a pulse, Big Jack Conway opened his eyes once more. His hand squeezed Jessie's until she nearly cried out.

"Promise me something, Jessie."

"Anything, Pa. Anything."

"I want you to take the boys back East to my brother's. Sell everything and make a fresh start in Boston."

"Pa..."

"Promise me." The words were ground out between clenched teeth. "I want a future for my babies."

"I'll do it," she whispered, feeling the lump growing until she could no longer speak.

"That's my girl." He relaxed his grip. His eyelids flickered, then opened. He tried to say something more, but though his mouth moved, no words came out.

Jessie squeezed his hand and felt the tears sting the back of her lids. "Pa," she whispered.

He didn't answer. She touched a finger to his throat. Even while Danny followed her example and reached for a pulse, Jessie was pressing her father's lids closed.

"You made it to Texas, Pa," she sobbed. "You made it home."

They buried Big Jack Conway beside the banks of the Red River. While Jessie gently washed the blood and dirt from her father's face, Danny dug into the soaked earth. With each shovelful of dirt his features hardened, his grim mouth tightened. So much for his dream of becoming a doctor. He had failed his own father. Failed miserably. How could he possibly think he could save others?

When at last the hole was wide enough and deep enough, he pulled himself up and wiped his mud-stained hands on his pants before walking to where his father's body lay.

The three of them struggled under the deadweight, but at last the hide-wrapped body was laid to rest in the earth.

"I think we should say some words." Jessie's voice was hushed.

"Do you know any?"

She searched for the appropriate Bible verse, but her mind had gone blank. While she twisted her hands, little Thad's voice broke through her thoughts.

"You used to read to me from the Book of Psalms. Do you remember?"

Jessie nodded, and Thad's childish voice recited the words she had so often read by candlelight in their little sod house.

"'And he shall be like a tree planted by the waters of the river. And he shall bring forth his fruit in his season. Through his children and his children's children, his leaf shall not wither.'"

As Jessie stared at the grave, she felt the tears well up and begin to spill over.

And then the little boy's voice grew stronger. "'Yea, though I walk through the valley of the shadow of death, I will fear no evil. For thou art with me.'"

His words unleashed a torrent of tears in Jessie. She stood in the rain and wept, feeling a terrible welling of emotions.

Beside her, Danny stared at a spot of dirt, refusing to look at the body of his father deep in the earth. As he reached for the shovel, Thad touched a hand to his sleeve.

"Danny, it's all right to cry."

"Men don't cry." He pulled away and lifted the first shovelful of earth.

"Cole told me that when his ma died, his pa cried like a baby. And Cole said his pa was the strongest man he'd ever known."

"Cole told you that?"

"Yeah." The little boy watched as Danny's lower lip began to tremble.

"What did he do while his pa cried?"

Thad swallowed. "He held him in his arms and cried, too."

"Oh, Thad." Danny fell into his little brother's arms and wept as though his heart would break.

Stunned, Jessie took a step toward her brothers and wrapped her arms around both of them. And while they held each other, they cried until there were no tears left.

Chapter Twenty-Four

The three slept beside their father's grave because they couldn't bear to leave him alone in the rain. And in the morning, they unhitched the travois and laid it in the grass beside the grave, knowing that the Comanches, watching from across the river, would retrieve it when they were gone.

They bid a last tearful farewell to their father, then rode south, leading his horse.

Though their hearts were heavy, they never looked back. They were criminals now, hunted in their own land. There was no more time for grief. If they were to survive, they would have to be alert to every danger.

They traveled by night and slept by day, keeping away from familiar trails. When at last they reached the border of their neighbor's land, they breathed a sigh of relief.

"We'll stop by the Starkeys' place and see if they'll make us an offer on the ranch."

Danny shot his sister an incredulous look. "You're really going to sell our ranch?"

"We have no choice. I promised Pa. Besides," she added grimly, "we can't stay here. We're wanted by a federal marshal."

She saw the look in her little brother's eyes and said softly,

"You're too young to be held accountable for what was done, Tadpole. But the law would take you away from me. And that would be worse than any prison."

She wheeled her mount, unable to bear the look in his eyes, and led the way to the Starkey ranch.

Jed and Sara Starkey and their three brawny sons came together from various parts of the ranch to greet their long-absent neighbors.

"Come on in," Sara said, pulling off the apron that struggled to span her ample girth. "There's cold buttermilk and fresh biscuits."

As she dismounted, Jessie was caught in a great bear hug. She inhaled the fragrance of flour and spices and felt a fierce longing for home.

"You've gotten even thinner," Sara said before releasing her. "I'm going to send my boys over with some of my home-made molasses cookies and see if I can't fatten you up a bit. Now," she said, turning to plant wet motherly kisses on Danny and Thad before leading them inside, "tell us where you three have been. We've been keeping an eye on your place and still haven't seen a trace of that father of yours."

Jessie explained their journey and their father's death, while leaving out the part about the jailbreak.

"And so," Jessie said when she had finished her story, "I thought you folks might like to buy our ranch and herd."

Jed Starkey leaned his sparse frame back in his chair and drew on a pipe, then watched the wreath of smoke curl above his head. Around the big oak table his three boys glanced at each other and smiled.

"It just so happens that Amos here has found himself a woman," Jed said with a grin. "And he's been talking about bringing a bride to live at our place. This could be a windfall for us. Your place adjoins ours, and we'd be close enough to lend a hand to each other."

Jessie stared at the table, unable to bring herself to look at Danny or Thad. "How much could you afford to pay me, Mr. Starkey?"

The older man glanced across the table at his wife, who nodded her approval. "I can give you two hundred dollars now. When we've had a chance to build up the herd, we could send you another two hundred dollars."

Jessie swallowed. Four hundred dollars for a lifetime of labor and love, laughter and tears. They were bartering away her life, her dreams. "That's fine, Mr. Starkey. I can send you an address as soon as we get settled. When can you give me the two hundred dollars? We'll need it for the trip East."

"I'll come by in a day or two. I expect you'll need a little time to pack up." He shoved back his chair and extended his hand. "I'm sorry you and your brothers are leaving. You've been fine neighbors." He glanced at Thad. "But I suppose life will be better for a youngster in the East."

Jessie nodded, keeping her gaze averted. "Yes, sir." She thanked Sara for the food and nodded toward her brothers. "I guess we'd better head for home."

Home. The word brought a fresh stab of pain.

The Starkeys walked them to their horses. Sara thrust several linen-wrapped packages of cold meat and biscuits into Jessie's hands.

They exchanged final words and waved as they rode away. Jessie and her brothers rode over twenty miles in silence, each lost in private thoughts.

When at last they stood on a ridge and gazed down at their ranch, Jessie felt a welling of such deep emotion she could hardly contain herself.

Home. For all of her seventeen years, this had been the only home she had ever known. This rough, barren landscape and this poor sod shack were more beautiful than any mansion. And she was coming home for the last time.

Jessie's horse, sensing its familiar corral, broke into a run. Jessie gave him his head and turned to see the others galloping behind her. Within minutes they were turning the horses into the corral and filling a trough with water. They walked arm in arm toward the sod shack and stepped inside, squinting against the unaccustomed gloom. Behind them, someone slammed the door and threw the bolt. Before Jessie could re-act, she felt the cold steel of a pistol against her temple.

"It's about time you got here, girlie," a man's voice said. "Where's Big Jack Conway?"

Shock waves jolted through her. "Who are you? What do you want with us?"

"I said, where's your father?"

"He's—" she ran a tongue over lips gone suddenly dry. "—dead."

She heard an angry hiss followed by a stream of savage oaths.

As her eyes adjusted to the dim light, she felt a wave of terror. Facing her was a tall man with long stringy hair and gaping yellow teeth. The man who had attacked her when she had first set out on her journey.

"Knife." His name was wrenched from a throat constricted with fear.

He laughed low and menacingly. "You remember me, do you, girlie? Well, you and me are going to get to know each other a whole lot better before we're through. I still intend to brand you with this little baby—" he held up his knife with the intricately carved handle and pointed the blade at her heart "—after I'm through having some fun with you."

"Enough, Knife," the other man said. "Business before pleasure. My name is Y. A. Pierce."

Jessie felt her heart tumble. The man was dressed in a fancy black suit and wide-brimmed hat. No wonder Marshal Smith had been dazzled by him. He had the appearance of a very successful rancher. Not at all the cold-blooded killer Pa had described.

"Since your father has met with an untimely demise, I will have to assume that he told you his secret before going to the grave. Now you're going to tell us where he hid my gold. Or I will be forced to let Knife have his way with you."

Cole knelt in the dirt and examined the still-warm trail. Since his odyssey began, Cole had become an expert at tracking killers. And the two men he was tracking were vicious killers. They had exchanged horses twice since leaving Abilene. The first time, they had slaughtered six Comanche warriors, along with their squaws and children, just for the sake of two horses. The last time was at a ranch about a hundred miles from here. They'd broken into the ranch house and shot the rancher and his tiny infant daughter. Even now Cole could not get the image of the rancher's wife out of his mind. She had not been as fortunate as her husband and baby. She had been brutalized before they had finally, mercifully, killed her.

Cole pulled himself into the saddle and urged his horse into a trot. As he scanned the landscape, he found himself thinking once more about Jessie. With a sense of sorrow he tried to banish the thought from his mind. Jessie was lost to him. That part of his life was forever gone. She and her brothers had been a brief, wonderful fantasy. Now it was time to face the harsh reality of life. Since he had first witnessed the death of his father at the hands of this man, Cole had dedicated himself to putting an end to his reign of terror. He had earned a reputation as the toughest lawman in Texas. He would not rest until the man was stopped.

Cole thought about his beautiful ranch here in Texas. Since he had accepted this thankless task of searching, hunting, he had not been home. A year. One whole year, and he had not slept in the big feather bed or watched the peace of a sunrise or the beauty of a sunset over his vast holdings. He'd been denied the frenzy of a branding and the touching miracle of a calf being born. The ranch was now in the hands of a foreman, a friend who would do his best to keep it the way it had always been. The graves of his parents and brother and sister lay on a steep hill overlooking a lush, fertile valley. He yearned to visit them, to draw strength from the land that had been in his family for three generations. But he could not rest until this thing was finished. By then, Jessie could be anywhere, he thought, running a hand wearily across his eyes. He would have to be content with the memories. But, he knew, she would haunt him until his dying day.

How she would have loved his ranch. She was born for such a place. In no time, a woman like Jessie would have it humming with life, with laughter, with—children. He closed his eyes for a moment, savoring the vision of Jessie walking toward him in the creek, offering herself in love. She was magnificent. She hypnotized him. She thrilled him. He frowned suddenly. She infuriated him. Marshal Smith had reported that they'd found no trace of her or her family. The little witch had spirited her father and brothers away to Indian Territory. Once there, Cole knew, the Comanches would shield her from view.

Be safe, Jessie, he breathed. Wherever you've gone, be safe.

He pushed on, keeping his gaze on the fresh trail. Soon, soon he would catch up with the man who had shot his father in the back. The same man who had cheated and killed ranchers from one end of Texas to the other. And when he did, only one of them would walk away.

As he topped a ridge, he stared down at the little sod shack, the poor neglected ranch. In the corral stood several horses. He would stop here a minute and refresh himself. And he would ask if any strangers had passed this way in the past day.

Jessie stifled a scream as Knife held the blade to Thad's throat.

"You'd better hurry up and tell Mr. Pierce what he wants to know."

Her mind raced. She knew that the minute she told these men the location of the gold, she would seal the death of her brothers and herself. A man as prominent as Y. A. Pierce would never be foolish enough to leave witnesses to his crime.

She had to find a way to keep her brothers alive.

"Please." She held up a hand and the two men watched her through narrowed eyes. "Pa mentioned the gold. But we were trying to stay one step ahead of the marshal. There was no time to talk about it."

"Don't play games with me, Miss Conway," Y. A. Pierce said coldly. "You're a very clever young lady. A man as stupid as Knife here might believe your lies. But I'm no fool. I know that a man like Conway would want to provide for his children's futures. Even in death he would have found a way to tell you where he buried my gold.''

Knife gave an evil leer. "Give me a few minutes with her alone, Mr. Pierce, and I'll have the information you want.''

Pierce seemed to consider that for a moment, noting the fear that crept into the girl's eyes. "Perhaps you're right, Knife. You do have a—knack for getting what you want.''

The long-haired man grinned and began walking toward Jessie. "Come on, honey. You and me are going to have a real good time.''

"Tell him, Jess.'' Danny's voice stopped him.

Jessie shot a look toward her brother that pleaded with him to be quiet, but he persisted. "I mean it, Jess. Tell him what he wants to know. We don't want the gold. You know you'll never use it.''

"Smart boy.'' Knife grabbed Jessie by the hair. He pulled hard, jerking her head back painfully. "Looks like your brother doesn't want to see my initials carved into his sister's pretty skin.''

"I don't know where the gold is.'' She spoke each word carefully, staring directly into Knife's narrowed eyes.

"I'm about to make a liar out of you, girlie.'' As he fastened a hand around her throat, they heard the sound of a horse's hooves.

Instantly Y. A. Pierce aimed a gun at Jessie. "Expecting anyone?''

She shook her head.

"Knife. Keep the boys out of sight. If either of them makes a sound, slit their throats.'' As Knife motioned for the boys to move to a corner of the room, Pierce caught Jessie roughly by the arm and dragged her toward the front door. "I'll be standing right behind you, Miss Conway. Unless you get rid of whoever this is, you'll be dead before he can step inside.'' He dug the pistol into her back and hissed, "Is that understood?''

Jessie nodded.

She stood at the door and listened as booted feet moved nearer. A knock sounded. Jessie threw the bolt and pulled open the door. And found herself face-to-face with Cole Matthews.

Cole felt as if he'd just taken a blow to the stomach. For a minute he was speechless. Then, finding the words, he said, "Jessie."

Was it really his Jessie? For long moments he simply stared at her, drinking in the tumble of golden curls, the mouth pursed in a little meow of surprise.

She couldn't speak. She felt a wild rush of emotions as she stared into the face of the only man who would ever hold her heart. Cole. She wanted to weep, to throw her arms around his neck and beg him for help. She wanted to cry out that their lives were in danger. He was a gunman. A cold, calculating gunman. She'd seen the look in his eyes when he'd first encountered Knife and the others threatening her. He'd killed three of them without a moment's hesitation.

But now. She felt a sudden rush of sheer terror. Even Cole couldn't save all of them in time. Some would have to die.

"Is this your ranch?"

She made her decision instantly. She couldn't risk it.

"Yes." She felt the pistol pressed between her shoulder blades and flinched. Her mind raced. If Pierce discovered that there was a federal marshal outside her door, he would shoot Cole before he even had a chance to defend himself. She had to be as cold as possible and get Cole away from here before his identity was discovered. Even though it meant that she and her brothers would once again have to face these men on their own.

"Are you alone?"

"My—brothers are here with me."

"Where are they?"

"Out on the range right now."

"And your father?"

She swallowed. "Pa died. We buried him on the banks of the Red River."

"I'm sorry, Jessie." He reached out a hand to touch her and she drew back, resisting his touch.

Feeling her rejection, Cole experienced a thrust to his heart as painful as any knife wound. He couldn't really blame her. He'd kept his identity a secret. In fact, he'd shared very little of himself with her. They had loved. Desperately. But he had kept himself, his life, apart from her. She had every right to hate him. But he owed her the truth.

"Your father's name has been cleared, Jessie."

Her eyes widened. "How? Why?"

"I met privately with the federal judge and testified that Jack Conway couldn't have been the cattle thief."

"How could you know that?"

"It doesn't matter now. All you need to know is that the Conway name has been cleared of all criminal charges."

Tears blurred Jessie's vision and she blinked them away. "Thank you for that, Cole. At least Pa has died with a clean record."

"You weren't listening. The record of the entire Conway family is clear. Your name's been cleared, too," Cole said softly. "The judge is convinced that you and your brothers acted out of desperation to save your father's life."

She let his words sink in. "We've all been cleared? We're no longer wanted criminals?"

The warmth of his words washed over her. "You were never a criminal, Jessie. But let's just say that the marshal has more important things to do than chase an ornery little woman and two kids through Indian Territory. He figured it was easier to clear your record than to chase you halfway to hell and back."

The beginnings of a smile on Jessie's lips faded as Y. A. Pierce jammed the pistol against her back and whispered, "Get rid of this trail bum. Or he dies."

"Thank you, Cole. For everything."

She made a move to close the door, but he stopped it. "Wait, Jessie."

For a brief moment their fingers touched. Jessie felt the heat and closed her eyes, absorbing the shock of his touch.

Cole studied her, drinking in the haughty upturned nose, the eyes the color of a stormy sky. "Is everything all right?"

"Everything's—fine."

She said the words quickly, the way she always did when she wanted to be convincing. Cole lifted an eyebrow and tried to peer beyond the slightly open door. But all he could see was Jessie barring his way. He felt the familiar prickly feeling and knew that something was wrong. Very wrong.

"I thought I might stop here a while."

"I'm sorry. I've sold the ranch and there's a lot to do before we leave for the East."

"East?" He experienced an ache around his heart that left him stunned.

"It was Pa's last request before he died. He asked me to sell the ranch and take my brothers East for a proper upbringing. My neighbors, the Starkeys, have agreed to buy the ranch."

He stared deeply into her eyes and saw a flicker of emotion. Just as quickly, it was gone.

"Then I guess I'd better be on my way." He touched the brim of his hat and turned away.

"Cole." She spoke his name with a sense of desperation. But as soon as the word was out of her mouth, she realized her foolishness. Jessie sucked in her breath as the gun was pressed so hard against her back she could feel the heat from the gunman's hand.

He turned. "Yes?"

She bit her lower lip to keep it from quivering. "Safe trip."

"Thanks."

Jessie stood a minute longer, staring hungrily at the width of his shoulders, the slope of his waist, the power in his thighs as he moved. And then the door was forced shut, and she was slammed against the wall of the shack.

"You're testing my patience, woman." Pierce slapped her so hard her head was snapped to one side. With a growl he added, "We'll just wait a minute, to make certain your cowboy leaves."

Everyone in the room grew silent, listening to the sound of fading hoofbeats. Knife stood by a window and watched as the rider disappeared over a rise.

"He's gone. Wish I'd had a look at his face. Something about his voice bothers me."

"A passing cowboy doesn't worry me." Y. A. Pierce motioned to Knife. "It's your turn. Do anything to the girl you'd like. Just get me the information I want."

Chapter Twenty-Five

Cole urged his mount forward until he was safely over the rise. Then, sliding from the saddle, he turned and studied the little sod shack and the surrounding countryside. Though everything appeared quiet and normal, he sensed that something was very wrong here.

It was true that Jessie had every right to treat him with disdain. But her conversation had been too stilted. With the shock of her father's death and the ordeal of selling the ranch, even a strong woman like Jessie should have displayed some emotion at seeing him.

Emotion. That was what was wrong. She neither laughed nor cried. Merely listened to his words and made polite responses.

As he studied the land, he realized that the tingling sensation hadn't ceased. It was still there. And so was the danger.

Taking his rifle from the boot, he made his way back toward the sod shack.

He'd been so sure of himself. He'd planned everything— the way he'd track the killers, the way he'd confront them. But suddenly everything had changed. He had no plan now, no way of knowing how he would react. Because he hadn't counted on seeing Jessie. The sight of her left him confused, disoriented.

Jessie. His hand clenched firmly around the butt of the rifle.

If she was in any danger, if so much as a single hair of her head was harmed, he'd track the ones who did it to the ends of the earth.

He bit down hard on the rage that seethed inside him. She was so good, so decent, and she'd been through more than most people suffered in a lifetime. He had to be certain she was safe.

When he drew near, he crawled on his stomach and inched closer until he reached the ranch building. Circling the shack, he paused beneath the only window.

Slowly, carefully he straightened until he could peer inside. What he saw from his narrow vantage point made his blood run cold.

Thad and Danny were seated on the floor in a corner of the room, staring tearfully toward Jessie, who was facing a man with a knife. The same long-haired man who had once before held a knife to her throat.

The man moved closer to her, reached out with the blade of the knife and held it to the top button of her faded shirt. With one quick motion he cut away the fabric and moved the knife lower to the second button.

Cole's hand tightened around his gun.

"Now, honey." Knife's words filtered through the window, causing a chill to course along Cole's spine. "We're going to see just how long you can keep your little secret." He turned to Danny, who sat frozen in horror, and Thad, whose cries sounded like the bleating of a lamb. "If either of you two boys knows anything about the gold, I'd advise you to speak up now." He laughed with a low scratchy sound that stretched their nerves to the breaking point. "Or you'll get to see how much fun a pretty thing like your sister can be."

Gold? Cole had no idea what the man was talking about. At the moment, it didn't matter. All he cared about was Jessie. This crazed gunman had somehow found her and was tormenting her again. The fury inside Cole erupted. Racing around the shack, he kicked in the door, startling the occupants.

"Drop the knife, or I'll blow you away where you stand."

Knife whirled and stared in surprise at the man who had once before held a gun on him. "You. I knew I recognized that voice."

Cole's words dripped venom. "Drop the knife and step away from the woman."

Jessie's eyes widened and she cried out a warning, but it was too late.

A voice behind Cole said, "I'm afraid you're the one who'd better drop the weapon."

Stunned, Cole turned to find himself staring at a face he'd carried in his memory for over a year. The face of the man who had shot his father in the back like a coward.

"You'll drop your gun," Pierce said, grabbing Thad and pressing his pistol to his head, "or the boy dies."

Cole remembered a time when he would have calmly shot the man's gun away without even giving a thought to the boy in his arms, and would have spun around and killed the knife-wielding madman, as well. But that was before Jessie's love had touched him in a special way. Knowing what Jessie and her brothers meant to him now, he couldn't risk harming them.

Cole's gun fell to the floor.

"Knife," Pierce shouted, "take up his weapon."

Instantly Knife picked it up and grinned. "This is the cowboy who spoiled all my fun the last time. And the one who was with the girl in the hotel in Fort Worth. Now," Knife said, his lips curling in a sneer, "let's see how brave you are without your gun."

"I don't have time for your little game of revenge," Pierce barked. "Finish with the girl and get the information. I'm tired of waiting for my gold."

"What's this about gold, Jessie?" Cole turned to her and cursed himself for the terror he could read in her eyes.

"This man is Y. A. Pierce."

Pierce. At last, he had a name to go with the face he'd carried in his mind for so long.

"When Pa found out that he was cheating the ranchers, he

stole Mr. Pierce's strongbox filled with gold. To get even, Mr. Pierce accused my pa of cattle rustling.''

''And my little plan was working perfectly until you came along and spoiled everything with that jailbreak. Now, Miss Conway, for the last time,'' Pierce said with a low growl of anger, ''tell me where I can find the gold. Or would you rather have Knife persuade you?''

''Tell him, Jessie.'' As he spoke, Cole stared around the little sod shack, his mind alert for anything that could be used as a weapon.

''I can't tell him.'' Jessie's mouth was a thin taut line of anger. ''As soon as he has the information he wants, he'll kill all of us.''

''I'll get it out of her, Mr. Pierce. Let me have her.'' Knife dropped Cole's pistol on the small kitchen table and turned toward Jessie.

Cole mentally gauged the distance between himself and the pistol on the table and realized he was too far away to make it before Pierce could shoot him. There had to be another way. In the meantime, he had to keep everyone talking.

''Maybe you should think of the consequences, Jessie.'' Cole studied the man who still held a gun on them. He was a big man, who, from the looks of his portly middle liked to eat well. He would be slow, but the gun gave him a distinct advantage. If he had to run at one of them, Cole decided, he'd take the one with the knife. The man would be quicker than Pierce, but there might be a chance to wrestle the weapon from his hands. And in the commotion, maybe Pierce wouldn't be able to get off a shot in time.

Jessie saw the way Cole's gaze shifted about the shack and felt a faint glimmer of hope. They'd been beaten before and managed to survive. Maybe, just maybe...

Lowering her gaze, she took a step toward Knife. ''Maybe, if you promised to spare my brothers, I could be persuaded to tell you where the gold is.''

For a moment Knife's eyes widened with disbelief. Then a

slow smile crept across his ugly features. "You think you can sweet-talk me into saving your hide, too?"

She swallowed her feelings of revulsion and kept her tone as soft as possible. "If you do, I'll stay with you."

"Don't be a fool," Pierce snapped. "The girl is just trying to buy a little time."

"So what? It's been a while since I had a warm, willing woman."

"Like the rancher's wife?" As Knife reached out toward Jessie, Cole charged forward, throwing all his weight against him.

Both men went down in a tangle of flying fists.

"Stop. I said stop." Pierce aimed his gun and shouted a second time, but Cole and Knife continued fighting, rolling about the floor. Suddenly there was the horrible sound of a gunshot, and blood spurted from the head of Knife. The bullet had missed Cole's head by inches.

As Knife lay lifeless, Pierce crossed the room to stand over Cole. "I certainly don't need you, cowboy," he hissed. "Or the boys. The only one I intend to spare is the girl. And when I've finished with the rest of you, she'll tell me where to find my gold."

Cole came to his knees and faced Pierce. "I've been searching for you for a very long time."

"Searching for me?" Pierce hesitated. "Why?"

"My name is Cole Matthews. You're the man who killed my father."

The man studied Cole closely, noting for the first time the steel-gray eyes and the firm jaw so like another he'd known. "Matthews. Of course. Colin Matthews. Owned the biggest ranch in Texas. Trusted me to drive his cattle to Abilene over a year ago." Pierce chuckled. "Your old man bankrolled my success."

"You shot him in the back like a coward."

"I'm no fool. I knew his reputation with a gun. If he'd seen me, I'd be lying in a grave right now instead of him."

"But I saw you. Though I didn't know your name, I saw

you for one moment before one of your men split my skull and left me for dead. That's how I convinced the judge that Jack Conway couldn't have been the rustler.'' Cole's voice was edged with steel. ''I vowed I wouldn't stop until I made you pay.''

''Really?'' Pierce's smile grew. ''If you know any prayers, you'd better say them. You're about to join your father.''

As he aimed the gun, the silence was broken by the sound of gunshot. For a moment Y. A. Pierce seemed to turn toward the sound with a look of complete surprise on his face. As he lifted his gun, a second gunshot echoed through the room. Y. A. Pierce slumped to the floor.

Everyone turned to stare at the one who had pulled the trigger. Little Thad stood beside the kitchen table. In his hand was Cole's gun.

''You said some day you'd teach me to shoot.'' His voice trembled. ''Did I do it right?''

Cole crossed the room, took the gun from Thad's hand and drew the little boy firmly into his arms. Against his tousled hair, he whispered, ''You did just fine, Thad. You did just fine.''

''I'll be back in a couple of days to take possession of your ranch.'' Jed Starkey climbed up to the seat of his wagon and picked up the reins.

Jessie nodded, avoiding the pained looks in her brothers' eyes.

The Starkeys' wagon rumbled away from the little sod shack toward the nearest town, over a hundred miles away. Inside the wagon were the bodies of Y. A. Pierce and Knife, along with the papers Cole had signed and sealed, notifying the federal judge that he was resigning his position as federal marshal. From now on he would be Cole Matthews, rancher. Also in the wagon was a letter from Jessie explaining where her father had buried the gold. She'd added that she hoped it would be turned over to the ranchers or their widows who had been cheated out of their money by Y. A. Pierce.

Cole stood with Jessie and her brothers, shielding the sun from his eyes.

When they had all recovered from the shock of what had happened, he had listened quietly as Jessie prepared her brothers for their imminent departure.

Cole thought of all the words he wanted to say, but through it all he kept his silence. She had a right to want a better life for all of them. Look what this harsh land had done to her. And look what it was doing to Danny and Thad. Danny's only hope of becoming a doctor was the education offered by the schools in the East. And Thad. The seven-year-old had already killed a man. In defense, of course. But nevertheless, he had fired a gun and killed a man. Maybe in the East, Cole thought with a frown, the boy would have a chance to grow up gently.

When the wagon topped a ridge and drew out of sight, Jessie turned toward the shack. Cole began saddling his horse.

"You're leaving?" Thad's voice quavered.

"Don't worry," Cole said, dropping an arm about the boy's shoulders. "You're safe now. Mr. Starkey said his boys would be over later tonight with some supper." He glanced toward the towering buttes in the distance. "And the Comanches have been true to their word. They would never defy their chief and cause you any harm."

"I'm not worried about Indians or gunfighters," Thad said. "I'm worried about Jessie."

"Your sister is one fine woman." Cole's eyes narrowed thoughtfully. "She's a survivor."

"Not always. Not this time," Danny said bitterly, coming up behind them.

Cole turned and studied the tall youth. "Mind your sister, Danny. She's got good sense."

The three turned and watched as Jessie walked from the small shack carrying some linen-wrapped food. She handed it to Cole. "This will keep you until you reach a town."

"Thanks." He stowed the food in his saddlebags and turned back to her. "Sure you won't change your mind about heading East?"

She shook her head firmly, avoiding his eyes. She had already waged a terrible battle with herself. But in the end, it was her promise to Pa that had won out over the ache in her heart. "I promised Pa."

"Yeah." He bent and touched his lips to her cheek. Instantly he felt the rush of heat and cursed himself for his weakness. Even now when she was lost to him forever, he wanted her as he'd never wanted anyone in his life.

She took a step back in order to break contact. The touch of him was so painful she wanted to cry. Instead she lifted her chin in a defiant gesture.

"Safe journey, Cole," she said, avoiding his eyes.

"And safe journey to all of you." He shook hands with Danny and Thad and pulled himself up into the saddle.

There were things he wanted to say, but he knew they'd sound foolish. How could he tell them they'd become the family he'd lost? How could he tell them that his life would be one long endless stretch of empty days and lonely nights without them? How could he tell Jessie that she had spoiled him for any other woman?

He touched the rim of his hat in a salute and wheeled his horse. Without a backward glance, horse and rider headed out in a cloud of dust.

Danny turned on Jessie with a display of fury she'd never seen in him before.

"I can't believe you'd let him ride out of here."

"What right have I to stop him? He has a home to go to. It's time for him to put his life together again."

"And what about us? Don't we have any rights?"

She touched her brother's arm in an attempt to placate him. "Danny, I promised Pa, remember? You wouldn't want me to go back on a promise, would you?"

"Pa didn't now what he was asking of you. He never would have asked if he'd known how you felt about Cole."

As she stared in openmouthed surprise, he went on, "You know what's wrong with you, Jess? You're just too stubborn for your own good. You never listen to what we want. You just go on doing what you want and expecting us to live with it. Like that damnable trip across Texas.''

Jessie started to reprimand him for his swearing, but his anger stopped her.

''You expected Thad and me to just wait here until you came back. But you were wrong. You needed us.''

Blinking, she said, ''You're right, Danny. I did need you. Both of you.''

Thad grinned. It was the first time he'd ever heard his sister admit to a mistake.

Danny added, ''You're crazy if you head East just for me and Thad.''

''A promise is a promise.''

He threw his hat down in the dirt in frustration. ''Hellfire and damnation! Can't I get you to listen to anything without interrupting?''

''Don't swear. You know how I feel about swearing.''

''I'll swear if I want. And you listen, Jessie Conway.'' He grabbed her by the shoulders, towering over her. ''I've grown up a lot in the last months. What I really want to do is go East and study so I can return to the West as a doctor.''

''Then why are we arguing?''

''Because you and Thad don't belong there. Thad can get just as fine an education in Texas, and a whole lot more love from you than from an aunt and uncle he's never met.''

''But I—''

''You promised Pa you'd look out for us. And the way I see it, Cole Matthews would be a better man for Thad to imitate than any man I know. On Cole's ranch Thad would be surrounded by the horses he loves and the people he loves— you and Cole. And that brings me to the most important thing, Jess.''

She tried to interrupt, but he held up his hand.

''Whether you want to admit it or not, Jess, you love Cole Matthews. And he loves you. And if you don't tell him now, he's going to be gone from your life forever.''

''Since when did you get to be an expert on love?''

"Since I saw the way you and Cole were with each other. It's the way I remember Ma and Pa when I was little."

At the mention of that, tears sprang to her eyes, and she brushed them away with the back of her hand. "Oh, Danny. How can I tell him? It's already too late."

Danny awkwardly patted her shoulder, straightened and handed her the buffalo rifle. "I guess you'd better think of something fast, Jess."

He and Thad grinned as Jessie studied the rifle for a minute before breaking into a run across the dusty yard toward a small rise. From that position she could just make out the form of a horse and rider topping a distant ridge. Aiming the rifle at the sky, she pulled the trigger. As she toppled backward, a terrible explosion thundered across the heavens.

She got to her feet, rubbing at the tenderness in her backside, and saw the horse and rider drawing nearer. In her excitement she began to run toward them. When they were close enough, she could read the worry etched on Cole's brow.

"Jessie. What's wrong? Are you hurt?"

"Yes." Tears sprang to her eyes, and she blinked them away.

He slid from the saddle and grasped her by the shoulders, staring down into eyes that were clouded with pain.

"What's wrong? What's happened?"

"It's my heart," she whispered.

He touched a hand to her breast and felt the wild beating of her heart.

"If you leave me, it will never heal."

"I thought… Hell…" As he bit back the familiar oath, he saw her eyes light with a smile of surprise. For the first time since he'd heard the volley of rifle fire, Cole relaxed. He took a steadying breath and drew her close, pressing his lips to her temple. "Are you trying to tell me you love me?"

She nodded and felt the warmth of his laughter against her hair.

"I'm so glad, Jessie. Because I love you, too. So much that I would have moved all of Texas to hear you say the words."

She caught his head and pulled his face near until his lips hovered just above hers. ''I love you,'' she whispered against his lips. ''And I want to stay with you forever.''

''Oh, Jessie. I intend to hold you to that.'' He moved his mouth over hers and felt the first wild stirrings of passion. ''I know you've sold your ranch here and that nothing will take its place. But you'll learn to love my ranch, Jessie. It's been needing a woman's touch for a long time.'' Suddenly lifting her in his arms, he pulled himself into the saddle and nudged his horse toward a grove of trees.

Her eyes widened. ''What are you doing? Where are we going?''

''Have mercy on a starving man, Jessie. Before we join your brothers, I deserve to spend an hour alone with you.''

''Umm.'' She brushed her lips over his and felt the barely controlled passion in his kiss. ''And then?'' She was laughing openly now, and he felt the warmth of her laughter wash over him, healing all the wounds.

''We're going to find a preacher, Jessie Conway. I'm going to tie you to me forever. Your heart belongs here with me. In Texas.''

''My heart is already yours, Cole. It's been yours since the first time you touched me.'' She brought her lips to his throat and felt his sudden intake of breath.

As the horse and its riders disappeared beyond the circle of tree branches, the two young boys clapped each other on the shoulders and let out whoops of glee that echoed on the crisp autumn air.

It had been an amazing summer. They had experienced so much on their journey, had lost almost everything they valued—home, father, childhood. But in losing, they had also gained.

And now that Cole and Jessie were reunited, they knew somehow that the real adventure had only just begun.

* * * * *

MILLS & BOON®

Makes any time special

Enjoy a romantic novel from Mills & Boon®

Presents™ *Enchanted*™ *Temptation*®

Historical Romance™ *Medical Romance*™

Perfect
Summer

The perfect way to relax this summer!

Four stories from best selling
Mills & Boon® authors

JoAnn Ross

Vicki Lewis Thompson

Janice Kaiser

Stephanie Bond

*Enjoy the fun, the drama
and the excitement!*

Published 21 May 1999

FREE!

2 Books
and a surprise gift!

We would like to take this opportunity to thank you for reading this Mills & Boon® book by offering you the chance to take TWO more specially selected titles from the Historical Romance™ series absolutely FREE! We're also making this offer to introduce you to the benefits of the Reader Service™ —

- ★ FREE home delivery
- ★ FREE gifts and competitions
- ★ FREE monthly Newsletter
- ★ Books available before they're in the shops
- ★ Exclusive Reader Service discounts

Accepting these FREE books and gift places you under no obligation to buy; you may cancel at any time, even after receiving your free shipment. Simply complete your details below and return the entire page to the address below. *You don't even need a stamp!*

YES! Please send me 2 free Historical Romance books and a surprise gift. I understand that unless you hear from me, I will receive 4 superb new titles every month for just £2.99 each, postage and packing free. I am under no obligation to purchase any books and may cancel my subscription at any time. The free books and gift will be mine to keep in any case.

H9EB

Ms/Mrs/Miss/Mr ....Initials ....

BLOCK CAPITALS PLEASE

Surname..

Address..

....

....Postcode ....

Send this whole page to:
THE READER SERVICE, FREEPOST CN81, CROYDON, CR9 3WZ
(Eire readers please send coupon to: P.O. BOX 4546, DUBLIN 24.)

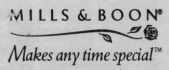